Catacomb

Flora's path now took her through an ever-widening vault, lined on both sides with carved architectural motifs. Above these were artful arrangements of skulls and pelvises and leg bones, formed into shapes that conserved space far better than laying out each body in its own niche. Clearly this was one of the elaborately decorated sections the tour guide had promised them.

She hustled up shallow steps to the upper level. Suddenly Flora found herself at a crossroads where three tunnels branched. Which way had her tour group taken? She listened hard. The only sound she heard was the quickening footfalls of the approaching stranger who was no longer concerned about concealing himself.

Flora took the left fork, praying for side chambers or deep niches. She saw two before she took the third one, hoping her pursuer would either take another path or assume she had chosen the first available hiding place. As she moved away from the main path, the electric lights faded. She turned on the tiny penlight on her key ring--good for finding keyholes but not much else.

The ceiling lowered and the rough tufa walls scraped against her thin cotton sweater. It was chilly down here. The passage twisted, hiding her little light from the man behind her. It narrowed until she could scarcely pass. Despite the cold, little beads of sweat rolled down her torso beneath her clothes, and her breath grew short. Was this a dead end?

Other Works From The Pen Of
Sarah Wissemann

The Dead Sea Codex, December, 2015
Two archaeologists working in Israel race to find an ancient manuscript about the teaching of Jesus' female disciples before Christian fanatics destroy them.

The Fall of Augustus, 2010
When Victor Fitzgerald is killed by a falling statue, Lisa Donahue becomes Interim Director of her Boston University museum. Suddenly she's juggling murder, artifact theft, and a complicated move into a new building. Then the treacherous Dean announces her replacement: a vicious woman from Lisa's past.

Catacomb

Sarah Wisseman

A Wings ePress, Inc.

Suspense Novel

Wings ePress, Inc.

Edited by: Jeanne Smith
Copy Edited by: Joan Powell
Executive Editor: Jeanne Smith
Cover Artist: Richard Stroud

Wings ePress Books
www.books-by-wingsepress.com

Copyright © 2016 by Sarah Wisseman
ISBN 978-1-61309-750-2

Published In the United States Of America

March 2016

Wings ePress Inc.
3000 N. Rock Road
Newton, KS 67114

Dedication

For Peri

Acknowledgments

As always, I am grateful to my critique partners Molly MacRae, David Ingram, Steve Kuehn, and Julia Kellman for their thoughtful comments. Also to the Writer's Café led by author Frank Chadwick at our local Osher Lifelong Learning Institute for allowing me to read drafts and receive useful criticism. I thank Dianna Graveman for copyediting and formatting, the Wings staff for everything they do, and my husband Charlie for his helpful suggestions on plot complications—and, of course, for putting up with me while I was writing.

One

It was a fine day for an argument.

"You did *what*?" Flora yelped.

"I called your boss and got you some time off," boasted Vittorio Bernini.

"Why on earth? And who are you to jeopardize my new job? Why, you interfering so-and-so!" She refrained from calling him a bastard as the blood in her veins heated up.

"Calm down, *cara*." Vittorio stopped and put his hands on her shoulders, holding her steady in one place. "There's a good explanation."

Flora, normally susceptible to the warmth of his hazel eyes, fidgeted under his hands and glared at him. "So explain. And it had better be good."

He took her arm. "We can't talk here." They were in the middle of a piazza in Trastevere, the old part of Rome "across the Tiber." He steered her to a café with spindly metal tables outside, choosing one at the back where other conversations would muffle their own. "Espresso for you?"

"Make it a *macchiato*." She preferred strong Italian coffee with a little swirl of milk.

Flora Garibaldi drew out a chair and sat, looping her purse around one knee. The soft air of late April wafted around her, lowering her internal temperature. Maybe she wouldn't boil over—yet. Vittorio had just done what he always accused her of doing, acting first and not thinking about other peoples' reactions until it was too late. Now she was on the receiving end, and she didn't like it.

As she waited for him to fetch their coffees, she decided that despite the occasional clashes of personality and inherited expectations, their first few months together as a couple had been quite satisfactory. They'd found a small but charming apartment, a third-floor walk-up with a tiny balcony, in Trastevere. Flora loved the area, with its cobbled streets and sunset colors on the painted stucco buildings: burnt orange, pale red, salmon, and gold. The non-existent grid plan of Rome no longer bothered her. Now, she reveled in the odd, triangular piazzas where she least expected them, the meandering streets, and the quiet, flower-filled corners of residential neighborhoods. She'd even adopted the Italian custom of putting out leftover dishes of pasta for the stray cats—some of the thousands of cats who weren't living in the ruins of the Colosseum but stalked the unwary small rodents in every corner of Rome.

The heavenly aroma of fresh coffee made her turn around. Vittorio approached, his compact body moving smoothly like an experienced waiter's between crowded chairs and café tables. He balanced the two cups of coffee in one hand and a couple of pastries in the other. *Ha!—does he plan on sweetening my temper with sugar and fat? Think again, buster.*

He might behave like a domineering Italian male, but she had to admit he was good-looking. Not for the first time, Flora admired his narrow face, framed by dark brown hair with a little wave in the front. He looked more like a scholar than a policeman. Not so odd, really, since he'd begun his career as an art historian, just like Flora. She was still trying to figure out what had attracted him to policing, beginning with the Siena murder squad.

Flora took the almond pastry and bit into it as if she hadn't just had breakfast an hour before. "Now tell me. Why did you call my boss, and why didn't you discuss it with me first?"

Vittorio took a sip of coffee and then met her eyes. "The assignment came up very suddenly yesterday. My boss threw it in my lap and told me to get busy recruiting help, because it's a huge job."

"What's a huge job?"

He deflected her question with one of his own. "What do you know about the Monuments Men?"

She stared at him. "Ah, they were a special unit deployed to search for art stolen by the Nazis during World War II, right? An American unit." Flora sipped her coffee. It was delicious, much better than the slightly muddy stuff they made at home in the little pot that boiled coffee from the bottom.

"Yes. Actually, the unit was formed by the Allied armies. The official name of the group was 'Monuments, Fine Arts, and Archives.' The Monuments Men did most of their work between 1943 and 1945 under very difficult circumstances. They weren't military men, most of them—"

"I remember. They were museum directors, curators, conservators. Art historians. There were about three hundred of them."

Vittorio's mouth tightened. "More than that. And their work continued long after the war. About sixty of the Monuments Men remained in Europe, serving as art detectives, searching for caches of stolen art that were hidden in caves, churches, villas, and even salt mines."

"So why are you suddenly spouting history of the Monuments Men? And you haven't told me why you found it necessary to call Ottavia."

He took a sip of his coffee and lowered his voice. "Because *il primo capitano* Moscati suggested it."

Flora, feeling an odd tingle between her shoulder blades, waited.

"There's a rumor going around that the Monuments Men missed a significant cache of art stolen by the Nazis somewhere under Rome. Art stolen from prominent Jewish families."

She froze. "They did?"

"Apparently."

"In the catacombs?"

"Yes. Somewhere in the six hundred kilometers of catacomb tunnels that go under the city and into the suburbs of Rome. The catacombs have been only partially explored by modern people since they were rediscovered in the sixteen hundreds."

Stunned, Flora leaned back in her chair. "That does sound like a huge job. How on earth will you cover all that territory?"

Bernini grimaced. "With difficulty. But Captain Moscati says I can recruit helpers. You, for example, since you are a paintings conservator and an art historian. And I figured, with your connections, you can help me find some experts in archaeology, architecture, painting, sculpture, Roman history... every discipline that touches on the looting and conservation of art."

"So that's why you called my boss! Wait. Why do you need conservators? This is a search mission, right? Will there be any actual work for conservators?"

"Probably. We don't know yet. The thinking is that having a few conservators along will help us evaluate different conditions underground as we search and also help sort out the art that needs immediate treatment when—if—we find it."

"Hmm. Underground conditions: dampness, mold, water damage, chemical damage from leached-out stuff in the water—yes, you will need us. Okay." Already Flora's brain was churning, throwing up possible names and professions. "I know of at least two American conservators and museum specialists. Can some of the recruits be Americans?"

"Yes, whomever we want. We will have a much more generous budget than the original Monuments Men. This commission comes from the highest level of the Italian government, and there is support from the European Union. We'll be working with experts from other countries, especially France, Austria, and Switzerland."

"What's the time frame?"

"Three months or less. Moscati implied we might get an extension of funding after that, but it's not guaranteed."

"You'll need the time extension—and more money—if conservation is involved." Flora smiled at him, her anger over his intrusion into her job dissipating. "Sounds like a promotion in the works for you."

Vittorio patted her hand. "Maybe. I'm not buying a grand piano or anything on the expectation." His unit of the Carabinieri was affectionately known as "The Art Squad," but its real name was the *Comando Carabinieri per la Tutela del Patrimonio Culturale.* Vittorio Bernini had joined the unit quite recently after his transfer from the Siena murder squad.

Flora focused her gaze on the dripping purple flowers suspended from the awning over the outdoor portion of the café. Romans excelled at planting things in urban settings just where you wouldn't expect greenery. "I think Lisa Donahue in Boston would come, if she can get away. She has extensive archaeology in her background, with a specialty in the ancient Mediterranean. And her friend Ellen

Perkins is an excellent objects conservator. Ellen works with all the stuff I don't, such as jewelry, ceramics, metal, and wood."

"Good start." Vittorio sipped his coffee. "What about the Villa Giulia curator who helped us with that damn statue? Assunta something—"

"Assunta Vianello. She'd be great, especially because she's not only a scholar in a high position; she's also a native of Rome. I bet she'll have specific ideas about where to look. And she's senior enough in her museum job to have useful connections."

"Excellent. I'd like to talk with her again. We will also have officers from the Carabinieri on the team. Astorre Orsoni, for one." His eyes flickered and one hand clenched.

"Astorre? He was really helpful last time. But I get the feeling you find him less of an ally and more of an irritant since you work with him every day."

Bernini sighed and drained his coffee cup. "You're right. I haven't figured out why, but our interactions are strained."

"Maybe he liked working with you when he was top dog here, and you were a junior officer located safely up north. He could be jealous of your new position and how you seem to have the first captain's ear." Flora pulled a tissue out of her pocket and blew her nose. Spring allergies dogged her even here, in a major city. She guessed it was just bad genes, since her mother suffered every year.

Vittorio stood. "Maybe. Whatever it is, I have to figure out how to work with him. Shall we go?"

"Yikes, yes." Flora yanked her cell phone off the table and stuffed it in her pocket. "It's almost nine. I need to finish restoring the triptych before I get involved in your project. And smooth out a few details with Ottavia. Even if she agreed to your scheme, she'll still have her own agenda."

Vittorio grabbed the battered leather bag he wore slung across his shoulder, like so many European men. "That's pretty much what she said on the phone. You'll get some time off every day to work on my stuff and be expected to put in the rest on your usual projects."

"Lovely. Two jobs instead of one. When will I sleep?"

Two

Ottavia Palmiere did not exactly ooze sympathy over Flora's increased responsibilities. "When will you sleep? That's your problem, sweetie. Your cute boyfriend negotiated some time off from the lab for you, but he didn't wave a magic wand and change our paintings conservation workload. I don't care how you do it; just meet your deadlines. We'll give you a key and the alarm code so you can work evenings and weekends if necessary."

Ottavia ground out her cigarette. She regarded Flora with a hint of amusement in her dark eyes. "You're a hard worker. Organized, too. You'll manage."

Flora sighed and took a slug of water from the aluminum bottle she always carried with her to keep herself from drinking too much coffee. "Yes, I will manage. I'm not quite sure what I'm getting into with the *Carabanieri*, but I couldn't say no to Vittorio." She gazed at her boss, admiring the dark hair piled on top of her head, the clean line of her nose, and the determined mouth. Ottavia's attitude projected "business first," but her lithe figure and attractive garb suggested she had a lively life outside of work.

Ottavia laughed. "Of course not! He is very persuasive, that one." She studied Flora's face for a moment. "Actually, I think you will enjoy it. Cloaks and daggers in the catacombs? Working with an international team? Sounds like a movie thriller." She lined up her red pen and her notebook, the one where she kept track of everything, on the desk in front of her.

"Well," said Flora with a little smile, "it will make a nice change from fiddly painting and working with smelly acetone."

"Oooo! So that's what you think of your job here..." Ottavia's tone was half teasing, half serious. She leaned back in her swivel chair and touched her black hair with one hand.

Deciding she didn't know her boss well enough to get away with making fun of her profession, Flora amended her comment. "You know I'm addicted to the smell of acetone and to painting conservation. I just couldn't help responding to what you said about the thrill of exploring under Rome. I've always wanted to explore the catacombs, but they're so extensive, I've only been down twice—in the more public sections. I can't wait to see more."

"The catacombs are amazing; there are frescoes down there, and tons of symbolism, both Christian and Jewish. I'm a conservator, too, remember. If your Vittorio needs more personnel, I'd be happy to take a turn sometime. Or if you find paintings that need repairing, we can work out a deal to squeeze them in here."

Flora nodded, surprised her boss would even consider getting involved. Ottavia's five-year-old painting restoration business had taken off in recent months, and she had so much work that she'd been making noises about hiring another conservator. Of course, if the catacomb team discovered some Old Masters, there would be decent money in it for Ottavia... and maybe a bonus for Flora.

Ottavia twisted her pen as she thought out loud. "You know, Flora, the area you have to search may be much larger than you think. Did you know how many different kinds of tunnels there are underneath the city? Sewers, aqueducts, slave tunnels, all kinds of stuff. And as far as I know, they've never been mapped completely."

Flora frowned. "I had the impression from Lieutenant Bernini that the information received by the Carabinieri pointed to the catacombs specifically."

Her boss smiled like a sphinx. "Tunnels are tunnels. They meander, intersect, and even collapse. I bet it's a labyrinth down there."

"I'm sure you're right. I'll ask him for more details. But he did tell you, didn't he, that we're not supposed to discuss this search with anyone else?"

"Oh, yes, he told me that." The expression in her brown eyes said that not all rules applied to Ottavia Palmiere.

Perhaps Ottavia was a little too interested in *carabinieri* business? Flora resolved to keep her mouth shut as much as possible.

They discussed a few more details about how Flora would manage her time, and then Flora left Ottavia's office and crossed to her own desk at the back of the laboratory. Gazing out the big window, she reflected that most bosses would not be keen on an employee taking time to do anything outside of the work at hand. Ottavia had not only blessed the undertaking, she'd offered to participate. Flora wasn't used to this—her last boss, the legendary Beppe Lorenzetti of Restauro Lorenzetti in Siena, had resented anything that distracted his workers. Giving out extra assignments was his prerogative. Too bad that job hadn't worked out, but Flora was happier in Rome.

Flora was grateful that moving to Rome had proven to be both a great career move and a chance for her and Vittorio to live together, away from his disapproving family. Naturally, they approved of Vittorio; but Flora, a half-American girl from an unknown family was another matter. Then there was the fact that they were living together, unmarried.

What makes you think your own family approves of your living with a man, a man the family doesn't know at all? Who were his parents, for starters?

Flora smiled at the voice of her mother that always lived in her head. Mamma Garibaldi had plenty to say about everything, especially Flora's boyfriends. Well, at least Mamma couldn't bash her this time for having no boyfriend at all...

Yes, bambina, it's nice you have a boyfriend, finally. But we haven't even met him! Who is his family? What is he doing in the police?

Oh, be quiet, Mamma.

Okay, time to get busy. Flora grabbed her favorite size of yellow paper pad—large—and made two lists: the left column for all the tasks she had to complete to stay employed. In the right column, she jotted down the names of Lisa Donahue, Ellen Perkins, and Assunta Vianello.

She glanced at the time displayed on her cell phone. Only eleven, plenty of time to reach Assunta before the curator took a lunch break. The other calls she'd reserve for late afternoon, when the Americans would be starting their work days.

Punching in the number of the Villa Giulia and the extension for Assunta, she waited.

"*Pronto.*"

"Assunta? It's Flora Garibaldi."

"Flora! How are you? Any more fake Greek statues on your horizon?"

"I sure hope not; one was quite enough for my lifetime! But I've got something even more interesting to worry about now. Have you got a few minutes to talk?"

"Sure. Fire away."

Flora described her new project, emphasizing how helpful Assunta Vianello could be to the team.

Silence.

"That is very, very interesting. Actually, I heard a rumor recently about a trove of Nazi-looted art in the catacombs. I never expected it to be verified so quickly, or at such a high level. Maybe I should speak with your Vittorio Bernini."

How interesting—Bernini should know the rumor was already circulating outside the Carabinieri.

"I'm sure he'd be glad to be of any help, especially if it includes sources of reliable information," Flora said. "He said specifically that he looked forward to talking with you. So, can you join us?"

"I would certainly like to. It may have to be part-time if I can't get away more than half a day at a time. I need to talk with the head of the museum and a few other people about reassignments. I will call you back either late today or tomorrow. I understand time is of the essence here."

Flora thanked her and clicked her phone off. She remembered the tall, model-thin curator with her blond hair and stylish clothes. A great job and the looks to go with it. She sighed. How many years would it take her to land an enviable position like that? She returned to her to-do list.

Triptych: finish in-painting
Martini painting: strip old varnish, stabilize paint layers.
Lorenzetti: deal with cracks, consolidation of paint layers.
Caravaggio: mix colors for in-painting.

Get to work, Flora.

She donned her painting smock, grabbed some new gloves from the dispenser, and moved to the other end of the laboratory to the giant worktable where her paintings waited.

Flora had been at work only a few minutes when her colleague, Roberto Salvi, arrived to finish treatment on a painting at the table across from her.

"Hey, Roberto. How are you?"

"Fine." He shrugged into an old, oversized shirt to protect his good clothes and laid out his paints, solvent, scalpel, and brushes. "I heard a fascinating lecture last night, all about archaeology underneath the city."

Flora looked up from her painting. "Who gave it?"

"A woman from a group called *Sotterranei di Roma*. She was an archaeologist, but the group has geologists, spelunkers, all sorts of people in it. They organize scientific research underground, dig archaeological sites, map ruins and tunnels, and even give tours."

Maps! Geologists who knew their way around underground! She experienced the thrill that serendipitous information appearing at just the right time always gave her. Flora struggled not to ask a flood of questions or betray too much interest. "Are the lectures public?"

"Sure." Roberto eyed her. "When the archaeologist finished, a geologist spoke about the geology of Latium."

"Oh, yes?"

"He told us all about how Rome is built on limestone and volcanic tufa, with Karst formations—"

"What on earth is 'Karst'?"

Roberto smiled. "Good question. Maybe you should say 'under the earth' since so much of it is underground. Karst terrain means soft rock, such as limestone and tufa we have around here. It was shaped over time by slightly acidic rainfall. The rain causes the rock to dissolve, forming fissures and caves and sinkholes." He paused again, as if to assess Flora's level of interest.

"Go on."

"Before the Karst formed, this part of central Italy was below water. It lay beneath an inland sea with lots of marine animals and shellfish with calcium-rich shells. Combine that with significant volcanic action nearby, and you have volcanic ash and hot lava, layering and mixing with limestone, hardening into tufa, or *tufo* as we call it in Italy. Great building stone. Ancient builders used the lighter portion of the ash to mix in mortar.

"Then you have the Tibur River with its huge drainage area, and you have a perfect landscape for amazing underground tunnels, chambers, and pools."

"And catacombs." Flora said, "You sound like a geologist yourself. Is that part of your background?"

"I took several geology classes at university before I became a chemistry major and then a conservator."

"This stuff is really interesting to me. Do you know some good websites on geology of Rome? And the *Sotterranei* group?"

"Yes. Shall I zap you a few from my cell?"

"Please do. And the lectures would fascinate me. Let me know the next time you go, okay? I'd like to come." Flora made a mental note to spend some time cruising the Internet that evening.

The *Sotterranei* could be really useful to the Carabinieri's search. But would Bernini give any of their members security clearance? Maybe they didn't have to know exactly what the Carabinieri were looking for, but just provide some guidance. And their maps.

~ * ~

At lunchtime, Flora made a brief foray to a corner café-bar that sold coffee and sandwiches and grabbed a couple of cheese-and-tomato *panini*. She added packets of mustard and mayo and returned to her desk to munch, drink coffee, and cruise the web on her tablet to learn more about the Monuments Men.

The story of the systematic looting by the Nazis of art from all over Europe mesmerized her, particularly when she found letters from various German officials authorizing theft on a grand scale. The key villains were *Reischmarshall* Hermann Göring and Alfred Rosenberg, the head of the *Einsatzstab Reichsleiter Rosenberg* (ERR). Initially, they prettied up their objective by calling it "safeguarding" material "valuable to Germany," but the language in their dispatches quickly changed to "seizure" of anything deemed Jewish cultural property.

In October 1940, the ERR, the Nazi Party's official art-looting wing, began confiscation of art from prominent Jewish families such as the Rothschilds of Paris. Alfred Rosenberg's small army of art historians sought out, photographed, and valued some four thousand artworks over the next year, securing them in locations provided by (commandeered from?) the Louvre Museum in Paris. Catalogues of the best paintings were sent to Hitler for his perusal, and then selected masterpieces were shipped to Munich in two railroad cars. And this was just the beginning.

Shaking her head, Flora picked up the second sandwich and followed links to individual Monuments Men. She discovered that famous British archaeologists such as Sir Mortimer Wheeler, Sir Leonard Wooley, and J. B. Ward-Perkins were among the founders of the group. During World War II, these men revised standard military practice. Instead of allowing tanks to rampage over archaeological sites first and ask questions later, they advocated education about the ancient sites soldiers might encounter so ruins could be protected. The group's initial goal was to prevent the further destruction of ancient cities like Cyrene and Leptis Magna in North Africa. Eventually they formed a monuments protection unit and recruited like-minded colleagues to become the first Monuments Men.

After the war, the goals of the Monuments Men shifted from protecting sites to retrieving Nazi-looted art and artifacts, finding the owners, and returning them to their original museums and private collections.

Flora finished her sandwich, thinking about what she'd just read and poring over old newspaper pictures of the Monuments Men inspecting and removing art from German hiding places. Some of the most spectacular pictures showed piles of art stacked up to the ceiling in the apses of churches.

So it was fair to say that the Carabinieri's Art Squad was continuing the work of the Monuments Men. Plenty of World War II looted artworks were still out there, hidden and undocumented, and it was now the job of men like Bernini to find them.

Her head whirling with new facts and plenty of speculations, Flora waded into her To Do list for the lab. She chose cleaning the heavily yellowed Martini painting as the most urgent task that was least likely to require brain power. She could gently remove the old varnish with cotton swabs and solvent while continuing to think about the massive operations of the Monuments Men and the upcoming search.

Finally, four o'clock arrived. A good time for a break and an excellent time to call Lisa Donahue in Boston. Or was it too early in the morning in Boston? If so, she'd call Lisa's home phone. Flora stripped off her gloves, discarded her grubby painter's smock that protected her clothing, and sat at her desk. She rummaged around in her files to find the phone number for the Director's Office at the Boston Museum of Archaeology and History. *Aha, here it is.* She extracted a sheet of white paper and laid it on the desk in front of her and punched in the numbers on her cell.

"Lisa? Surprise! It's Flora Garibaldi calling from Rome."

"Holy cow! What a long time it's been. How are you, Flora?"

Flora grinned and filled in her friend about recent developments in her personal and professional life since she'd seen Lisa at a conference two years earlier. "... so we moved to Rome. I'm working in a private conservation business, and Vittorio joined the *Carabinieri's* Art Squad."

"Well, I can't top that," said Lisa with a characteristic chuckle. "My life is dead boring right now. Too much administrative crap at work and carting our kids all over the landscape instead of relaxing at home. What can I do for you?"

Flora took a deep breath and gathered her thoughts. This would be a tough sell to a busy museum director who had her own agenda on the other side of an ocean.

"Vittorio's boss called him in to his office yesterday, and he has a really important project we need help with..."

Lisa asked a few questions and then said, "Catacombs and skullduggery in the art world! Sounds absolutely fascinating. As it happens, I am in between projects and would welcome a change. And I adore Italy. But I still have to check with my staff and make arrangements. And there's the little matter of expenses. Can the Carabinieri help with my airfare? I can't justify this trip on our puny Boston museum budget."

"Airfare, accommodations, and a per diem are all included. I wanted to ask your objects conservator, Ellen Perkins, if she could come, too. You're her boss; what do you say?"

"Well! I will need to make some arrangements to cover for two of us being absent. But I think I can swing it. How about I call you back in a day or two?"

"The sooner, the better. Vittorio will be breathing down my neck."

They disconnected. Flora's face broke into a smile; this project might even be fun! Working with old friends and treasured colleagues she hardly ever got to spend time with... drinking some wine in the off hours... maybe finding something priceless. All of a sudden, she was excited.

She glanced at her cell phone again. Only sixteen-twenty. She had plenty of time before Vittorio would be home for dinner. How about a quick visit to one of the catacombs she hadn't seen, just to get a feel for the terrain they'd be searching?

Flora pulled out her Rome map booklet and figured out which bus would get her to the Via Appia Antica, where several of the most popular catacombs were located. She grabbed her cell and her all-purpose satchel, figuring she'd made enough progress on her conservation work to justify leaving early.

And if Ottavia didn't like Flora's new, flexible hours, she'd sic Bernini on her again.

Three

Flora took a city bus to the stop closest to the Porta San Sebastiano in the Aurelian Wall and walked from there along the Via Appia Antica, one of the original roads leading south out of Rome. Parts of the ancient road were surprisingly well preserved. Massive pavers of volcanic rock from the Alban Hills ran between sidewalks, flanked by low stone walls, overhanging trees that provided shade, and twisting vines. In gaps between the trees, Flora enjoyed vistas of green, dotted with the villas of the rich, unidentified ruins, and clumps of tall, spindly cypress trees. In less than an hour, she'd left the crowded city behind and whisked herself away to the country.

After paying for her ticket at the entrance of the San Callisto (St. Calixtus) catacombs, Flora joined the last official tour of the day. She found herself accompanied by a rowdy American family with several small children. The mother wore capris and thongs, the worst possible shoes for venturing underground.

"The catacombs of Saint Calixtus are among the most important of all Rome," began the petite Italian tour guide in English.

"Who's Saint Calixtus?" asked a small, T-shirt clad boy. "Is he like Saint Nicholas?"

His brother and sister giggled. The little girl, who sported bright pink sneakers with twinkling lights, smiled at Flora. "Are you from Italy?"

"Yes, I am. But my family is half American." Flora smiled back, charmed with the child's friendly face.

"We're *all* American!" said the little girl.

The guide plowed on, ignoring the fact that some of her charges were not listening to her spiel. "Beginning about the middle of the second century A.D, the catacombs were part of a cemetery complex. Christian martyrs were buried here, along with sixteen popes and many ordinary Christians."

Ah, so this was one of the Christian catacombs. Good for absorbing the underground atmosphere, but maybe not the most likely section to house stolen Jewish art. Flora would make a point of visiting one of the Jewish catacombs, if she could obtain the necessary permission.

"The catacombs in this part of Rome are named after the deacon Calixtus, who, at the beginning of the third century, was appointed by Pope Zephyrinus as the administrator of the cemetery. Later the catacombs of St. Calixtus became the official cemetery of the Church of Rome. Okay, people, we're going down deeper—"

Shouts of glee from the children.

"Follow me down the staircase to the second level, but watch your step. We will visit the Papal Crypt and see many frescoes."

Once on the lower level, they proceeded to examine Greek inscriptions for the various popes and visited the cubiculum of St. Cecilia. Flora paid more attention to the guide when she heard the story of how Cecilia became a martyr at her house in Trastevere in 230 A.D.

"Cecilia was shut up in her own caldarium so she could be scalded to death, but she emerged undamaged," the young guide said with relish, speaking directly to the two American boys. "Then she was beheaded, but the executioner was inexperienced. He didn't kill Cecilia with one blow, but he cut her neck with several sword strokes. Cecilia lived for three days, long enough to demand that her home be made into a church."

The little boys turned round-eyed at the grisly story, and their mother looked annoyed.

Poor Cecilia! What a way to become a saint! thought Flora, smiling at the reactions of the American family. She remembered that Cecilia had been a patroness of music who refused to consummate her marriage, which was forced upon her by her parents. It was professing Christianity and seeing angels that got her killed.

Once past the frescoes of the Raising of Lazarus and the Loaves and Fishes, Flora allowed the others to pass her so she could examine her surroundings in detail without being jostled. The tour guide's voice faded; that was okay with Flora. She could look up the rest of the Christian history later.

Knowing she was deviating from the standard tour path, Flora took the next stairway down to the third level. A new tunnel took her past several burial *loculi* on her right, once occupied by skeletons. She shuddered as she imagined empty-eyed skulls grinning up at her. As the tunnel grew narrower, wet stone left moisture on her hair as she stooped lower. Her nostrils twitched at the smell of mildew.

What they sought couldn't, or shouldn't, be here under such conditions. But, then, perhaps this part of the Roman catacomb had been dry sixty years ago. Or perhaps the Jewish art owners hadn't had time to choose the ideal hiding place with the Germans arriving any minute. Note to self: since they were Jewish, they might have preferred a Jewish catacomb to a Christian one. Unless, of course, they lived right on top of a Christian catacomb and knew how to get in.

As she strolled along, her painter's eyes automatically noted the colors of the underground passages. Just like the city of Rome above her, the soft, easily carved tufa and limestone echoed the earth tones of umber (raw and burnt), sienna, and tawny gold, with patches of viridian green and dark brown where water had flowed recently.

She moved past stone and brick niches with very little decoration to elaborate chambers, with stucco and frescoes, pictures of saints, and delicately carved Christian symbols of fish and peacocks. The variety of decoration struck Flora as particularly interesting—did each family have its own section of the catacombs? How many different artists were represented down here?

Flora reveled in the feeling of being on her own in a place so rich in history and art. The group was not so far ahead of her that she couldn't catch up if she wanted to, but she'd have to backtrack and climb stairs to be sure of finding their route.

After a five-minute stop to take pictures with her cell phone of some niches that looked deep enough to hide something, she became aware of footsteps behind her. A latecomer for the tour? Unlikely; the tour had started at least half an hour ago. She didn't think the tour managers let single people in; most tourists traveled in groups with a guide. And Flora was two levels down from the tour route.

Flora felt a frisson of unease. Then she couldn't hear anyone in front or above her, only the single man—or woman—behind her. She walked a little faster, fingering the cell phone in her pocket. Probably it wouldn't work down here—too far down for decent reception.

The footsteps kept pace with her.

Then she thought of pickpockets, who were plentiful in the Eternal City. So were Italian men who made a sport of following and harassing women.

She should catch up with the tour group with no more stops for photos. But now she couldn't retrace her steps without running smack into her stalker. She'd have to keep going and hope for stairs leading to the upper levels or a good hiding place.

A chill ran down Flora's spine like a cave spider as another possibility occurred to her. What if it wasn't a lost tourist or an Italian Romeo hunting females? What if it was another searcher for lost art? At least one person or group outside the police knew about the rumor of a Nazi cache; there could be others. She hurried forward, the thin soles of her sandals slapping against the soft tufa stone, and then stopped abruptly. She heard two footfalls and then silence. Flora repeated her maneuver, traveling at least ten paces before she stopped. The footsteps halted, too. She heard nothing except dripping water ahead of her. No voices at all.

Okay. No question about it; someone—surely a man—who didn't want Flora to see him trailed her. She pulled her bag closer to her side and increased her pace to a half-run. Perhaps the group ahead of her had paused for another mini-lecture about the Christian burials in the catacombs or for taking photos of an architectural detail. She could catch up with them and then the follower would melt away.

Maybe. Perhaps not, if he sought the same treasure she did.

Flora remembered a tip given to her by a karate instructor: use your keys. Thread the keys through your fingers, sharp ends pointed outward, so you have "tiger claws" to rake the skin of an unwary attacker. Still walking, she stuck her right hand in the outer pocket of her satchel and grabbed the keys.

It might make sense that her follower knew about the Nazi-looted art. But if he did, how did he know Flora was down here looking for the same thing? Had he followed her from the bus stop inside the city walls? The possibilities haunted her, especially when she thought about how much money might be involved if lost European masterpieces were recovered. Renoir, Titian, Caravaggio—the paintings of such artists fetched millions at auction.

Flora's right sandal caught on an irregularity in the floor and she pitched forward. Her hands saved her from all but a scraped knee. She picked herself up and wiped her hands on her skirt.

Her gaze flicked from side to side as the tunnel widened to show a new set of burial niches on either side. If she slid into one of those openings, would she be invisible to the man following her? What if there were still bones at the back of what looked like an empty niche? Could she then cover herself with bones and pretend to be a two-thousand-year-old dead Christian? She shivered and walked faster.

Try the cell phone, Flora thought. She pulled it out and pushed the "on" button. No reception.

The footsteps sounded a little closer, with only a bend or two of tunnel between him and her. Now her only interest in side tunnels was a place to hide. No stairs and no other passageways had appeared for at least a half mile, maybe more. A side tunnel leading to a disused part of the catacombs; that's what she needed.

Instead, Flora's path took her through an ever-widening vault, lined on both sides with carved architectural motifs. Above these were artful arrangements of skulls and pelvises and leg bones, formed into shapes that conserved space far better than laying out each body in its own niche. Clearly this was one of the elaborately decorated sections the tour guide had promised them.

She hustled up shallow steps to the upper level. Suddenly Flora found herself at a crossroads where three tunnels branched. Which way had her tour group taken? She listened hard. The only sound she heard was the quickening footfalls of the approaching stranger who was no longer concerned about concealing himself.

Flora took the left fork, praying for side chambers or deep niches. She saw two before she took the third one, hoping her pursuer would either take another path or assume she had chosen the first available hiding place. As she moved away from the main path, the electric lights faded. She turned on the tiny penlight on her key ring—good for finding keyholes but not much else.

The ceiling lowered and the rough tufa walls scraped against her thin cotton sweater. It was chilly down here. The passage twisted, hiding her little light from the man behind her. It narrowed until she could scarcely pass. Despite the cold, little beads of sweat rolled down her torso beneath her clothes, and her breath grew short. Was this a dead end?

Again, the tunnel changed without warning. She popped into a larger space. Flora remembered her cell phone and used the light from its screen to survey the space, identifying two human-sized openings in the walls. She nipped into the one that looked like it might have more room at the back and flicked off the cell. Groping against the rough rock walls, she moved as far into the opening as she could. As she shifted her weight and leaned against the wall, the cavity opened again on her right. Flora scooted a little further into what felt like a small, round cave. Cool and dry, no bones.

She concentrated on slowing her breath. In. Out. In. Except for her breathing, the silence reminded her of being encased in a down sleeping bag.

Muffled. Suffocated.

Wrong image—she need to calm herself, not freak out. Breathe. In. Out. In.

Where was her pursuer? She heard nothing. She decided to wait a few minutes and then emerge and do her best to retrace her steps to the entrance of the catacomb. No point in going on to get herself really lost.

The minutes crept by. Flora felt her legs stiffening and shifted her weight sideways, hoping the stone would provide a softer place to lean. Instead, her thigh hit something hard. It fell over with a clang. She grabbed her cell phone, but its battery was dead. She flicked on her penlight and saw a shovel, its blade covered with crumbled tufa. She followed the trail of stone debris to the right and found another opening at the height of her waist. Flora swept the tiny light around, frustrated that her light was so inadequate.

As far as she could tell, there was nothing in the little side chamber. It looked like the digger had penetrated the wall but she couldn't tell if he—or they—had discovered anything.

She must tell Bernini.

Four
Isabelle's Rossin's Diary, Part 1

(*N.b. Brackets are used to indicate letters filled in later by the Carabinieri.*)

May [17,] 1940. My name is Isabelle Rossin and I am twenty-two years old. I was born in Paris, France, in the Marais district. We live in a large apartment just off the Rue des Rosiers, and I thought I would live here with my family for many years, perhaps forever, as an old maid! But today I met Sal [vatore]. He walked into the fruit and vegetable shop where I shop every day. I was choosing *aubergines* [eggplants] when I turned around and saw him near the checkout. I admired his strong shoulders and the way his brown hair flopped over his forehead—so handsome! Then those dark eyes met mine over the tomatoes and I felt a shiver all the way down to my toes. I was so glad I had on my blue dress. When he smiled at me, I knew I had met my future husband.

June [... 1940]. Sal is Italian, from a little town north of Rome. It is called Cassino and is near an important monastery. He comes from a big family, like me, and he dotes on his little sister Maria. We have met several times, always casually at the same shop where I pick up vegetables. Today we went for coffee. He is such an interesting man, a trained art historian. I too have a great interest in art, and I want to learn much more so someday I can be a guide at the Louvre.

I am crazy for him. I have never felt this way before—the other boys were just crushes. This is the real thing. I feel transformed. Anything is possible now.

So far we are keeping our relationship secret from my parents. They will explode when they learn I have fallen in love with a foreigner, even if he is Jewish. What will Papa say? Will Mama disown me? She is already so upset over my sister's boyfriend.

Thinking about this wonderful new love takes my mind off the war; the Germans have invaded France and the news is terrible. Our men are dying. My family talks about leaving Paris, but Papa says we must stay in the Marais. It is our home. All our relatives are here. It would be cowardly to leave just as things get worse.

June 10 [1940]. Everyone is afraid. The resistance has collapsed under the German advance, and Sal says Paris will be next to fall.

We met for coffee again today. Sal asked me to marry him. I want to, so badly, but my parents' anger will blast us as high as the tallest tree in Paris! No, maybe all the way as high as the moon! I know they want me to be happy, but they want me to marry in their way, in the same close community of Jews living in Paris so everything will stay the same. I feel they are like the cat, *Choux*: he hates changes of any kind, especially in his food.

Sal says we should marry and do it soon so we can get out of France before *les Boches* sack Paris and take charge of all transportation. They are already limiting trains, stealing fuel.

I do love him, and I know we could have a happy life. If only he could live here, in Paris, with us! He is sure he can get that job back in Cassino. There is nothing for him here, especially not in war time.

I hate the idea of leaving my home, but even considering that possibility means this is the real thing. I am ready to marry Sal.

June 12 [1940]. My parents just about had heart attacks, both of them, when I told them about my plans. Papa turned red in the face, then very white. "How can you think of leaving us, of moving to another country? This war is terrible; we must stay together. Family is everything." Mama stormed and ranted, throwing up her hands and crying.

"We are from a distinguished French family! We are important, we are art collectors!" She grabbed my shoulders. "You must marry someone of equal status, not some nobody from Italy! Think of the children you may have. Where do you want them to grow up? Will they learn our culture, or someone else's? Isabelle, you are so foolish, so shortsighted! You think of no one but yourself..."

My shoulders hurt where she gripped so hard, my stomach aches, my heart hurts. If only I were not the younger daughter... my older sister Estelle is so much better at persuasion.

The fact that Sal is an art historian wraps no cheese with them. Who is his family? Who was his father? Only an Italian businessman, a different class from the doctors and lawyers and art collectors on the Rossin side. And Sal has no employment now. How will we live if he has no job?

[page lost]

... Sal and I, we do not care what they say. With the German takeover of Paris, it is dangerous to stay in France. We will marry next week and are moving to Italy, southeast of Rome. Sal has written to the monastery [of Monte Cassino]; he is sure they will take him as a librarian and curator. We can live on his uncle's farm and we will manage. I have learned how to economize, which is a good thing since new clothes are already hard to find and we've heard soon there will be food rationing. Everyone says the Germans [will take everything], especially from the Jews. Living on a farm means we will have good or at least plentiful food. We may eat better there than here in the city where there are so many people, so little fresh food...

June 14, 1940. The megaphones. The fear. The sound of hateful German in our ears as we listened to their announcement. The Paris we knew is gone—taken by *les Boches*.

I found the marching Germans, so haughty with their arms stuck out, absolutely terrifying. How can they admire that man, that Hitler? He is such a little man, so puny, so angry. I am afraid for my family, afraid for those who stay behind. Paris will never be the same. My family will never be the same. How long will I have to wait to see them again?

Sal says the train office is mobbed; everyone tries to leave. He will go every day until he gets our tickets. It may take weeks...

Five

Vittorio Bernini settled at his desk and lit his fourth cigarette of the day. Despite all the hype in the news about the dangers of smoking, most of his colleagues still smoked and would until Rome burned down to the last centimeter of tufa. Bernini did, too. *Someday,* he thought, *when I'm not under so much stress, I'll quit.*

Ha, ha, when will that ever happen?

He was relieved that Flora hadn't burned like an overheated thin-crust pizza when he told her he'd gone over her head with Ottavia. Well, Flora had been upset, but not enough to stop speaking to him. He felt sure she'd recruit some good people to the team. Professionals in their fields, some with detailed knowledge of the labyrinthine terrain they'd be searching.

Actually, the Carabinieri had already in their ranks men and women who would be better suited than college professors to the underground work, both in terms of native knowledge and physical fitness. He wasn't sure how fit he could expect some of the scholars to be. Then there was the problem of how to split the team up, and which police officers he could rely upon to lead small groups and keep the investigation moving.

Vittorio puffed and inhaled carcinogens, scribbling notes on a pad with his other hand. One of the abilities he'd developed as a child was writing notes with either hand. True, the notes from his right hand, the non-dominant one, weren't as pretty, but they were legible. Being a leftie had earned him a lot of teasing as a child, but he was used to his physical self and rather enjoyed testing his agility on the right side every now and then.

First, he had to line up permissions from various governmental and municipal agencies. This would require firmness and diplomacy, since officials of all stripes were masters at excuses. "No, you can't have those maps! We are repairing a sewer this week..." Or, "Private records? Who says the Carabinieri have access? Your *generale*? Get him to talk with my boss..." Bernini knew he'd have to do some of that sweet-talking himself, but he needed at least one other officer to help speed things along.

He planned to divide the team of police and civilians into subsets of explorers and archivists, depending on individual abilities. They needed all the information they could gather on what *might* be down there as well as where, exactly, along the hundreds of kilometers, they should focus their energies. Several libraries in Rome had archival material left over from both world wars, and the art reference materials contained images and lists of what had been recovered since 1945 and what had not...

"*Come stai*, Bernini. How's the catacomb project going?"

Bernini looked up from his notes at the skinny redheaded man, Astorre Orsoni, leaning over his desk. Orsoni was one of the few men in the department he already knew when he moved to Rome; they'd worked together on a case involving smuggled Greek statues and forged paintings only a few months ago. But their acquaintanceship had never progressed to friendship. Quite the contrary. "Okay,

Orsoni. Flora's helping me recruit some conservator and museum specialists, and I'm making lists of what we'll need."

"What do we need academic types for? This is a police investigation."

"Evaluating the art we find, if we find it. Identifying artists, titles of works, and original owners. Matching up artworks with lists of stolen property—"

"Okay, I get it. Who's going to be on the search team from our department?" Orsoni's flippant tone of voice didn't match the tight way he held his body.

"You, Marino, Costa, Romano, De Luca, Lombardi, Ricci, and Gallo. At least that's the initial list of senior officers. We'll probably add people as we go along."

"Do we need that many people? What's Moscati say about using so many personnel?"

Bernini examined Orsoni as the older man perched on the edge of his desk. What was bugging him? Was it just being passed over for leading this venture? "The boss gave the search top priority. And we need lots of men to search the hundreds of kilometers of tunnels down there."

"Surely we can rule out the public areas?" Orsoni meant the public portions of the catacombs where tour groups were allowed to go. They both knew that scholars, scientists, and explorers with proper credentials had more extensive access to unlit and undocumented areas.

"Not entirely. Have you seen all the stairs and little side passages that branch off some of the main tunnels? Who knows where they lead, and when they were last visited by anyone?"

"True." Orsoni was Roman born and bred, so his knowledge would be useful. Particularly on where some of the less well-known access points to the underground city were located. "When's our first meeting?"

"I'll get the local team together tomorrow morning. We can't really get going until the international people arrive, which will take at least to the end of the week, maybe longer. Not everyone can just drop their day jobs and their lives and fly to Rome." Bernini turned around in his swivel chair as he heard footsteps behind him.

"Hey, what's up with the catacomb project?" The speaker was a swarthy man in his mid- thirties. Benedetto Gallo hailed from Naples originally, but his family had moved to Rome when he was a teenager so his father could advance to a higher position in the Carabinieri. Gallo never let the others forget that his father had retired at the rank of *generale di brigata.*

"Just trying to get more information out of Bernini here," Orsoni said.

Gallo chuckled as if Bernini were a closed spigot that never released water. He was buddies with Orsoni, but he was generally easy to work with. A good officer.

Bernini's eyebrows lowered. "Now hang on, you two. I already told Orsoni here that our meeting's not until tomorrow. I'm still planning our attack and gathering what we'll need. I can't discuss what I don't even know myself."

"Yeah, sure," Orsoni responded. "Or maybe you just don't know how to delegate responsibilities like Moscati does."

"Delegate what, exactly? I don't have a full team yet, let alone knowledge of the full scope of the job. It's developing hourly. Give me a break!" Bernini's raised voice attracted attention from the other staff. He was behaving badly just when he needed to set an example of cool and calm leadership.

Emilio de Luca wandered over, a full cup of coffee in hand. "Maybe you should move the meeting up to today," he suggested, glancing sideways at Orsoni and Gallo. "Stop the flood of questions and share some info."

Bernini appreciated De Luca's talent for diplomacy, but he needed more time before he gathered the gang together. "We'll sort it all out tomorrow morning. That's a promise." He shoved his chair back, glancing up at the wall clock as he did. "I have a meeting with Moscati in five." He grabbed his pad of paper and moved away from the gathering clump of over-curious cops.

"What's eating Bernini?" Orsoni muttered.

"Girlfriend trouble, I bet." Gallo sounded smug with knowledge he didn't have.

Bernini shook his head vigorously as if he could shed his irritating colleagues like cold raindrops from his hair. This catacomb search was shaping up to be a real pain in the backside. Corralling a bunch of different people and forcing them to play nicely together was never easy, and this was Vittorio's first big command.

He tapped on *il primo capitano's* door frame.

"Come." Moscati's dark good looks complemented his impeccable attire, currently a charcoal gray suit and discreet maroon tie. "Sit down, Bernini. I just got off the phone with the senior man in Austria," he said, pinning Vittorio with his I-know-what-you're-thinking gaze. "They're sending someone to join our team. Paris is doing the same; here are their names." He shoved a slip of paper across to Vittorio.

Vittorio was not surprised. His boss had already told him that the arts and antiquities police of other countries would be involved in sorting out any major find. Nazi looters had lifted artworks from Jewish collectors all over Europe, stashing them in private homes, churches, and all sorts of unexpected hidey holes. Determining ownership of the paintings and statues after almost seventy years would require extensive collaboration among different governments. Original owners must be tracked down, or if they had not survived, their descendants must be located. Wills must be located and examined, lawyers consulted, and so forth.

"When do they arrive, sir?"

"This evening. We're putting them up at the Pensione Medici, near the Spanish Steps. They'll be here in time for your meeting tomorrow."

"Great." Vittorio's flat tone of voice failed to hide his lack of enthusiasm for interacting with high-level strangers, and his boss smiled.

"Don't worry, Bernini. They will be here only as consultants. Their role is to contribute information about art objects that were never recovered and to report our progress back to their governments. They won't interfere with your operation on the ground."

Vittorio made a face. "Right. I'll believe that when I see it."

Moscati laughed. "So cynical, at such a young age! You'll go far with that attitude." His face turned serious as he leaned across his desk. "Now, what you really have to worry about is funding. You have a limited budget from the general, and you have to produce results quickly."

~ * ~

Benedetto Gallo poured more coffee from the pot that squatted near the sink in the Art Squad's lounge. He leaned against the table where the officers ate lunch when they weren't traveling around Rome, and thought about how much he loved the Carabinieri.

Since childhood, Benedetto knew he wanted to follow his father into policing. The grandparents still lived in Naples, but his parents and uncles had relocated to Rome where their jobs were. Giuseppe Gallo had started at the lowest rank, just like his son, but rose to one of the highest ranks with commendable speed. Benedetto was determined to succeed like his father and make the entire family proud.

Now he thought about the meteoric rise of Vittorio Bernini. He was relatively new to the Roman division, and already Moscati had given him a big command. While Gallo didn't mind that for himself, he resented Bernini's promotion on Orsoni's behalf. Orsoni was the most senior; he should have gotten the appointment and command of the catacomb project.

He wandered over to the tall window, carrying his coffee. Outside was a relatively traffic-free piazza, studded with trees and municipal plantings.

Gallo was single. He loved socializing, but making friends at work was difficult at the best of times. You had to work with colleagues no matter what you thought of them or their methods. He preferred to hang out with his cousin Guido, who worked in the *Polizia di Stato,* rather than with work buddies.

Orsoni was the exception. They both enjoyed watching American gangster movies and westerns, so Gallo stopped at the Orsoni apartment for a meal with Astorre's young family most weeks and lingered to watch a video. He found Astorre's wife attractive to look at, but her constant carping about her job, her family, and Astorre's imperfections was hard to bear. Benedetto wanted a woman of his own, but someone nicer, more pliable. He wouldn't meet one among his colleagues; the female officers of the Carabinieri were tough as the volcanic rock used to pave Rome's streets.

Gallo didn't know Vittorio Bernini well. But he was okay as a boss. Bernini radiated dedication and fairness, and he excelled at organization. Orsoni really had no cause for complaint—yet.

Maybe it was up to Gallo to smooth the way a bit and not chime in every time Orsoni said something antagonistic. But Orsoni relied on Gallo to be his sidekick, so he'd have to tread delicately.

After all, this search would require most of them to go underground, an environment that made Gallo distinctly uneasy. He was a bit claustrophobic; he'd learned that on a school trip to a church crypt where one of his fellow students had closed a trap door on him as a joke. Gallo had screamed himself hoarse before a harassed teacher arrived to let him out. Now he hated all small spaces, even closets in his own house.

Orsoni's demeanor had changed in the past few weeks. He seemed preoccupied, surly. Gallo felt sure it wasn't just being passed over for Bernini; it was something in Orsoni's personal life that bothered him deeply.

Gallo resolved to be a better friend to Orsoni and keep his eyes and ears open. And if he was helpful to Bernini, he might learn more.

He could play both sides and win.

Six

Flora waited until she couldn't stand being underground a moment longer and retraced her steps. After a couple of false moves, she found the stairs that took her up to the entrance level again, and soon after that, the tourist gate to the catacomb.

It was locked. She'd been down there longer than the last visitor.

Flora yelled as loudly as possible and waited. After an interminable time during which she realized she needed a toilet, she examined the gate. The builder had left a decent gap between the gate and the hinge. Only a thin person could manage it, but she was very slender. She removed her sweater and stuffed it in her bag. Then she squeezed herself through, turning her shoulders and hips sideways, and pushing centimeter by centimeter. After one horrible moment when she stuck in the middle, her body popped through the gap.

The relief made her giddy. She found a friendly tree by the side of the Via Appia and did her business behind it, and then walked quickly back to the city gate to look for her bus.

After a futile wait of twenty minutes, Flora asked a passerby if the buses were running.

"No. They went on strike at seventeen hundred."

"*Oddio*! This city! I suppose we'll have a train strike next."

"Or a garbage one, like Naples. You should have seen the streets, piled high with rotting food and other stuff."

"Glad I don't live there."

"*Ciao.*"

Flora was lucky to find a taxi, but her cell battery had finally died. Once back in Trastevere, she found a bar owner who let her use his phone and called Vittorio.

"Bernini." He sounded tired and harassed.

"Vittorio, it's me. I took a catacomb tour at San Callisto—"

"How did you find time to do that? I thought Ottavia would have you hard at work."

"I fudged it a bit," she confessed. "I accomplished quite a bit this afternoon and I wanted to visit the underground and get a feel for it. I found something..." She explained, leaving out the parts she was sure he'd disapprove of, such as taking stairs to lower levels alone and squeezing through the gate at the end of her trip.

She talked so fast that he had to make her slow down. "... So I think someone else has been down there, recently."

"Hmm. I imagine there's more to this story than you're telling me, but that can wait. Can you find the place again?"

"I think so. I thought about leaving a trail of crumbs like Hansel and Gretel—"

"*Che cosa?*"

"Oh, sorry, that's a reference to a German fairy tale about two children lost in the woods—you wouldn't know it. Anyhow, I tried to memorize the turns as I came out. Then I sketched a little map." Some map, sketched as it was in nearly illegible pencil on the edge of her Rome map booklet.

"If you are right, Flora, you took quite a chance going down there alone."

"Why? I was with a tour group!"

"Yes, but you let yourself be separated from them, and you said yourself you were scared."

"Well, I thought more of girl-chasers than possible art thieves!"

"Start thinking about how dangerous this search may become. If there really is stolen art that's worth millions down there and someone is competing with us to find it, anything could happen."

Flora gulped as she heard the strain in Vittorio's voice. Maybe he was right to be worried about her. Perhaps she'd have to change how she did things, just a little.

"I was just getting a feeling for the territory. I didn't anticipate any danger."

He sighed. "We'll talk it over tonight..." She heard voices in the background. "I have to go. I'll be home around seven thirty or eight. I hope."

~ * ~

Flora arrived home first. She jammed the groceries between her hip and the door frame while groping in her purse for the keys. Immediately, a small black streak shot into the hall.

"*Gattino*! Get back inside!" Flora dropped her bags in the open doorway and ran after the kitten.

The little black cat danced away from her down the hall, pursuing an invisible adversary. He might have been born feral, but he'd learned quickly how to bend his human slaves to his will.

Flora scooped him up and kissed him on the silky dark fur between his ears. "Silly thing! When we get around to naming you properly, it will have to be something that matches your skittish personality."

She grabbed the string bag containing their supper and pushed the door shut behind the two of them with her foot. The kitten, on the floor looking hopefully up at Flora, mewed his interest in being served smelly fish mush as soon as possible. His scrawny tail twitched sideways across the floor and his tiny paws flexed and curled. Flora filled his bowl with salmon-flavored cat food and set out on the tiny worktable the chicken and tomatoes she'd purchased

Remembering her difficult conversation with Vittorio, Flora decided she should make an especially tasty supper. She rummaged in the pint-sized fridge and pulled out half an onion, carrots, zucchini, and fresh basil. Quickly she assembled a stew with oregano, pepper, and chopped veggies and put it on the stove to simmer. She gazed at her product with amusement, thinking that she was getting better at making what her mamma called "refrigerator-cleaner" casseroles and stir-fries.

Flora had been seated at the table with a glass of red wine only a few minutes when she heard the key in the door and Vittorio entered the apartment.

Gattino flew at his legs and swarmed up to his shoulder. "You crazy cat!" Vittorio yelled as he detached twenty claws from his arm and put the kitten back on the floor. He eyed Flora. "When are you going to train this creature?"

Flora laughed. "Kittens are untrainable in how they treat their human slaves. They can be taught to use a litter box and stay off the table—"

The kitten hopped on the table and butted her hand.

"—but that's about it. Guess I'll have to buy a water spray bottle to teach him manners."

Vittorio dropped his bag in the corner, draped his suit jacket over a doorknob, and poured himself a glass of wine. He took the chair opposite Flora and leaned his forearms on the table.

"You're not really mad at me for going underground, are you?" she said, noting his rumpled hair and the tiny creases around his mouth.

He looked at her with a mixture of exasperation and affection. "No. But I am concerned about your safety. And your tendency to charge into new situations without telling anyone, without backup—things I tell my new officers never to do."

"Good thing I'm not a policeman, then."

"True. But if you're going to be a member of my team, you have to behave like one. You're a civilian, but you have to be a civilian who abides by the rules. And because you're also my girlfriend, you must set an example for the scholars and other specialists of how to work with police."

"I see. I really do." Flora realized he had never been more serious. And this was his first big command in a new job. Of course he was concerned about her behavior if it reflected on his own competency. "I'll do my best. Look, here's the map I made." She spread out the notecard on which she'd sketched the map.

He examined it carefully and asked her to describe her route again. "You didn't catch a glimpse of the man following you?"

"No."

"And you are sure it was just one person?"

"I heard the footsteps quite clearly. It was one man, or I suppose it could have been a woman with heavy feet."

He smiled, but his smile did not touch his eyes. "Next time you want to explore underground, you'll go with me or another Carabinieri officer. Someone who's armed and not afraid to use a gun to protect you. Okay?"

"Okay."

Vittorio slumped in his chair and took a sip of wine. The tension between them had eased, but Flora still felt like she was on probation. She realized that however independent she felt, she'd have to follow his lead in the catacomb search, or risk their personal relationship. Separate her public and private roles a little more carefully. She rose to stir the stew, asking, "So how was the rest of your day?"

"Not wonderful. Some of the officers are being uncooperative, and we haven't even had our first meeting yet. And I could strangle Orsoni."

"Tell me."

He filled her in and then said, "Our meeting's tomorrow at ten a.m. Can you come?"

"Me? Are you sure you want me there this soon, when you haven't even made assignments yet?"

"Yes, I do. I want them to see you as a full member of the team from the beginning, and I want to make them understand both your qualifications to be there and the added value of the other scholars and conservators you're bringing on board." His eyes twinkled, anticipating her reaction. "Yes, they will all think, 'She's his girlfriend; why should we listen to her?' but as soon as you open your mouth, you will establish yourself."

Flora was surprised and gratified that he thought she came across that well to strangers. She herself was not so sure, being a little shy in new situations and always conscious that her small and delicate physical stature didn't immediately project authority. Since her undergraduate days, she'd struggled to school her facial expressions and body language so her emotions didn't show. This was after a roommate told her she was totally transparent: any fool could read Flora's face.

"You mean, your colleagues won't immediately write me off as a lightweight, decorative female just along for the ride?"

"Ha! You said it, not me. But yes, exactly. Hey, what are you cooking? It smells great."

"*Pollo con verdure.* Or, as my mamma would say, 'Refrigerator-cleaner stew.' It's not ready yet, so have some more wine."

Vittorio fetched the bottle and poured more *vino rosso* into both their glasses—not proper wine glasses, but jam jars they hadn't gotten around to replacing with something more fashionable.

Flora remembered something. "Vittorio, there's something you should know."

"Yes?"

"When I called Assunta Vianello earlier today, she said she'd already heard the rumor about lost art in the catacombs."

Silence.

He looked at her somberly. "That means—"

"Yes, I know. The more people who know about it, the more dangerous the search will become."

His mobile rang.

"Mamma, how are you?" Vittorio abandoned his wine and reached for a cigarette, which Flora lit for him so he could pace.

She watched his lips thin as his mamma berated him about something. He moved away from the table, opening the door to their balcony. *"Si, si, Mamma..."*

Flora rose and stirred the stew, adding some chopped basil leaves and more pepper. She tasted it and decided tomato paste would enhance the flavor, especially when thinned with a little of the red wine. While she hunted for the last can in their inadequate pantry, she heard Vittorio's tone of voice change.

"No Mamma, I cannot come this weekend. Maybe in a couple of weeks. My job has accelerated. I have a new assignment, and Flora is helping me..." He crossed the kitchen again, his face darkening with suppressed emotion. "Mamma, if you complain about my 'living in sin' every time we talk, I will cut short the conversation. Flora is not just a casual girlfriend; she is long-term, special..." He returned to the balcony and his voice faded.

This was familiar territory. Both mothers were upset their children were "living in sin" in a city where their families had no representative, no relative who could visit them and monitor how Flora and Vittorio behaved. Flora suffered weekly from her mother's hostility to someone who wasn't from a family she knew, preferably Florentine aristocracy with old money. Certainly not a policeman!

Vittorio's mamma was very religious and certain her favorite son would go to hell if he lived with a girl he did not intend to marry *immediatamente*. And furthermore, Italian men were supposed to become fully established in their careers and then marry someone already vetted by the parents in consultation with the aunts and uncles. No one seemed to care what Flora and Vittorio wanted, what they felt for each other.

Flora thought it likely they would marry, eventually, but neither had met the other's family yet, and the way things were going, she wanted to avoid those meetings as long as possible. The only bright side was Flora's father, who had told her, "Be happy, do good work, and don't worry about what your mamma says. I will handle her."

If only my father could make my mamma shut up, thought Flora, turning the flame down low under the chicken.

Vittorio returned, sliding the cell phone into his pocket. He sat down with a plop. "My mamma wants to meet you."

"What?"

"She's decided she wants to meet you soon."

"Why? So she can berate me about living in sin with her oldest son? So she can push us into marriage before we're ready?"

He gave her a slow smile. "Come on, *cara*. Just think about it."

This usually had a devastating effect on Flora's insides, but this time she resisted. "Don't think you can manipulate me with that smile. I don't think I'm prepared to meet someone who disapproves of the very idea of me."

Vittorio leaned forward and captured her hands. "Flora. She's trying to get used to the idea that perhaps my choice of a life partner is out of her control. The fact that she wants to meet you at all is an enormous concession on her part. Only two weeks ago, she told me she would never invite you into her house."

"Concession?" She pulled her hands away. "That makes me feel like I'm a bargaining chip, not your girlfriend! I wish I could believe that meeting her would accomplish something useful, but I don't. I think we should wait until she's had more time to get used to the idea."

Not to mention until she, Flora, had more time to acclimate to the looming reality of yet another set of parents trying to run her life. Everything she'd learned about Vittorio's mother so far made her wary; she sounded so much like Flora's mamma. Bossy and interfering, convinced that only she knew how things should be done, how young people (especially young women) should behave.

"*Cara*, please listen. My mamma is a strong woman, like you. She is Italian, like your mamma. She wants only the best for me as her son. No matter whom I choose, she would have reservations; she would kick and scream at any woman she hadn't chosen herself. Once she meets you, I know she will love you. I have to show her that—"

47

"Show her who's boss, you mean? I'm sorry, Vittorio, but now I feel like a hot potato that's getting tossed back and forth. I don't want to meet her right now!"

He sighed and rose from the table. "Maybe when the catacomb project is over. In the meantime, think about what you really want in this life. Haven't you ever heard the word 'compromise'?" He crossed to the door and opened it.

"Where are you going?"

"Out."

The door slammed and Flora slumped in her chair.

"*Merda.*"

Seven

The dream started in the pre-dawn hours.

Flora, now a giant bird of the prehistoric variety, flew over the landscape, watching it change beneath her enormous wings. At the beginning she saw a huge inland sea, sprinkled with volcanoes to the north and south. The shorelines expanded and retreated, the mountains belched fire and ash. Lava flowed down the sides and subsided under the water.

Gradually the land emerged, coated with layers of limestone made from the carbonate shells of marine creatures and other matter that had been squeezed, heated, cooled, over time. Rain came and went, forming acidic pools in the limestone that ate away the stone. An earthquake or two thrust up folds and created depressions, one filling with water to become a mighty river.

The acidic water continued its work, eating away limestone and shaping chambers, tunnels, pockets, until the terrain resembled coarse peasant bread. River water found entry points and flowed underground.

The holey landscape disappeared as layers of mud and gravel dumped by the flooding river covered them over. An enormous swamp grew, rich with water birds and tall grasses.

Then men came and drained the swamps with tunnels and channels—

She awoke when the alarm went off and lay still for a few minutes, remembering her dream. A full-scale, Technicolor version of the landscape under Rome. Flora was enchanted with what her mind had concocted while she was asleep; someone should do a three-dimensional computer model of her dream for geology classes! Most of what Roberto had told her, supplemented with her Internet searching session, had been woven into the dream. And flying dreams always made her feel good.

She rose and made coffee, still thinking about it.

Vittorio had left her a note. "Don't be late, *cara*. I need you at the meeting."

Flora's spirits rose. She was still "*cara*" then, whatever differences lay between them.

She toasted two pieces of bread and made a cheese sandwich. Protein and optimism, that's what she needed. It might be a very long time until lunch.

~ * ~

Three hours later, Flora sipped more coffee and looked warily around the long, rectangular table.

Vittorio had introduced her to the other major players: Astorre Orsoni and his buddy Gallo Benedetto, the Neapolitan; Emilio De Luca; and three female officers, Adele Marino, Giovanna Romano, and Irene Costa.

Flora was particularly interested in the other women, who had arrived where they were professionally through hard work and dedication to the job. She tried to picture herself going through the tough physical and emotional training needed to join the Carabinieri.

Adele was a round-faced redhead with lush curves restrained by rigorous physical exercise. She could have been plump; instead she looked fit and competent.

Giovanna's short blond hair sported a purple streak. Her no-nonsense clothes proclaimed her disinterest in looking feminine, and her fine gray eyes bore no makeup.

Irene's toughness showed in the contours of her face. A lean jaw, distinct cheekbones, and large brown eyes suggested intelligence and dedication. She too looked fit, and although she was thin, her biceps bulged from her sleeveless top.

At the other end were two men in impeccable gray suits, the representatives of Zurich and Paris who were supposedly "just observers." They looked like they'd dressed purposely to fade into the background, but Flora knew Vittorio was worried about their possible interference in how he conducted the search.

Bernini began his introduction to the catacomb project. "You've all heard of the Monuments Men. They were a group of art historians, museum curators, and other specialists recruited to locate art stolen by the Nazis from private collections, especially those belonging to Jewish families, during World War II. The Nazis also set their sights on collections belonging to major museums in occupied territories, such as the one in Naples. They tried—and in many cases succeeded—to seize valuable art and ship it to Berlin. They hid caches of paintings, sculpture, and valuable books in churches, villas, salt mines, and other unlikely places to be recovered later."

"And they cherry-picked the best stuff to send to Hitler," Adele added.

Bernini nodded, but his sharp glance at Adele indicated he'd prefer not to be interrupted again. "It wasn't until 1943 that the Allies became aware of just how systematic the Nazi looting campaign was, with authorization and funds provided from the very top."

Bernini looked at his notes for a moment and smiled. "Here's a tidbit you'll enjoy. An American soldier with a toothache found a former SS officer—the son-in-law of the dentist he and his companion visited near Trier, Germany—who told them how the looting was controlled by Hitler and his top man, Hermann Göring. Göring hid art in a hunting lodge as a monument to his dead wife. Meanwhile, Hitler planned to create his own 'super' museum in his boyhood town of Linz, Austria, after leveling the city and rebuilding it to his own specifications."

Several officers fidgeted, obviously tired of the history lesson.

Bernini noticed their impatience and dropped his notes on the table in front of him. "So why am I telling you this? Because our superiors in the Art Squad have heard a credible rumor that the Monuments Men missed a critical cache of art hidden in the catacombs of Rome—"

Orsoni broke in. "We know all this, Bernini. What are we going to do about it?"

Bernini stared him down. "Some explanation is necessary for the people who just joined our search team. Not all of them are Carabinieri, and we also have international observers here."

Flora could finish Vittorio's unspoken thoughts: "So shut up, Orsoni, and let me get on with it."

Bernini switched to describing the scope of the project and the large number of people needed to achieve success. "...So that's why I need two teams initially, one to search in the catacombs and one to do the archival work."

"Do we switch tasks at some point?" asked Irene Costa. Her cryptic glance at her seatmate Adele Marino said she knew darn well that the men would do most of the underground exploring and the women would be stuck with the paperwork.

Bernini's brown eyebrows snapped together. "I'm assigning you to one team or the other based on your demonstrated talents so far, Costa. But yes, team members will move around as we progress, and—"

Orsoni cut in, "I'm not spending my time in any goddamn library."

Gallo sniggered his agreement. Then he rearranged his facial expression to look attentive.

Flora could feel the tension reverberating around the room, but she wasn't sure of the source of it. Why were Bernini's colleagues being so difficult? Was this just office politics as usual, or was it more than that? She vowed to notice every small detail of the interactions so she could tell Bernini.

Bernini sighed. "Orsoni, who's in charge here?"

Flora watched as the two men locked gazes like bulls preparing to charge. Next they'd be pawing the sand.

She let out the breath she didn't realize she'd been holding as Astorre Orsoni broke the gaze and looked down at the table. Vittorio hadn't exaggerated when he'd said his former ally had a problem.

"Tell us our assignments, then." Emilio De Luca spoke in a conciliatory tone, and Bernini shot him a grateful look.

"We start this afternoon," he said to the assembled officers and visiting reps. "Right after lunch. Costa, Gallo, and De Luca will proceed to the *Biblioteca di archeologia e storia dell'arte* in Piazza Venezia. The rest of you will come with me to the office of the catacombs to study their maps. Signorina Garibaldi will show us the catacomb route she explored yesterday off the Via Appia Antica. By next week, we'll have two American museum professionals joining us."

Flora wondered why Bernini said nothing about her discovery of someone digging in the San Callisto catacomb. Perhaps he wanted to confirm her story first? That made sense. After all, they had no evidence that her adventure had anything to do with lost art, and no way to tell how recently the opening she'd found had been dug.

De Luca asked, "Doesn't it make more sense to put all personnel on hunting for the loot? I mean, we can check the libraries and archives after we find something."

Flora decided it was time to assert herself. "Actually, the library work will help us determine where to search and save us time. Christian and Jewish families used specific sections of the catacombs to bury their dead in Roman times. It's possible that their descendants' families used the same areas to hide their art during World War II. So, if we go underground armed with maps of old neighborhoods, we can perhaps narrow down search areas. Then, when we find something, we need lists of what was stolen from whom." She noticed that one of the two men, the Austrian, made a note on his pad.

Adele Marino picked up on Flora's remarks. "There are probably more than just paintings down there. I've read about statues, vases, metalwork—all kinds of stuff the Nazis looted from prominent Jewish families—"

"Show-off," muttered Orsoni, who sat in a tipped-back chair across from her.

Adele pretended he didn't exist. "The other thing to keep in mind is that the objects we seek could take many forms: boxes, cloth-wrapped bundles, single objects thrust in among bones..."

"Ugh." Irene Costa shuddered. Her glance met Orsoni's and he smiled slightly.

Flora's mental television immediately flashed an image of her own hand groping for art under the dusty bones of someone's ribcage in a dank tunnel. Ugh, indeed. But Adele's comment made her think of new criteria for finding the lost artworks: size, material, colors—everything the team could use to sharpen their search skills when they went underground. She spoke her thoughts aloud. "Adele's right. When we're looking at crumbling walls and holes in the tufa, we need to keep our eyes peeled for different sizes, shapes, and textures. So a marble statue will take more space than a small box of jewelry, and a wrapped, framed painting has a certain shape."

Orsoni let his chair back down with a thud. "An unframed painting has a rolled-up shape. And think about matching material to parts of the Catacombs according to moisture or lack of it: you'd want organic materials to be stored in dry places—"

"But can we assume the conditions down there today are the same as they were in 1943?" Adele interrupted. "And did people hiding valuables have time to be picky? If they thought the Nazis were on their heels, they might have just shoved paintings and statues and figurines into the first available hiding places."

"Probably not," Orsoni agreed. "I know from my spelunking friends in *Sotterranei di Roma* that conditions keep changing. Areas that were dry two years ago suddenly have water trickles; walls come down, arches tumble."

Aha, thought Flora. *Someone here already knows about* the Sotterranei.

"Not surprising, considering that some of the tunnels and cemeteries date back to at least the First Century A.D. And there are multiple layers of building," Bernini said. "We're talking about hundreds of kilometers worth of underground structures. And they're not all on one level; they are stacked up like a *torta*."

Flora stuck her oar in again. "All the more reason we visit the archives in all the possible libraries where records from World War II might be stored. We may find hand-drawn maps, diaries, sketches of tunnels, all kinds of stuff that could be helpful as we search specific areas."

"Yeah, we may find those things," agreed Irene. "But it could take months or years. Do you have any idea of the condition of many of our archives? Stacks of old documents and photos. Mountains, even. Not organized in neat folders with labels. And not digitized with any regularity."

"True. But there are online resources," added the ever helpful Adele. "There's an amazing website I found with computer-generated maps of underground Rome." She turned her laptop sideways so the people on her right could see her screen. "Also an academic journal, *Forma Urbis*, where scholars have been publishing work on individual underground sites."

"I doubt any single mapping project is complete. What we will be doing is assembling an enormous jigsaw puzzle—with half the pieces missing," Bernini said. He nodded at Adele Marino. "Given your level of knowledge about resources, I think you should join the archival team, at least for starters."

"Fine with me."

"Can I switch to the underground exploration team, then?" asked Irene Costa.

"Okay," Bernini agreed. "Time for lunch, I think. We'll split up this afternoon and have our first progress reports tomorrow morning at nine, here at the Comando."

~ * ~

The two of them walked briskly to the nearest café-bar to order *panini* and coffee.

"So now what do we do?"

"Pass along every hint we get to your brothers and cousins and let them know which areas have already been searched with no finds. Do everything we can to stay one step ahead of the Carabinieri team."

"Maybe I should send someone to do archival work, too. We need as much information as we can get, as quickly as possible."

"How much do you think the cache of stolen art is worth?"

"If it's there, which we can't count on, it's worth millions. And it won't be easy to turn into cash."

"I'm not worried about that part."

"Why not?"

"Because I have plenty of contacts in the black market."

They paid for their lunches and ate them at a small, pigeon-filled park, unobserved by anyone who knew them.

Eight

Bernini's plans for Tuesday afternoon were thrown into disarray by a request from his boss for another meeting with Art Squad's senior officers. Since that group consisted of five generals of ever increasing rank, he could hardly say he'd rather be in the catacombs.

By the time Bernini got out of that inquisition, it was too late to go to the Via Appia and talk with the staff there. Paperwork kept him in the office late, and Flora spent the afternoon at the conservation lab.

A coolness like the rising breeze before a storm persisted between Flora and Vittorio. They were talking to each other, but only about practical matters like who would stock the fridge and feed the kitten. The organization of the catacomb search consumed Bernini, and Flora's conservation work was piling up. By unspoken agreement, they'd shelved any discussion of mothers and families until things quieted down.

Over the first cup of coffee, Flora told Bernini about her discussion at work with Roberto. A little shyly, she suggested that the underground group might be useful to the Carabinieri. Far from ignoring her idea, Bernini called the *Sotterranei* group right away and asked if someone could meet with them immediately, before they went underground. The woman at the other end sounded surprised, but she agreed to send a colleague to a meeting within the hour.

They left the apartment and walked to their favorite café to wait. Flora enjoyed the freshness of the air and the sounds of Trastevere waking up: a motorcycle revving, someone on a cell phone, the clatter of a louvered door being pushed up. Aromas of hot pastries and rich coffee overlaid the smells of drains and dog poop underfoot.

A young man with brown, curly hair approached Flora and Vittorio as they chose a table. He bounced slightly as he walked, and his thin, wiry build suggested the strength and flexibility of a dancer.

"Hello, my name is Fabio Greco. I'm from the *Sotterranei di Roma.*"

Bernini introduced himself, and Flora and scraped a third chair up to their table. "What kind of work do you do for the *Sotterranei?*" he asked after he placed their order for coffee and pastries.

"I'm an archaeologist. I work with teams of other archaeologists, geologists, and spelunkers to explore and map parts of underground Rome most people never see."

Flora leaned forward. "Not just catacombs, then?"

Greco smiled at her. "No, not at all. There's a fabulous layer cake down there of structures made at different times. Chambers carved out by water—the sea, the Tibur River, acid rain. Tunnels and burial places carved out by man. Churches, crypts, storage places, you name it. It will take many years to explore it all."

Bernini's shoulders sagged. "How much of the underground territory is mapped?"

"Only a fraction of it. Scholars and explorers over time have made attempts, but their maps are often filed in strange places, in no particular order. We find many of the early documents by accident. A large part of our job, as we see it, is to consolidate information in one place so other researchers can find it."

Bernini's position shifted and his face held a little hope. "I can't tell you why I want the information, but I hope your organization will share what maps you do have."

"It shouldn't be a problem. We are volunteers, for the most part. People who care about historical accuracy and good documentation. We follow in the footsteps of Antonio Bosio, who spent decades exploring and researching tunnels and catacombs for his book, *Roma Sotterranea.* He finally published it in 1632. Oh, the only people who might not share stuff right away are scholars who have been funded by universities or private organizations. They want to publish their results first; later they usually make them public." Greco pulled out a notebook, tore out a page, and wrote down a couple of phone numbers and website addresses for them. "Here are some contacts for you."

Bernini took the piece of paper. "Thanks."

Flora glanced at Vittorio and then back at Fabio Greco. She chose her words carefully. "If someone told you that something was hidden in a certain area under the city, how would you organize a search?"

Greco eyed her, his lips twisting into a grimace. He answered with equal care. "Depending on the source of information, I'd assume the hiding place could be in one of multiple places in that part of Rome. The Christian and Jewish catacombs cover over two and a half square kilometers, and galleries and passages are stacked about twenty meters high. But it's not just catacombs and subway tunnels down there. If you include sewers, crypts, early aqueducts, tunnels made by slaves and men quarrying stone, you have to search through a maze of thousands of kilometers. It would be a terrible job."

"*Thousands* of kilometers!" Bernini's shoulders sank again. "What are conditions like down there? I've been in the public parts of the catacombs, but never the less traveled areas."

Their new friend smiled. "It ranges from easily walkable to crawling on your belly. Wet areas and dry ones. Safe tunnels and those on the verge of collapse. The city sends experts down periodically to block tunnels they think are unsafe by pouring in mortar. In many places, you'll see the tufa peeling off the ceiling like weak plaster. It changes constantly. All I can promise you is that a tunnel may be passable one week and hopelessly jammed up the next."

"Any more advice?" Flora asked with a smile.

Greco gazed at the two of them with some skepticism, as if he couldn't believe the police were up to the task. "You must take good equipment and lights down there. And drinking water, lots of it—I won't drink any flowing water down there, it might have sewage in it from leaks in the Cloaca Maxima. You'll need the fresh water. It may be cool down there, but you can really work up a sweat crawling."

~ * ~

After their conversation with Fabio Greco, Bernini and Flora picked up Adele Marino and Davide Ricci, another officer, and they drove to the entrance of the San Callisto catacombs.

Flora fidgeted in the car. She wasn't at all sure she could find the place with the shovel again. Her little map had been created in haste, while she was in a state of shock. She'd been in such a hurry to get out of the catacombs after the nasty experience of being followed.

Bernini parked the Carabinieri's Alfa Romeo in the small parking area outside the catacomb entrance. They all climbed out, grabbing their water bottles and cell phones.

Soon they were in the tiny office of the supervisor for that section of the catacombs. She rifled through a file drawer and pulled out a map. It was a basic map, standard issue, the same one that tourists were given.

"Here," she said, pointing out where they stood at the entrance to a labyrinth of tunnels that crossed each other like embroidery.

"Don't you have anything more detailed, such as for maintenance of the tunnels where tourists aren't allowed?"

"Er, no. I'm guessing the Vatican office has them."

"Any other entrances?" asked Bernini.

"Probably, but nothing is guaranteed safe and passable except this one," the young woman replied.

"Okay, thanks for your help."

Flora and the three officers entered the catacomb, retracing Flora's footsteps from the evening before.

She walked briskly along the main tunnel, which was well lit and easy to navigate. Flora longed to explore slowly again, taking note of details in wall decorations and symbols she'd missed the first time. But her police colleagues encouraged her to move along.

Flora descended the first wooden staircase, and the others followed. Soon they arrived at the small flight of crooked stairs carved out of tufa that Flora had taken to the second level down.

Flora stopped at the remembered intersection of three tunnels and consulted her little sketch. "To the right here," she said, with more confidence than she felt.

This section marked the first time she'd heard footsteps behind her. Flora slowed her pace so she wouldn't miss the next turn.

"Okay?" Bernini asked. He paced right behind her.

"Okay so far," she said.

About fifteen minutes in, Flora reached an intersection that gave her trouble. Had she turned left here, or taken the middle tunnel? Her sketch was grubby from handling and hard to read.

The three Carabinieri waited. "Didn't you leave crumbs coming back?" joked Adele, trying to lighten the atmosphere.

"Let's take the left-hand tunnel. If I'm wrong, we can come back to this point and take the middle one," decided Flora.

After a couple of false turns, she located the niche and the little cave where she'd hidden herself.

The shovel was gone.

Someone had been there before them, between yesterday evening and this morning.

Nine

Flora navigated the ring-road toward Fiumicino airport with her heart clawing its way up her throat. She still wasn't used to driving in Rome. She would never get used to it; even Chicago drivers hadn't prepared her for the lane-less chaos of Italian driving. Vittorio said the rules were different here, that she had to imagine she was playing bumper cars without ever touching another vehicle. She replied that there were no rules at all; it was kill or be killed. Take the horrible ring around the Colosseum. No lanes there, just lots of little cars with hardly any metal between you and the next vehicle jockeying for position.

As a pedestrian, you were supposed to step off the curb, amble slowly and evenly toward the monument island in the middle, without ever stopping or flinching, trusting that no one would hit you. Bernini made her try it—once. Flora's mostly American upbringing meant she had all the wrong reflexes. Her flinch reflex took over, every time.

She wondered what time it was, but it would be suicide to take her eyes off the traffic, even to push the little protuberance on the side of her cell phone that brought up the screen. On the highway, drivers stayed in lane some of the time, but they didn't bother to signal and switched lanes at high speed and with mere centimeters between cars. Lisa Donahue and Ellen Perkins were due at eleven thirty, so in theory Flora had plenty of time to park and get into the terminal to meet them after they passed through customs.

Flora glanced at the rearview mirror. Italians tailgaters were more aggressive than Chicago drivers, and that was saying something. Wait a minute; wasn't that the same car she'd seen behind her right after she entered the highway? Was the driver following her? She risked a second glance. A dark, thin person. Could be either male or female. Crap, she could do without this!

Stai calma, Flora, she told herself. Don't freak out. Just because you were followed in the catacomb doesn't mean you're being followed now. Or just because someone moved that shovel and seems to know everything you're doing, before you do it.

But it's not paranoia if they are out to get you...

A sign caught her attention. Only a few more kilometers and then she could exit. *All right, let's see if the other guy follows me into the airport,* she thought.

He (or she) did not. Probably the person tailing her didn't want to pay for parking. Or, he figured Flora's trip had nothing to do with stolen art. Or, he had followed her just because she was Bernini's girlfriend...

She didn't like the way her mind was throwing up spooky possibilities. Maybe she wasn't cut out for a cloaks-and-daggers game underground after all.

Twenty minutes later, Flora paced the lobby outside customs along with what appeared to be half of Rome, milling around waiting to greet friends and relatives. Some bore signs (those were the businessmen greeting strangers); most juggled small children, babies, cell phones, and coffee cups. One good thing about being in an

Italian airport—or most European ones for that matter—was you could buy an excellent cup of espresso.

According to Vittorio, she didn't need to be here at all. But Flora had driven herself for several reasons. She wanted to meet Ellen Perkins on her own to assess what she'd be like to work with, and she wanted to share her version of the catacomb investigation with Lisa without Vittorio leaning in and correcting her, or coloring the attitudes of the two Americans. Flora figured she'd need friends and allies for this project; she planned to make sure Lisa and Ellen were fully on board with both facts and feelings. She also hadn't seen Lisa for two years and needed to refresh their connection.

Suddenly she spotted two women coming through the swinging door. One was short and a little chubby, with curly blond hair streaked with lime green, but the other was taller and wore her long hair in a distinctive braid flipped over one shoulder. Lisa's honey-gold braid.

"Lisa!" Flora broke into a big grin and waved.

Lisa smiled back and touched Ellen's arm to indicate which way to look.

Flora hugged Lisa and shook Ellen's hand. "Welcome to Rome! How was your flight?"

"Awful," Ellen said. "We had a mom with two children right behind us. Those darn kids didn't quit yowling until about an hour before we landed."

"You make them sound like cats," Lisa said. "At least it was better than having the baby across the aisle vomit in your lap."

"I've often wished for a cocoon on overseas flights—you know, like a science fiction movie where they put you in suspended animation while your spaceship travels to another solar system," Flora said as she led the way to *Ritiro Bagagli.* "Someone wakes you at the other end with fresh coffee, and you just skip the journey."

"I like that idea," Lisa said. Her expressive face sobered. "Then we'd feel readier for this underground adventure of yours, Flora. I've been thinking about all the ways it might be dangerous."

"Rock climbing is dangerous. So is caving. But we should be safe if we take good equipment and reasonable precautions." Ellen tossed her curls and hastened to claim a space next to the luggage carousel. She might be a bit pudgy, but she looked fit. Also edgy, like someone who hated to sit still for long.

"That's not the kind of danger I was thinking about," Lisa said.

Flora met her gaze. They were on the same page already; other humans could be more dangerous than the hazards of an underground environment. She said, "I hope you two brought hiking boots and clothes for exploring narrow and chilly places?" Flora asked.

"Oh, yes," Lisa said. "Ellen made sure I did. I've got a light jacket, a fleece, skid-proof shoes, everything I'll need."

Of course. Lisa and Ellen were both New Englanders, and Flora remembered Lisa saying she and her husband vacationed in the mountains of New Hampshire. Prime hiking territory.

"I brought a waterproof jacket and my best boots," Ellen said with a gleam in her blue eyes. "I'm picturing slimy walls and cave spiders."

Flora laughed. "Well, the touristy part of the catacombs is mostly dry and not too cave-like, but it is cool down there. And we will be exploring tunnels where tourists don't go, where we'll need hard hats and miners' headlamps, and there may be some wet areas. We're going to team up with some of the explorers in the *Sotterranei di Roma*—that group includes professional spelunkers and climbers."

"Hmm," Lisa said. "Hope I'm in shape for this. I kept myself pretty fit until my promotion to museum director. Now I'm exercising by rising from my chair to get more coffee. It's leading to administrative spread."

Ellen scoffed. "You're not that bad, Lisa. You walk a lot in Boston, and you do a lot of walking on weekends." She turned to Flora. "So how will the catacomb search be organized?"

"My boyfriend—Vittorio Bernini—says we'll be splitting into two teams. Some of us have already started with archival work, and I bet he'll put Assunta in charge of that group."

"Assunta?"

"Assunta Vianello, the curator at the Villa Giulia Museum. You remember, I told you how she helped us last time."

"What about Internet searches?" Ellen asked. "I'm pretty good at ferreting out information online, especially about conservation literature."

"I'll make sure Vittorio knows that," promised Flora.

"Why is our baggage taking so long?" asked Lisa when nothing happened at the carousel.

Flora looked for an airport employee but couldn't find one. She asked a bystander.

"*Sciopero*. General strike of airport workers."

Lisa groaned.

"Give me your baggage slips. I'll take care of it." Flora strode over to a young policeman trying to placate a group of irate travelers. She spoke with him briefly, turned over the luggage slips, and returned to Lisa and Ellen.

"The state police will see that your baggage is transported to your hotel by evening, when the strike is over." She grinned, feeling a small rush of accomplishment. "That's the first time I've used my connection to the Carabinieri to get something done. Shall we have a coffee before we get on the road?"

"Sure," Ellen said. "But will the coffee shop be open?"

"Fortunately for us, the café-bar is controlled by a private company."

"Maybe an espresso will keep my eyelids propped open a little while longer," Lisa replied.

The three women stood in line for coffee and found a small, round table with chairs near the back of the airport café. A good, anonymous place for a private chat.

Ellen added an obscene amount of sugar, stirred, and took a swig of the hot, sweet brew. She closed her eyes and then shook her curly head like a dog coming out of water. "Wow, I needed that!"

Lisa smiled at her colleague, sipping her espresso slowly as if she wanted to make it last as long as possible. She turned her gaze to Flora. "Flora, why don't you brief us? I've told Ellen what I remembered from our phone call, but I bet you know more now."

Flora didn't answer right away. She stared over Lisa's shoulder.

"What is it, Flora?"

"That man. I've seen him before. He's sitting close to the espresso bar, almost close enough to hear us." Was he the same dark, thin man she'd seen in that car before she took the airport exit? Did he come in a different entrance and..." Her thought trailed off.

"You are jumpy, aren't you?"

"Well, I've been followed in the catacombs already, and I may have been followed to the airport."

By unspoken agreement, they moved their chairs closer together and lowered their voices. Ellen's normally chipper expression darkened. "Now you've got my attention."

"Tell us everything that's happened so far, Flora," Lisa said.

"That's exactly why I wanted to have coffee with you guys, away from the distractions of Rome and the people on the team. Here goes." She gave them a rapid summary of what she knew, from

Vittorio's high-handed phone call to Flora's boss to her catacomb walk.

Lisa and Ellen looked at each other.

"Creepy," Lisa said. "I'd have been worried too in that situation."

"Now what?" asked Ellen. "And who's on the team besides us?"

"We'll be working with officers at the Art Squad, part of the Carabinieri branch based here in Rome. The team includes both men and women with different talents: knowledge of the city, archival and photographic skills, and so forth." Flora listed the names of officers she'd met. "We'll be divided into teams. I'd like to say you'll be kept together, but Vittorio may move us all around depending on what needs to be covered any particular day. Lisa, I'm guessing you are very good at library research work?"

Lisa made a face. "Anyone who does a doctorate in archaeology or art history has to have good research skills. Won't much of the material be online?"

"Not as much as you'd think. The Carabinieri has its own IT department, of course, and we have the fastest computers available. But our problem will be personal letters and journals and lists from World War II that have never been digitized. Or catalogued properly. Our archival libraries simply don't have the funding to employ many people at a time, so it takes forever to organize stuff."

"Ah. Good old-fashioned digging among old paper manuscripts. My favorite kind of work, actually," Lisa nodded.

"I'm hoping to go underground as soon as possible," Ellen said. "I've joined a hiking group in the Blue Hills outside of Boston, so I'm in reasonable shape for long walks. And I love caves."

Flora waved a hand at Ellen. "Don't worry, you'll get your chance. The other thing I wanted to warn you about is the tension among our team. There's some bad feeling because Vittorio was put in charge of the operation while Astorre Orsoni—that's our most senior lieutenant—was passed over by *il primo capitano* Moscati."

Lisa's blond eyebrows rose. "How does Vittorio feel about it?"

"All in a day's work, I think. But of course he wants the search to succeed, and it is his biggest assignment ever."

"And what about you?" Lisa said. "How is it for you, being yanked off the conservation job that was going so well?"

Flora's mouth turned up at the corners. She'd always appreciated Lisa's ability to empathize and pay attention to others around her. "I've mixed feelings. I'm glad Vittorio needs my help, and I think part of this experience will be fascinating. But I also have the feeling we're getting in over our heads before we've even started."

"Because you were followed at least once?" Ellen asked.

"Not just that. It's the vastness of the project that scares me. We have so little information about where to search, except where our adversaries have tried already."

"Who are they?" Lisa asked. "And are you sure they are after the same thing? You said you'd found digging debris and a shovel. That could be anyone."

Flora shook her head. "No. Just this morning, we got a call over breakfast. Vittorio's boss just confirmed that someone else with ties to the black market in antiquities smuggling is looking in the catacombs for a cache of Nazi-stolen art. But we have no idea who it is."

Ten
Isabelle Rossin's Diary, Part 2

August 28, 1940. The move from France took forever because all the trains were delayed and unbelievably crowded.

We each had two suitcases, which was all we could carry. Even that was too much. The porters took our cases and shoved them into another car. Then they helped boost us into boxcars since the passenger cars were full to bursting.

It was a terrible journey. Forty or fifty people—men, women and children—stuffed themselves into our boxcar. The lucky people chose a corner where they could lean against a wall and take turns sitting down. After a couple of hours, we all took turns leaning against a wall or sitting. The rest of the time, the press of people held us upright. If you tried to eat or drink something you'd brought with you, a hundred eyes watched you accusingly. In the middle stood a smelly bucket that became our only toilet...

I hope I die before I have to travel like that again!

Now we are settled in Italy, if you can call living out of suitcases settled. We are at Uncle Riccardo's farm just outside Cassino, near the monastery. Our room is tiny, but we are lucky to have any space at all that is private. Giovanni, Sal's cousin, gave his room for us. He sleeps on a mattress in the living room now.

I was interrupted during my writing today by Sal[vatore]'s mother, who lives on the next farm. She wanted to borrow some flour. It was funny, because I did not know the word for "flour" in Italian, so she made motions of kneading on the table. Ah! I understood then. She is making more pasta. I know it is cheap, but if I have to eat nothing but pasta, I shall scream! Franco, Sal's father, says he will buy some chickens this week. Eggs and meat, variety in our diet!

[*pages missing*]

September [... 1940]. It is so different here in rural Italy. In Paris, I was used to city noises and smells. Automobiles backfiring, the screech of buses, the shouts of the milkman. Fresh cheeses and meats from the outdoor market around the corner, stale urine in the stairwells. Here, we have a rooster who crows all day and all night. Overwhelming odors of manure, stacked in piles around the farm, and pigs' slops. The chicken coop smells so bad, it makes me retch. I have to collect the eggs. One day I forgot I had eggs in my skirt pocket and leaned against the kitchen sink. You can imagine the mess...

Sal's uncle Riccardo grows olives and peaches and onions, so we will never starve, but the war up north comes closer every day and we know it is only a matter of time before it reaches our part of Italy. My Uncle Henri, who left Paris just before the Germans arrived, has finally reached Florence after a long journey by boxcar, hitchhiking, and walking tens of kilometers. He will arrive soon to visit us, perhaps on the back of a vegetable truck.

I must work on my Italian. Sal says his nephew can teach me.

Eleven

Vittorio Bernini felt jumpy and irritable, as if ants were walking all over his skin. He couldn't settle to any task at work. Time for a mind-clearing walk. This was his practice when things weighed too heavily on him. He told Paola, the Carabinieri secretary—*il primo capitano* Moscati's right hand—that he would be out of the office for an hour, but reachable on his cell. She nodded, used to the vagaries of policemen juggling multiple cases.

Bernini left the *Comando Carabinieri per la Tutela del Patrimonio Culturale.* Like many Italian ministries and governmental buildings, the Carabinieri Art Squad was housed in a historic building. This one, a spectacular Baroque palace in cream and pale orange, boasted a multi-part facade that undulated like a stage set. The colors and textures made the surrounding buildings look drab. Never mind that the interior of the *palazzo* contained ancient plumbing, tiny closets, and no air-conditioning; at least it had high ceilings and big windows.

He turned right and took off toward his favorite piazza, the Capranica. Big enough for pacing and pigeons, it soothed his mind while providing the visual stimulation of flower shops, busy cafés, and the legs of pretty women as they ran their daily errands. He walked steadily over uneven stone pavers for a few minutes, skirting café chairs and flower pots. He let his thoughts drift as he tried to unbraid the strands of his anxiety. When he wasn't thinking about work, he thought about Flora. Problems infested both his work and his love life.

Flora's impulsive habit of rushing into new situations without telling him, or even asking what he thought, concerned him. Would that change over time? He thought not. He loved her sense of adventure, her enthusiasm, but he also wanted to keep her safe. The classic dilemma of falling in love with a modern woman: he wanted to wrap her in cotton wool, but he could not.

Then there was her attitude about meeting his mamma. That surprised him; he'd thought their relationship was more mature, more committed. But he also understood that Flora had suffered over-management by her own mamma, so there was legitimacy to her wariness about subjecting herself to the control of yet another domineering Italian female.

Bernini turned right on Via delle Paste. The other part of it, he finally admitted to himself, was that he was ready to move to the next stage in the relationship and Flora was not. Or perhaps she was but didn't view the next logical step as Bernini did. The ultimate commitment: marriage. He yearned for that, despite his misgivings about joining a family that spanned the globe, with in-laws in Chicago he'd never met. But the occasional interaction with Flora's relatives would surely be manageable if he had Flora.

Then he spotted a young couple with a dark-haired baby in a stroller. They looked so happy, laughing at their babbling offspring. The image hit Vittorio with a visceral punch. He wanted a baby like that one. Flora's baby. Their child. Maybe two or three children. The very idea made him grin like an *imbecille*.

He crossed the Piazza Capranica, intent on purchasing a *macchiato* to bring his brain up to its preferred caffeinated level. A tiny café-bar under gaudy canvas drew his eye because it also had tables outside in a perfect spot for watching people. He'd sip his coffee for a few minutes, and then walk another twenty minutes or so through a different neighborhood on the way back to the Comando.

Coffee in hand, Bernini resumed his ruminations. Item two: the revelation from Moscati that someone else with black market ties was on the trail of the missing art. Not surprising, really. If the Carabinieri heard rumors, then surely other interested parties had their ears to the ground as well. Unless the searchers behaved in ways that attracted attention, it was perfectly possible for two or even ten different groups to explore underground Rome at the same time. When you included the sewers, crypts, and catacombs that Adele Marino and Fabio Greco had talked about, the territory was vast. So much of it was open to the public; the rest could be easily accessed by those who knew about the many entrances to all those tunnels.

How the hell would they be sure they'd searched all the possible hiding places? They needed a tracking system; he'd put the IT person on it. Each member of the team would report in every day, with specific notes and GPS coordinates.

Pigeons strutted beneath his table, looking for crumbs. "Sorry, birdies. I have nothing. But someone before me ate *panini*, so you're in luck." He brushed the crumbs onto the pavement and smiled at the surge of birds cheeping around his feet.

The tensions at the office certainly explained why Bernini wasn't sleeping well. He had expected outside competition in the search, especially when he thought about the probable value of some of the art they might find. What if there were another Klimt painting waiting underground, one like the gold-adorned portrait of the

Austrian aunt of Maria Altmann? Or another priceless Greek marble statue such as the Getty *kouros* now in California? What was down there could be worth millions. No, those exciting possibilities didn't keep him awake at night; rather, he had the niggling feeling that there was something right under his nose he had missed. Something that would help him steer the search in the right direction.

A young woman dressed in a very short skirt, with heels on her feet and cell phone stuck to her ear, rode by on her moped. He admired her legs until she disappeared around the corner, wondering how soon she would fall off or hit something.

Bernini turned his gaze to a nearby flower arrangement. He knew that focusing on what he could not remember—or hadn't noticed—would not work. Far more likely that the missing item would pop up later, while he was doing something else, or when he lay awake at night. Perhaps remembering would be the silver lining in his accumulating cloud of lost sleep.

Time to move on. He drained the coffee, clattering the cup down on the tiny saucer, and stood, rolling his shoulders to loosen them. He unbuttoned his suit jacket and took off down a cobbled side street, enjoying the variety of smells that assaulted his nose. Raw fish, with a tang of salt air from the port of Ostia. Fresh baked pizza with warm tomato sauce and basil. Dog shit. Flowers from the window boxes above his head. A whiff of what he called "Rome smell:" a compound of car exhaust, dank moldiness wafting up from underground crypts and aqueducts and subways, old urine, cigarette smoke, and garlic.

Just as Bernini turned into the entrance of the Carabinieri building, another thought occurred to him. What if there were no trove of lost art despite the fact that someone besides the police was searching? The very fact that the rumor was known to several people argued for a hoax, an urban legend. What if they were spending thousands of euros on a wild goose chase? The idea made him shiver. Surely their sources were reliable. If not, the *generale* and the colonel would look for someone to blame lower down the ladder of authority. Such as Bernini.

~ * ~

Gallo joined the team led by Davide Ricci in one of the two Jewish catacombs open to the public, under the Villa Torlonia. Five Carabinieri, a couple of police academy students, and a guide accompanied them. The plan was to orient the larger group by showing them the differences between Christian and Jewish catacombs, then splitting up into sub-teams to explore the other Jewish site at *Vigna Randinini*.

The group proceeded along a well-lit tunnel until they reached a *cubiculum*, a chamber full of burial niches and frescoes.

"Notice the Jewish symbols in here," Ricci said, pointing. "And Jewish families usually sealed their burials after wrapping the bodies." Gallo saw painted or carved menorahs, shofars, grapevines, and citrons, rendered in reds and blues, decorating the white plastered walls. Some burial niches were still partially sealed with crumbling walls of rubble or brick, plastered over to provide another painting surface.

Their guide said this area was still visited by Jewish families seeking the burial places of their ancestors. So maybe a World War II family trying to protect their art collection had come down here to find a hiding place.

Gallo was impressed by just how many possible hiding places there were. There were rectangular niches or *loculi*, with and without bones. Cavities that might have been used for lamps or other lighting during Roman and later times. Side tunnels and crude passageways galore.

Although this section of the underground network was dry, a whiff of mold reached Gallo's allergy-prone nostrils. He sneezed. Good thing he didn't have to sleep down here—not that he'd sleep much surrounded by burial niches.

A skittering sound caught his attention. Probably even the empty niches housed small rodents or insects or stray cats that liked the underground. But where did such creatures obtain food? The cats would eat the rodents, but the smaller animals wouldn't find much. Orsoni said some of these tunnels intersected with sewers and aqueducts, and animals probably had their own tunnels up to the surface.

Ricci and De Luca stopped ahead to examine something near the ceiling, flashlights turned upward. Gallo, almost the last in line, glanced back the way they'd come and noticed a dark figure step sideways into a side tunnel.

One of the students? One of his colleagues? Of course, there were no facilities down here; anyone might step aside to take a leak off the main walkway. But the stealthiness of the movement had caught Gallo's eye.

And Bernini seemed unusually concerned about secrecy, but it was difficult to keep this search secret. How many people already knew there might be a fortune in lost art stored down here?

On impulse, Gallo decided to turn back and see who it was. He could catch up with Ricci and De Luca easily since they weren't moving fast.

He walked rapidly back to the side tunnel and peered in. His flashlight showed a narrow, twisty passageway that turned left almost immediately. The ceiling was low and the rock roughly carved, with protrusions and depressions.

Gallo glanced back at the other Carabinieri, still visible as silhouettes, and stepped into the tunnel. His rubber-soled shoes made no sound on the stone floor.

Bent almost double, he felt like a crab scuttling forward. More than ten minutes of this would give him a backache.

A flick of light and soft voices showed someone was ahead of him.

Intent on pursuit of whoever had left their team, Gallo decided he'd go as far as he could without being seen, check out who was prowling the tunnels ahead of him, and report back to Bernini.

Ten minutes later, he stepped out of the passage into what was clearly a subway tunnel. The platform's dusty and crumbling condition indicated that it hadn't been used in years. He looked both ways and spotted a familiar figure talking with two young men.

Now what on earth was she doing here?

Gallo started forward, but he tripped on a loose rock. The clatter drew the attention of the three people on the platform.

Two of them came toward him.

Twelve

Flora walked home slowly through the early May dusk, carrying her shopping bag and her canvas work bag. Women hurried home with fresh meat and vegetables to prepare the evening meal. Every other person passed with a cell phone held to the ear, and she heard scraps of conversations in English and French as well as Italian. Glasses clinked, dogs barked, and a baby cried. A mangy cat followed her, no doubt attracted by the smell of the cheese and prosciutto she carried.

Her colleague Roberto at the lab had told her cats were revered in Roman times.

"Really? Why?"

"They were admired as symbols of liberty and as good mousers. Roman soldiers took them on campaigns to protect their grain stores."

"Makes sense."

"There's more. A Roman killed a cat by accident in 47 B.C. He suffered the punishment of the times: he was stoned to death."

"Jeez! Well, Rome's cats today don't look very revered. Most of them are sick-looking strays."

Roberto grinned. "A law was passed in 2001 protecting the over 300,000 feral cats as part of Rome's 'bioheritage.'"

"I don't believe it!" Flora was highly amused.

Flora paused and gave the mangy cat a tiny piece of cheese.

The skinny cat wolfed it down without even a mew of thanks and ran the other way.

Flora deliberately lingered near shop entrances and flower stands while she mentally composed what she'd say to Vittorio. Although they'd been talking with each other almost normally, she knew that issues still lay between them.

First, Flora running off to explore a catacomb by herself. In her mind, that was a perfectly innocent, non-dangerous move. At least, it started that way. She was familiarizing herself with new territory, as a writer must before writing about a new setting. But in Vittorio's mind, her adventure was a symbol of her tendency to rush off by herself and stick her nose into other people's business. And perhaps to test Bernini's control of her behavior: first as a lover, second as her boss in the catacomb search. Or was it the other way around? Either way, he had acted as if he felt threatened by her impulsive excursion. And scared.

And how did she feel about his acting overly sensitive? Touchy and irritated.

Then there was the issue of meeting his mamma. Flora stared at a symmetrical arrangement of fruit, kiwis teetering on top of a substantial pyramid of apples and pears. She eyed the peaches, stacked nearby. Surely it was too early for ripe peaches? But they looked so good, she bought one anyway. Flora sank her teeth into the fruit, making juice run down her chin. It was luscious, a slice of heaven and a promise of summer delights ahead.

Meeting a man's mother was a real milestone, meaning the relationship was serious and would probably end in marriage. Flora already knew she wanted that, and that Vittorio was the right man for her. But part of her yearned to be free of entanglements a little longer before making the final commitment. The other part, what she thought of as the little bird sitting on her shoulder before she fell asleep at night, told her firmly to get on with it. "What are you waiting for? If he is '*il primo capitano*' in your life, don't discourage him, don't send him away by pretending indifference!"

Her girlfriends had told her that pre-wedding nerves included attacks of doubt and procrastination that occurred over several months. It was normal, they said, to hesitate a little bit before leaping across the chasm into a lifelong commitment, even if that commitment seemed welcome. Everyone had to find the right balance between pursuing a career—or not—and raising a family. That there would be a family was hardly ever brought into question. Modern Italian women might wait a few years, but most of them eventually had the babies their more traditional relatives expected.

That she was half-Italian, half-American made it even more complicated. She could expect to encounter layers upon layers of different expectations, from both sides of the family, if she married Vittorio.

Flora fingered a bouquet of flowers, admiring the purples and blues, and debating buying it. Too obvious for a peace-making gesture? Who cared?

She bought it and inserted the bouquet into her shopping bag so most of the flowers waved in the breeze but the stems were protected by her other purchases. Walking on, she realized part of her hesitation came from the very nature of her relationship with Bernini: they'd arrived at a critical juncture without her even noticing. All the basic dating moves were complete. They knew each other's likes and dislikes, personal habits, sexual preferences... and it was far better than anything Flora had ever experienced.

She felt a sense of homecoming every day when she knew Vittorio would meet her within the hour that had nothing to do with sharing an apartment, arriving home for dinner. "Home" was where he was, whether it was being in the same room together, or the late night cuddle when she rested her head on his chest and he stroked her back. She could not imagine living without him.

This time, when she opened the door to the apartment, Gattino didn't escape. Instead, the little cat wrapped himself around her legs, doing his very best to trip her while she put away her groceries.

"Do you know cats were revered by the Romans?" she asked him. "Of course you do."

She'd just filled up a small crystal vase with water for the flowers when she heard the rasp of Vittorio's key in the lock. He walked in, carrying an identical bouquet of flowers, but yellow and gold instead of blue and purple.

Their eyes met and Flora began to laugh. "Great minds think alike... I almost bought that one!"

He put his stuff on the kitchen table and slipped his arms around her. "And I just wanted to say—"

Flora beat him to it. "I'm sorry about being such a brat the other night."

"I'm sorry for putting so much pressure on you. I just have to learn not to let my mamma set any timelines for me, or us. We will do things when we want to, not when she says."

Flora returned his hug and looked up into his face. "I think I will be ready to meet her, within a month or two, just not now when we have so much going on. Okay?"

"Done." He kissed her. "What's for dinner?"

"Oh, you! Sometimes I think food is all you think about!"

"You know that's not true," he said with a twinkle in his hazel eyes.

"I do. Pour some wine for us? I'm going to make pasta with *arrabbiata* sauce."

"I'm not angry, but I do love that dish." This was a private joke between them, since the literal translation of the name of the spicy tomato sauce was "in the angry style," referring to the liberal dose of red pepper in it.

Flora began to tear up romaine and arugula for a salad. "What happened today?"

"Well," Vittorio said as he lounged in his chair and picked up his wine, "we got more confirmation today from the source who claims someone besides us is hunting for stolen art in the catacombs."

She turned and looked at him. "Are you allowed to tell me?"

"Yes, I think so. Tomorrow you will swear an oath to keep everything about this investigation quiet outside the team, so we advance on your promise only a little."

"'Jump the gun,'" muttered Flora in English.

"What?"

"It's an American expression. From racing. We have a starting gun for many kinds of races—if you start before the gun sounds, you are 'jumping' it and may be disqualified."

"I got it. So, what I have to tell you is that the threat is a credible one, reported by our regular *Polizia di Stato*. A junior officer spotted a team of four people climbing a fence around one of the entrances to the catacombs two nights ago. Since they were armed and carrying shovels, he did not confront them, but took note of the time and location. Then he reported the incident to his captain, but of course, when others arrived to check, there was no evidence of a break in, digging, or anything else."

"What part of the city?"

"Not far from Metro line A, so now we have a new concern."

"What is that?" Flora asked as she whisked olive oil, balsamic vinegar, salt, and pepper together for a salad dressing.

"I need to find out how close the Metro lines are to any part of the catacombs. In fact, what the team needs to do is assemble an overlay of all the available maps—for catacombs, crypts, sewers, metro entrances, aqueduct foundations—and figure out where they overlap."

Flora stopped in mid-whisking. "You mean places where searchers can use the entrance to one system of tunnels to get into a second one?"

"Exactly. It won't be easy, because multiple agencies and government units control the municipal functions for the city of Rome—and they don't play well together. You wouldn't believe the difficulties I've already had trying to get complete maps of just the public part of the catacombs." He sighed and sipped his wine. "I may drown in paperwork before I get through this project. Permissions and forms are needed for everything we want."

"Make Orsoni do some of the legwork."

"Orsoni?"

"Yeah. Knowing his obnoxious attitude, he'd make you do it if he were in charge."

Vittorio's eyes glinted with amusement. "Do I detect a trace of vindictiveness there?"

"Who, me?"

"I just might do that. It gets worse. I talked with a sewer inspector today and instead of being helpful, he moaned and whined about how he has no funds and an impossibly tight schedule for sewer repair and—"

"Did he promise to share his maps?"

"No. I'll probably have to demand them from the Public Prosecutor, yet another delay."

"No chance of the whole underground system being in a computerized database?"

"Ha, ha. I wish. No, no one in the province of Roma has such a thing. Partial records, yes; complete records, forget it."

"Then added to all that, you have archaeological sites. The *Sotterranei* have some maps. Didn't you already obtain some from Fabio Greco's contacts?"

"Yes, but their maps are very specific, sites and tunnels their own people have explored." He sniffed like a little dog. "Is that pasta ready yet? The *arrabbiata* sauce smells wonderful."

"*Cinque minuti.*"

Vittorio rose to wash his hands, and his cell phone rang. He answered it.

Something flat and ominous in the tone of his voice made Flora turn from the sink where she was draining the pasta. His face turned pale as he listened.

Vittorio ended the call and slid the cell phone back into his pocket.

"One of my colleagues has been murdered," he said.

"*Oddio.* Who?"

"Benedetto Gallo. You sat across from him at our first meeting."

"Where—"

"*Cara,* I will tell you later. I must go."

"I'll save dinner for you."

"Put it in the fridge. I'll be hours." He kissed her firmly and left.

Flora sat down in her chair, knees weak and mind spinning with fearful speculations.

If Gallo had been killed, Bernini could be in danger... would she ever get used to living with a policeman who might be here today and dead tomorrow?

Gallo's murder must be connected to the lost art investigation. But how?

Who would do such a thing?

Thirteen

Bernini stood at the entrance of Metro Line B at the Circo Massimo stop, not far from the foot of the Palatine Hill.

The body of his colleague lay twisted on its side. Blood pooled in a dark ring on the cement from a knife wound to Gallo's heart.

He touched a gloved finger to the blood. Warm and liquid. The death had happened very recently.

Carabinieri officers of several stripes and ranks stood around watching while the crime scene team from the *Polizia di Stato*, the first responders, did their stuff. They took photos from several angles, took tiny samples of hair and blood and fabric. Then a man marked the perimeter of the crime scene and two others slid the body into a bag for removal to the morgue.

Vittorio Bernini's hunger had completely dissipated, replaced by a visceral loathing of the wretched beast who had committed the crime. Anger mixed with sadness that one of his few friends in the department was gone in such a brutal manner.

Benedetto Gallo had been a committed officer with a keen eye for irregularities, both in the art world and the more immediate environment of the Comando. He tended not to make many friendships at work because he knew the pitfalls; different assignments could test boundaries between colleagues, and it was best to keep an open mind and a professional attitude. Orsoni was the exception; Gallo and Orsoni had been close.

Bernini had appreciated Gallo's professionalism, and because of that, Gallo's occasional clumsy show of support for Orsoni seemed trivial. Now he wondered if Gallo's personal relationships had gotten him into trouble. Did someone demand his loyalty and silence, citing family or professional connections, only to be rebuffed? Did Benedetto know something about the investigation that he hadn't had time to share?

His musings were interrupted. The crime scene head officer gave his report and asked for permission to remove the body.

"Yes, of course." Bernini summoned Emilio De Luca and Astorre Orsoni to accompany him as he explored the subway station beyond the immediate crime scene.

Orsoni's face reflected more anger than grief. "How on earth did he get taken by surprise? And what was he doing here in the first place?"

"It's hardly the catacombs, it's just a Metro station. A fully functional one, not an abandoned platform. He could have been meeting someone for dinner. This part of Rome is full of restaurants," De Luca said.

"We must check the maps we have so far. I want to know if this location is close to any underground tunnel besides the subway route," Bernini said. He used his flashlight to illuminate a side niche full of electrical wires. "Gallo could have had a dinner appointment, true, but you both know what an enthusiast he was for scoping out anything connected with an investigation. I wouldn't be surprised if he was systematically checking subway platforms, planning to report back to us with any anomalies."

"And it got him killed," muttered Orsoni. His shoulders slumped. Bernini guessed that grief had overwhelmed Orsoni's anger.

"What's that?" De Luca pointed to the left where a bend in the tracks revealed crumbling masonry. The three men gathered around it while Bernini used his flashlight. A torso-sized hole led into a larger space whose full extent they couldn't see in the dim light. It reeked of cat piss, a hazard of all underground spaces near the surface.

"Looks like it might be a tunnel," Bernini said. He shone the light up at a mass of stonework that made him think of a church crypt. "I wonder if it connects to the catacombs. How about—"

His cell phone blipped in his pocket. He pulled it out and scanned the tiny screen. "Moscati's trying to reach me." Bernini pushed his speed dial button for the first captain, but nothing happened. "I have to go up above this level to get any reception."

Orsoni said, "I bet reception's going to be a problem during all of our underground explorations."

He's right about that, Bernini thought. *One more handicap to worry about.*

Bernini sighed as he pocketed his cell phone. "You guys take over. Do you have a decent light? Go as far as you can, see if this tunnel connects with anything else. If it looks plausible as a place to hide art, we should spend more time investigating and get someone down here with a GPS unit and add the coordinates to our map. See you back at the Comando."

He took off at a run. *Il primo capitano* did not like to be kept waiting.

At the top of the subway stairs, he tried his cell again. The connection worked.

"Moscati."

"Sir. I was down in the Metro."

"Ah, of course. What can you tell me? How did Gallo die?"

"Knife to the heart. Someone who knew basic anatomy got it right with one thrust. We've no idea whether Gallo was exploring on his own or just exiting a train on his way to dinner."

"Come back to the office as soon as you can. We need to reassign some people to the murder investigation while the rest of you pursue the Nazi trove."

"Yes, sir. *Subito*."

~ * ~

They crouched in a tunnel not far from Metro Station Circo Massimo.

"Did you have to kill him?"

"I didn't do it."

"But you know who did. And I'm willing to bet it was one of your brothers or cousins."

"They're not easy to control. Especially Franco, the youngest..."

"You must rethink your plan, your commitment to this cause, everything. Do you realize how much you risk if you are caught? Far from helping your family, you'll be in prison, in no position to earn money or do anything else useful."

"Oh, skip the lecture, cousin. I won't get caught; I'm too careful."

"That's what most criminals think."

Silence.

The first speaker sighed. "I want to help you; you know I do. But this path is madness."

"You promised!"

"I did. And for the sake of family, which is everything to you, I will continue to feed you information. But get your young men under control! Make them understand the consequences—for all of us."

"I'll do my best."

They split up, taking separate routes home.

Fourteen

Bernini drove as quickly as he dared, which wasn't fast enough. He joined the suicidal milling circle around the Colosseum, jockeying for position with all the other non-signaling drivers. Unlike Flora, he'd driven around central Rome enough since he started this job to know all the shortcuts.

When he pulled into the parking lot at the Comando, he saw Orsoni's little Alfa Romeo and two light blue *Polizia de Stato* vehicles. Okay, that made sense, since the state police had been first on the crime scene.

He walked into a meeting in progress led by *il primo capitano* and his equivalent rank from the state police. The scene-of-the-crime results were partially in; the digital photos of Gallo's body were projected on the wall. Fingerprints—if there were any—would take longer because someone had to check for matches in the database.

Moscati and Franconi listened while Bernini made his report, occasionally nodding and whispering to each other. Bernini found this amusing, since he knew they didn't really get along with each other. When they stood together at public briefings, the rigid shoulders of both men told the true story.

"... and so there is nothing to indicate whether this murder was connected to our catacombs investigation. Gallo was robbed and may have resisted—we'll know that when the autopsy results come back." Bernini swallowed as his mind skittered over the image of his friend and colleague brutally cut open with the pathologist's saw.

"What was stolen from his body?" Moscati asked.

"His cell phone and wallet, sir."

"Too bad. Calls to and from that phone might give us leads to the murderer."

"Actually, it was the police cell that was stolen. I recovered the personal cell." Bernini put it on the table. "And it's clear the body was moved from another location; there were drag marks on the pavement."

"So he was killed elsewhere. How was he stabbed?" asked Franconi. "And was it a professional job or a random stabbing?"

"Single wound to the chest, suggesting someone who knew basic anatomy. And since it was a frontal attack, I think that means Gallo knew and trusted the assailant."

"Rossi, start going through his contacts and text messages," Moscati ordered, handing the cell phone to a junior officer fresh out of Carabinieri training. He frowned at Bernini. "Who were Gallo's friends?"

"I don't know, sir. He was a bit of a loner. He wasn't married, but he had a brother with a young family living in Trastevere. I believe he spent a fair amount of his time off with them. Wait—I remember he did go on a weekend trip to Naples with De Luca."

"Gallo's retired father, the brigadier general, is going to give us trouble if we don't solve this murder quickly." The speaker was a tall, sturdy man with pepper-and-salt hair who had just walked into the meeting room. The colonel, Bernini realized, was taking a special interest in this case. That meant he would shortly be taken aside and told just how important the Gallo family was.

Moscati's scowl indicated he knew he would receive the same treatment from his boss. "That is true. I'm going to reassign De Luca to work with the *Polizia di Stato* murder squad since he probably has some insights on Gallo's friends and enemies. Bernini, you can have him back on your team in a few days."

"*Va bene.*" Bernini began frantic reshuffling of personnel in his head but quickly realized the jigsaw of assignments required the paper list he'd left in his office. If he could make his thumbs work faster on texting, he could keep all his notes on his cell phone. De Luca was on the archives team. Should he be replaced now, or later?

"Bernini. You were on the Carabinieri murder squad in Siena, right?" Colonel Brunesci asked.

"Yes, I was, sir."

Moscati anticipated his superior's advice. "Bernini, we may reassign you to the investigation of Gallo's death if we don't get results in the next forty-eight hours."

"Sir." Bernini hoped that wouldn't happen. He'd left Siena to get away from sordid wife-beatings and murders so he could focus on antiquities smuggling and art theft. The catacomb search was just gearing up. If Bernini got yanked off, Orsoni would be the most likely replacement. And once Orsoni got his mitts on the position he'd wanted in the first place, he'd stay in command.

Moscati took over the meeting, parceling out the tasks of notifying the family and tracing Gallo's movements over the last couple of weeks. He set a second meeting for eight o'clock the following morning.

Bernini pulled out his cell and texted Flora that he would be home well after midnight.

The meeting broke up fifteen minutes later. As he sidled toward the door, the colonel pulled him aside.

"Lieutenant Bernini, a word."

"Yes, sir." He knew what was coming.

"You know about Gallo's family? About his father's senior position in the Carabinieri?"

"I do." Bernini leaned against the wall and resigned himself to hear the history of the force all over again. He was not disappointed.

"… the *generale di brigata* took over the Art Squad and made it what it is today. His influence is still felt in the way we do things. This death is a disaster, not just for his family, but for the reputation of the Carabinieri. We must move carefully… '

Bernini listened soberly, his mind racing ahead to the probable consequences if they failed to solve the murder. A head or two would roll. As one of the officers in charge, he was directly under the sharp eye of the colonel and the generals above him.

He remembered an English expression Flora had taught him: "Handle with kid gloves." That was what he must do with the people and activities under his domain. His own private expression was "Tiptoe around trouble."

Starting now.

Fifteen
Isabelle Rossin's Diary, Part 3

September 22 [1940]. My mother writes that food rationing has begun in Paris. She must stand in long lines to get any cheese or meat, and they are eating horrible-tasting, gray bread and vegetables that are not fresh. Mama saw a poster that said, "Save bread! Cut it in thin slices and use the crusts for soups!" I ache for them. Some people are so desperate they are eating their pets, their cats and dogs! My relatives are going hungry while we have relative abundance here—true, it is not the food I am used to, but we do fine...

November 2 [1940]. I miss my family. They write that things are very bad in the Marais district. The Nazis find every excuse to arrest Jewish storekeepers or to raid the apartments of people known to have art. Sooner or later, they will come for our collection. My father is so worried. He says he may [ship some of] it to us and we will keep it until the end of the war.

The nausea is gone. I am getting as big as a cow, and my appetite is huge. I wonder if my baby is getting enough nutrition?

December [... 1940]. My father wrote that Nazi officers came and took all our paintings and art [except the objects] he sent to us... He tried to resist the seizure and argue with the Nazis, but Mama stopped him. People have been shot for much less. *Les Boches* knocked over furniture, broke things. They were so rude. The officer in charge threatened Papa, saying, "All you Jews will have short lives. We shall see to it."

January [... 1941]. Our first baby has been named Salvatore after his grandfather, a tradition here. I will push for the next baby to be named after one of my family members and see how far I get. Little Sal is thriving, despite the war and the short rations.

Mama writes that she is becoming a very inventive cook as rationing gets worse. There is no flour so she uses mashed potato, and she is experimenting with making sour milk do for cheese! Most horrible of all, they can't get coffee very often, except when one of Papa's rich friends brings it, so she grinds together toasted barley and chicory! I cannot imagine the taste.

[gap in the diary]

Sixteen

Flora used her unexpected free time to call Lisa Donahue to see if she and Ellen wanted to meet for a glass of wine or dinner, if they hadn't eaten yet.

"I never turn down a good Italian wine," Lisa said. She spoke to Ellen in the background. "And neither of us has eaten yet. Still getting over jet lag, so our stomachs have no idea what time it is."

"I think you need a good introduction to the cooking of Latium," Flora said. "I will meet you at your hotel in about twenty minutes, okay?"

"We'll be ready."

Feeling only slightly guilty for choosing to spend money instead of eating her own cooking, Flora tipped the *pasta arrabbiata* into a bowl, covered it with plastic wrap, and shoved it into the fridge. If, as she suspected, Bernini grabbed a snack at the Comando's vending machine, the pasta would be there for tomorrow's meal. She'd go out with her friends and pretend, for a little while, that Bernini's friend and colleague had not just been murdered.

~ * ~

The three women descended upon a trattoria near the Pantheon that was known for its pizza *bianca* with divine cheeses, arugula, roasted red peppers, and also its innovative pasta dishes. Flora's favorite dish consisted of chopped mushrooms in a cream sauce over tortellini: *tortellini alla panna con funghi*. She'd had that dish before, but this version had an especially decadent cream sauce, spiced with something subtle like nutmeg. The restaurant was family-owned, staffed by brothers and sisters while the mother cooked and the father served as *capo cameriere* and wine steward.

Flora steered her companions to a corner table, perfectly positioned so the wonderful aromas from the kitchen wafted in their direction while the noise of dishes clattering was muted. She ordered a mellow red wine from Montepulciano, one she'd recently discovered and liked very much.

"How was your first day in Rome?" Flora asked.

"We slept in, then had a wonderful breakfast of coffee and pastries, and then walked our feet off—" Lisa began.

"And then we took a nap, had more coffee, and visited the Colosseum," Ellen said. "The ruins were impressive, and so were the gazillions of stray cats."

Lisa peered at Flora's face. "You don't look so hot, Flora. What's wrong?"

Flora looked up from moving her wine glass in little circles. "I probably shouldn't tell you this so soon, but you'll hear about it tomorrow anyhow." She took a deep breath and closed her eyes for a moment. "A colleague of Vittorio's was murdered tonight. I don't know if the death is related to our search for lost art, but the victim was on our catacomb team."

Both Americans gazed in consternation at her.

"His colleague, killed?" Ellen said. "Does that mean your boyfriend is in danger, too?"

"No more than usual," Flora replied. "He was on the murder squad in Siena. He's been shot at, but never injured. So far. If we stay together, I'll have to get used to being afraid every time he leaves the apartment."

Lisa winced. "Poor you. Will the Carabinieri share evidence with us? Will they fill us in if the murder is tied to the reason we are here?"

"I honestly don't know how much they'll share. Certainly the fact of the murder, but not all the material evidence or the strategies the police will take to find the murderer.

"Vittorio said earlier that we would be required to swear an oath of secrecy when he convenes our first team meeting with everyone present. My interpretation of that warning is we'll be required to keep our mouths shut about our major purpose and the details of the investigation in case our rivals get ahold of vital information. But the fact of a murder can't be kept secret—not from members of our team."

"Whew," Lisa said. She took a larger sip of red wine while she considered the implications. "Well, I think we all knew this job might be dangerous. Perhaps this just changes how we do things, like each of us pairing up with a cop, preferably an armed cop."

Flora smiled. "Good idea. Your idea makes sense for other reasons. Vittorio is already worried about fitness levels of scholars compared to Carabinieri officers—you're not a problem, Ellen."

Ellen grunted and Lisa smiled, silently admitting that she didn't look much like a buff young explorer.

"Now that we may have a murderer pursuing us, it would be smart if someone on each team has a gun. And part of the tunnels we'll be exploring will be unsafe structurally, so no one should be exploring alone in case there's a cave-in..." Flora said.

"Or your flashlight goes out. Or you run out of water, or get lost," added Ellen.

"Or your cell reception doesn't work underground," Flora said.

Lisa tipped a little more red wine into her glass and pushed the bottle toward Ellen. "Who is the person who was killed?"

"Benedetto Gallo. He's a man from Naples, a good officer. Vittorio liked him."

"And you don't know any details?"

"Nope. Vittorio will most likely be out most of the night, investigating. I hope he will tell us more tomorrow, when we have our team meeting."

The waiter arrived to take their orders, and all three ordered pasta and salad. Ellen defiantly added a small pizza with cheese and arugula which she claimed she'd share as an appetizer. "I'm starving."

"Actually, I am, too," Lisa said. "But wine always wakes up my appetite. Flora, what time is the full team meeting tomorrow?"

"Nine a.m., unless they reschedule because of the murder."

"Tell us more about your Vittorio. How's he doing in the new job?"

"He's a *tenente*, or lieutenant, now. He likes his senior captain, Moscati. His colleagues are interesting and not always easy to work with. Lieutenant Orsoni—that's the guy who helped us with the Greek statue investigation—seems to have his nose out of joint. Probably because he wanted command of the catacomb search and Moscati gave it to Vittorio. The team has several feisty women; you'll like Adele Marino and Irene Costa. That's about all I can tell you now, since I've only met them for the first time a couple of days ago."

"I bet you'll be glad to have reinforcements," Lisa said. "We'll watch your back."

Flora agreed. "That's exactly what I was thinking. We three should stick together."

"'The Catacomb Girls?'" suggested Ellen.

"Hmm. I'm not sure that name's a good omen," Lisa said.

Seventeen

Bernini hadn't gotten home until one thirty in the morning. He hoisted himself out of bed with a groan as Flora opened her eyes.

"I'll make the coffee," she said, swinging her legs out of bed.

"Thanks," said Vittorio, who usually did this. "I'm going to take a shower."

Over espresso, yogurt, and toast, he told Flora about the trauma of finding Gallo's body.

Flora shuddered. "How horrible."

Then he described the tunnel they'd discovered. "I got a call just as I was heading out of the Comando building after our late meeting. Orsoni said it didn't lead to another underground system, or at least not obviously. There was a caved-in ceiling about two kilometers in."

"So how will you know what's worth exploring and what isn't?" Flora asked as she inhaled the wonderful smell of fresh coffee and refilled her cup with dark brew and hot milk. Their morning mixture was more *macchiato* than *cappuccino*; they didn't own a frothing gizmo. Flora had adjusted the grind of the beans so the result was less like Tibur River mud and more like rich, Illinois soil.

"That is indeed the question," Vittorio said, rumpling his hair in frustration. "We have incomplete information, very sketchy maps, and not enough people on our team." His hazel eyes focused on her face. "That means your archival work is crucial. You can help me narrow down where to look underground."

"I know Ellen prefers to be underground, but she has really good computer skills. She could locate online records—the ones that are digitized—about stolen artworks from Jewish families. Maybe she could help me set up a database with types of art, family names, and any info about parts of the catacombs families used."

"Excellent. I'll loan her to your team for a few days. What did you turn up in your first library search?"

"There are some letters and diaries at the *biblioteca*, but they're buried in folders along with photos and documents in no pattern that I could see. They'll take hours to go through."

Vittorio grimaced and drank more coffee as if it would drown his worries. "We need to find shortcuts," he muttered, chin tilted down. "Quick ways to access information."

"I suppose you can't use students because of security risks," she said.

He raised his head. "Hey, that's an idea! I'll see if we can swipe some warm bodies from the police academy. Thanks, Flora! And then we need someone to supervise them..." He stared at her with unusual intensity.

"Oh, no! I'm not the one to supervise a bunch of cocky young Carabinieri or *Polizia di Stato*! Get one of your own to do it."

He smiled. "Yes, I know. But you would be very good at it."

"Except that I have zero authority. You need someone who can give orders and be obeyed instantly."

Vittorio's eyes danced. "I'm thinking you would make a very good officer, *cara*."

She felt a glow in her chest at the compliment. "Perhaps. Hey, it's eighty thirty. Didn't you want to be a little early for the meeting?"

"*Si. Andiamo!*"

~ * ~

Soon they were all seated around the long, oval table at the Comando building. The Italian team was complete, including Assunta Vianello and an art conservator from Florence named Giallo. Lisa and Ellen represented the United States, and a man named Baudin, who was an art historian specializing in Jewish works of art, had come from Paris. Also present were the two men from France and Austria who had lurked in the background at the first team meeting, before Lisa and Ellen arrived.

Bernini introduced the newcomers and moved quickly into the main agenda of the meeting. "Okay, everyone. The first order of business is security. Our secretary is passing around a form that we have all collaborators on Carabinieri investigations sign. It says that if you breach confidence or talk to reporters you will be instantly dropped from the team as well as face a stiff fine if you're not Italian and a police record if you are Italian." He glanced around the table and made sure everyone was paying attention. "I don't have to tell you how sensitive this project is, but we have a new development. One of our Art Squad officers was murdered thirty-six hours ago, and we don't know yet whether or not his death is related to our search. We have to assume it is connected and take appropriate precautions."

"What happened?" asked Baudin

"*Sotto-tenente* Benedetto Gallo was stabbed in a Metro station. It appears to have been done by someone who knew basic human anatomy. His wallet and police cell were stolen, but not his personal cell."

"Just the police cell?" Irene said.

"Yep. It is quite odd that the personal cell phone was not taken as well."

"So the murderer wanted information known only to the Carabinieri," Adele said.

Flora watched faces as everyone digested this unpleasant news. Vittorio had whispered to her, at the last possible moment before they started, to pay special attention to people's reactions during the meeting. Did that mean he suspected someone in the Carabinieri of murdering his colleague, or did he just want to make sure he knew where people stood in relationship to each other? *Allies, rivals, lovers—all were possible in this very mixed group of men and women from different backgrounds and politics. Most likely both,* she thought. She decided to look for surprise or anything else unexpected on the faces around her.

Orsoni added his two cents. "I was there at the scene with Bernini. We have no suspects yet, so anyone who knows anything about Gallo's friends and enemies—"

"Thank you, Orsoni, I was just coming to that." Bernini took over again, earning a scowl from Orsoni. "There was a meeting last night with the colonel and first captain. One or two of us may be pulled from the catacomb search to help with the murder investigation…"

Uh oh, thought Flora, watching Orsoni hunch his shoulders. Orsoni really does not like Bernini being in charge. A case of too many cooks? Maybe if Orsoni received command of part of the operation, he would be more cooperative. She'd ask Vittorio if that were a possibility—or maybe he would resent her suggestion. Flora sensed that this investigation, with its new role for her bang in the center of Vittorio's job, would test their patience and their emotional control over and over again.

"… De Luca has already been assigned to the murder squad because he knew Gallo pretty well and had recently taken a weekend trip with him. That means you, *Signor* Baudin, will join the archival half of our team."

Baudin nodded. Flora thought his thin, slightly stooped build and bespectacled face looked more suited to joining her at the library than walking miles underground. But he was a Parisian; people who lived in central Paris—and most modern cities—ran up and down subway stairs and walked miles on a daily basis. He might be fitter than he looked.

"Next item: personal safety while you are on the job. *Signorina* Garibaldi had a little adventure in the San Callisto catacomb this week. She was followed by someone unknown after she fell behind her tour group, and she found an area that appears to be recently excavated off the main tourist track. Someone broke through a tufa wall into a small chamber, but nothing—no art—remained there."

And the overturned bucket I saw had disappeared before Bernini got there, added Flora to herself. Looking at the neutral expression on De Luca's face, Flora realized she should also pay attention to the people who controlled their faces unusually well. Someone who betrayed no emotion at all could be hiding anything… De Luca wasn't the only one. Giovanna Romano kept her face bland and unconcerned, as did the two officials from other parts of Europe.

"Since then, we've had reliable confirmation that at least one other group with black market or antiquities-smuggling ties is looking for lost art underground," Bernini continued. "We don't know who it is yet, so finding out will be one of our objectives. So, if you are working in public places, including parts of the catacombs that are regular tourist routes, you may travel alone as long as you stay with a guide." His glance flicked to Flora.

"But if you are exploring after dark or in a part of the tunnel system that has poor maps or dubious cell reception—that's most of the catacombs unless you are very close to the surface—you need to be in pairs. One of you should be armed, which means civilians must team up with Carabinieri or *Polizia di Stato* officers."

"You mean you're adding men from the other police divisions?" Orsoni said.

"Yes," Bernini nodded. "We need all the help we can get. We just don't have the personnel in the Carabinieri alone for an investigation of this size—"

"But the state police have totally different training! And those young recruits don't know what they're doing yet!"

Bernini frowned and said in his most measured voice, "*Il primo capitano* has already approved my request for more men and women. We will also have some police training students helping in the archives."

"Isn't adding so many uncommissioned personnel to our team a security risk?" Irene Costa asked.

"The new folks will be reminded that keeping their jobs depends on keeping their mouths buttoned up outside this building. That applies to all of us." Bernini eyed his most talkative colleagues for a moment. "Now for assignments…"

"Sir." A young uniformed officer entered the room and whispered into Bernini's ear.

Flora saw his lips tighten.

"We have a problem," Bernini said, looking up from the note. "Digging has been reported in two other catacombs, at the Domitilla and Commodilla. We need to get a handle on this quickly. I want two pairs of people to check out these sites." He looked around the table. "Romano and Costa, each of you take a student and try to figure out why each site was attractive to the diggers. Is it a Jewish or Christian catacomb? Does it connect with anything else that might be a good hiding place? What is its underground position relative to neighborhoods above it? That sort of thing. Our adversaries may have some tips we don't."

Or, thought Flora, *someone within the Carabinieri is leaking information.*

"So you've eliminated the Christian parts of the catacombs?" asked De Luca.

"Not entirely. I just think it more likely that tunnels under Jewish-owned land will produce something."

"Hmm. Want me to check landowner records?"

"Yes. I know one area near the Palatine Hill was a popular Jewish neighborhood. I thought my team could start looking there."

"Okay. When shall we check in with each other?" asked Adele Marino.

Bernini replied, "How about seventeen hundred? Then I'll know where we stand, what needs to be done next."

~ * ~

Emilio De Luca scratched the top of his head. He had plenty to think about after the meeting with Bernini's team and his own meeting with the State Police's murder squad. So far, all they had was dead ends. Too many of them. The officers on the job of tracing Benedetto Gallo's friends and relations had reported back. Nothing unusual, nothing helpful. The man didn't seem to have an enemy in the world.

So what had Benedetto Gallo done to deserve an early death by knife wound? Had some furious family member come up from Naples to do him in? Or was the killer closer to home, a friend, relative, or colleague living in Rome? And where had Gallo been killed, exactly?

They'd searched the Metro station, Circo Massimo, and the tunnel leading away from the current platform. But had they checked the unused subway platforms within, say, a two-kilometer radius? There were at least two that De Luca knew about.

He placed a call on his cell. "Did anyone examine the disused subway platform halfway between the stations of Circo Massimo and Piramide on the Metro B line?"

The officer consulted someone in the background.

"No, not yet."

"See to it. Look for blood and drag marks. Let me know." De Luca pushed the disconnect button.

Now what?

He ambled to the coffee station in the Comando lounge and refilled his cup with dark sludge, adding two spoons of sugar to ease the bitter taste.

If Gallo's friends and relatives produced nothing, then they had to face the unpleasant possibility that someone within the Carabinieri had ordered Gallo's death. Bernini had dropped hints about an information leak, but De Luca thought Bernini was reluctant to investigate one of his fellow officers as a traitor, perhaps a murderer.

De Luca, who had been in Rome's Carabinieri for seven years, had seen enough of human nature to know that no one was immune from lust, greed, or jealousy. Having police training did not protect anyone from the emotions of daily living. Only two years ago, the Art Squad had arrested one of their own for embezzling a special fund set aside to help the families of officers killed in the line of duty. Naturally the scandal made the newspapers, and the Art Squad's upper ranks were not happy with the negative publicity.

He'd talked with his wife, Alessa, only the night before after they put the children to bed about the tense atmosphere at the Comando. De Luca didn't make the mistake of telling her any specifics about the search for lost art, just that it was a difficult case and one of his colleagues had been murdered. She'd already read about Gallo's murder in the newspaper.

"I don't like you being on the murder squad, Emilio. It puts you in danger. Whoever this is might target you next. When will you move back into the Art Squad?"

"In a few days, probably. *Cara*, don't worry so much. We've had extensive training for all kinds of situations, more than most police. We don't work alone; we always have backup."

He couldn't tell her he was afraid someone within the Carabinieri was working against his team. That someone he knew could be an informer, a murderer, or both. At some point, he would tell Bernini, but he wanted something solid to buttress his suspicions first.

De Luca lit a cigarette and sipped his sludge, feeling the jolt of caffeine hit his brain.

What motive would drive someone with a perfectly good job to search for lost Nazi art on the sly and find it before the Carabinieri?

Greed. Greed for more money, either because the person craved things he or she could not afford, or maybe because a close family member was in family trouble. Greed coupled with recklessness.

What did he know about his colleagues? Astorre Orsoni: pretty young wife, always well-dressed, young son who seemed to have all the latest toys and motorized devices. Giovanna Romano: butch appearance, no interest in clothes. Crazy about southern Italian food. No mention of family problems. Irene Costa: she didn't talk about home much, but she had mentioned a relative who could never hold down a job. Vices? Cigarettes and red wine. She liked fast cars; she dressed nicely but not in the height of fashion.

De Luca didn't see any obvious clues, but he had a hunch he was on the right track.

Dig deeper and keep your eyes open, he told himself.

Eighteen

Ah, Italy. Garlic, mangy cats, motor scooters, and divine coffee. Beautiful architecture, fountains, wonderful food, and indifferent service—for women over a certain age.

Lisa Donahue was delighted to be back in her favorite foreign country, but she'd love it more if she had gotten more sleep.

Their *pensione*, an older building with high ceilings and no air-conditioning, left quite a bit to be desired. While the price was right (the Carabinieri was paying for it), the amenities were more student-grade than well-heeled tourist, and the plumbing had seen better days. Attempts at a hot shower failed, and the paper-thin walls allowed Lisa and Ellen to hear far too much of the marital argument and subsequent lovemaking next door.

The revving of motor scooters late into the night and catcalls below her unscreened window kept Lisa awake.

Lying on the hard mattress, she watched the streetlight playing over the ceiling and felt a breath of cooler air wash over her jet-lagged body.

She had plenty to think about. The meeting at the Carabinieri's palace headquarters had been an eye-opener in many ways. The delectable Vittorio Bernini, in command of a rowdy team of hotshots and naysayers, overseen by a snappy *capitano*. A palpable tension between Bernini and Orsoni, the redheaded and red-tempered officer who'd been passed over. The interesting women around the table, and the ways they jockeyed for position.

Lisa's Italian was far from fluent, but the body language of the various players had filled in the missing words for her. She wanted to go underground to see the catacombs, but she accepted the fact that she'd be more useful in the archives.

Flora and Bernini faced a huge challenge. Not only did they have hundreds of kilometers of underground tunnels to search, they had different police agencies and municipal authorities to placate. Lisa had witnessed a small tussle between Bernini and an officer from the *Polizia di Stato* in the hall right after the meeting. From the wildly gesticulating hands and the way the other officer stuck his head into Bernini's personal space, she assumed it hadn't gone well.

Lisa flopped over onto her right side, facing the window, and bunched up her pillow into a more satisfactory support for her head.

How could she be most helpful to Flora and Vittorio in this very demanding situation? If she couldn't sleep, she could at least review every single thing she knew about the looting of art and antiquities during World War II.

Nineteen
Isabelle Rossin's Diary, Part 4

April [1942]. Baby Maria has arrived. Maria is her official name, after Sal's sister who died last year, but I shall call her Bella in private after my grandmother. She is indeed beautiful. Rationing is worse. I hope I will be able to feed her what she needs...

November 12 [1942]. My parents sent me two more paintings by special courier to keep for them until after the war. I am not so sure this was a good idea; the Nazis in Italy are just as bad as the ones in Paris. Whenever they hear of a well-off family with Jewish connections, they mount raids, take things, injure people. They are thugs and bullies.

Maria is seven months old now. She is thinner than she should be, but we are giving her extra eggs and milk to plump her up.

July 25, 194[3]. Mussolini is gone, deposed from power. The Allies have landed in Sicily. Soon their forces will move north, and what will that bring but more shortages? The Germans seize food and gasoline; will the Americans be any better? My husband says the ground battle will eventually arrive on our doorstep.

Sal is worried about whether the art and library collections at the monastery will survive the war. As librarian and curator, he is in charge. He says art from the museums in Naples is being transferred here and it will be stored in the monastery for the duration of the war. The Naples collection includes beautiful things: paintings, bronzes, statues, antiquities from Pompeii. In addition, the monastery holdings include a Library of Monuments and many priceless illuminated manuscripts and tapestries. They must not fall into enemy hands, or be subjected to bombing.

September 4, [1943]. Weather still hot. Rationing worse; I have no meat or fish so we are eating a lot of pasta (again!). I harvest vegetables from the garden to make the sauce, but we all find it tedious without the savory flavors we are used to. The boys are thriving; they are very brown and play outside whenever they are out of school...

September 20 [1943]. The art collections from Naples arrived at the monastery Sept. 9, the same day as one of the Allied landings at Salerno...

The Germans are everywhere, tromping through our town and lording it over the people at the monastery. Sal says they are planning a big operation directed by the Hermann Göring Division. The office where Sal works has a commanding view of the roads coming up the hill and the courtyard in the monastery. He sees more trucks arriving, lots of men gesticulating and arguing. Their German voices carry well in the still, hot air, but not clearly enough to hear what they are saying. Only the tone, which is autocratic and overly loud.

Twenty

Flora's world accelerated and tilted at crazy angles. Vittorio was never home; they were both overworked, and neither of them slept well at night. If she were a gnat perched on the spinning globe, any moment now she'd fly off into deep space, or become too dizzy to function. Her uneasiness stemmed from doubt in her abilities to deal with whatever they found. Was she really a competent art historian? A good enough conservator? At the same time, she trusted Vittorio Bernini and his Art Squad colleagues to guide the team in the most efficient ways find the art in the vastness of underground Rome.

If it was still there. Although Vittorio hadn't said as much, he'd hinted enough to let Flora know he shared her misgiving: any art trove left underground during World War II could have been moved, sold, or dispersed, long before the Carabinieri heard the rumor. They might be chasing their tails.

Since the part of San Callisto where she'd found the bucket had already been checked by the Carabinieri, Bernini had asked Flora to team up with Lisa and Adele Marino and return to the *biblioteca* with students from the police training school. Ellen would go with them to construct a database, and Assunta Vianello would meet them after she and a colleague checked out the archives at the Ministry of Cultural Heritage and Activities.

They rode in Adele's police vehicle, a standard four-door model. It was a tight fit for three at the best of times, especially with their cameras and laptops taking up most of the back seat.

Flora noticed the traffic was much worse than usual. "What's going on?"

"Another transit *sciopero*. The drivers are striking for higher wages. Again. You think this is bad, wait for the next garbage strike. Then whole streets will be blocked and the smell will drive you underground."

When they arrived at their destination thirty minutes instead of ten minutes later, Adele squeezed the car into an illegal parking spot and slapped her Carabinieri pass on the inside of the windshield. "There," she said with a smile. "No one will tow this car or make us pay a meter. This job has some perks after all."

Inside the library, Adele located the skinny young man with the odd gait who had helped them the first time. Scuttling sideways like a crab, he showed them to a room with a big table so they could spread out, and sent for an assistant to pull files for them. In about fifteen minutes, a young woman wearing a miniscule red skirt arrived pushing a cart stacked with folders related to Nazi-looted art and Jewish families in Rome.

Flora and Ellen sat at one end of the table to discuss the database format while Adele organized the five students. Lisa began sorting file contents into piles by family name and location within the larger Rome area.

Ellen opened the database program on the Carabinieri laptop and swore at the unfamiliar layout. After several unsuccessful experiments, she clicked the keys needed to bring up a blank database. "Stupid European keyboard," she muttered, referring to the rearrangement of the standard American keyboard she was used to. Then she quirked a blond eyebrow at Flora. "Search fields?"

Flora thought about it. Assuming they found an artwork, say a painting, they'd attempt to identify it. "Artist's name, name of artwork, medium, exact date or period of creation."

"Okay. Category: artwork. Fields: artist's name..."

Flora used her fingers to tick off categories. "Ownership, or better, provenance. Names of owners, addresses if known, dates of transfer from one owner to another..."

Ellen typed busily. "Provenance category created."

"Okay, dates of Nazi seizure, transfer, etc."

"That's part of provenance, isn't it?" asked Ellen. "The entire history of the piece, from the time it was created to when it turns up in a modern collection."

"Yes, of course, but add a flag or something so we can pull up the date when the Nazis got ahold of each piece. If we have that information," Flora said. She looked at Lisa, who was listening attentively. "What else, Lisa?"

"How about a cross-reference to known Jewish families? If an artwork was owned by a woman who then married and changed her name, you'd have at least two family names associated with the painting or statue."

"Excellent!" Flora nodded. "So the searchable fields will include 'owner,' 'dates of ownership' for each owner, and 'Jewish connection.' Right, Ellen?"

"Yes, got it. I'll list the years separately, so you can search on, say, 1943, and find out who had the painting or artwork at that time."

"Thank goodness the papers are already labeled with original folder names. That means we can re-organize the documents by any category we find useful and eventually they'll be put back in the original folders," Lisa said.

"Not by us, they won't," muttered Ellen, glancing at the teetering piles of files already on the table.

"Okay," Flora said when Ellen had roughed out the database. "Another idea: if underground hiding places are related to specific neighborhoods in Rome, we need a 'location last seen' category in the database."

"Or maybe 'storage or display location' should be added to each chapter of an artwork's history," added Lisa. "Not that we'll find that information most of the time, but if we do know where something was in, say, January 1944, that could be useful." She looked at Flora, who nodded.

Ellen clicked away. "Done."

The women looked at the huge piles of files. "What criterion should we use first?" asked Lisa, rolling up her cotton sleeves.

"Let's use location, as we just defined it," Flora said. "Group the folders first by neighborhoods, such as Trastevere, then by Jewish last names. Then we look for artworks owned by and stolen from those families."

By noon, the dust from the files had settled on all three women. Flora had a streak of black across her nose, and Ellen's formerly white blouse looked ready for the washing machine.

They had sorted papers into piles for the Buscichelli, Liebermann, Capuano, Castelnovo, Marino, and Romano families, all inhabitants of Rome during World War II and later.

Flora couldn't help noticing that the last two names corresponded with the family names of two of the team members, Adele Marino and Giovanni Romano. *Hmm. Something to keep in mind and pass along to Vittorio.*

Then they went to work.

~ * ~

Two days went by with what Flora called negative progress. The team waded through stacks of files, finding all kinds of diaries, letters, and lists of household furnishings. Most files were discarded as having no relevance to their search. Three family archives looked promising, with mentions of artworks stolen by the Nazis, but further research showed that the items had been recovered in the first decade after the war.

By day three, Flora was ready to tear out her curly hair in clumps if they didn't find something useful for Bernini. Everyone else was sick of coffee and *panini*, agitating for longer lunch breaks. Adele Marino made sure they kept at it, especially since the catacomb teams had turned up nothing useful as yet. They were a long way from narrowing down search locations underground.

Around five o'clock, Flora stood up to stretch her tight shoulders and wiped the dust off grubby hands. She gazed with hatred at the huge stack of papers still to be examined. Water, she thought, and another short break.

After a restroom visit and half a bottle of water, she decided to make a random selection. From the middle of the stack, she pulled out a folder labeled "Misc. Italian families, unknown surnames." It proved to be a collection of personal letters, photos, and other documents dating to the middle part of the World War II period, roughly 1940–1943. Most referred to families displaced from other parts of Europe who ended up in Latium or Tuscany.

A ragged-edged black-and-white photo of a young woman with dark hair was paper-clipped to a sheaf of paper. Flora stared at the tantalizingly familiar face. Where had she seen those eyes, the way the lock of hair arched over the forehead?

She unclipped the sheaf and discovered she held a partial diary, its pages ripped along the left edge where they'd been torn out of a binding. The pages were stained and filthy, and sections were illegible or missing. She turned the top page and read, *"Sal and Cl... (name unreadable) are up to something. I am so worried that they will get hurt, or killed. Then what will the children and I do if Sal doesn't return?"*

"Sal" was probably short for "Salvatore," who was presumably the husband of the writer. Flora hunted through the other pages for female names and found none. Perhaps the woman had introduced herself at the beginning of her diary, in a section that was missing. She jumped ahead to the next legible section. *"I feel they should listen to me since the paintings belong to my side of the family. Uncle Henri says..."*

Henri? Surely, that was a French name. So was part of the family French?

"He came down from Paris only three months ago to value the Renoir... and Monet paintings and he arranged for a specialist in Greek antiquities to come another time and assess the vases and bronze statue..."

Flora's pulse raced as she remembered Lisa saying once that most Greek bronze statues were melted down in antiquity for weapons. Statues that survived into modern times were therefore rare—and very valuable. Feverishly, she shuffled the other papers in the folder, looking for a list of artworks belonging to the mysterious French-Italian family...

Two sheets from the bottom of the stack, she found it.

1 Renoir study, woman in red at café

1 Monet cathedral painting
2 Matisse sketches
10 Greek vases: amphorae + one BF vse by Exekias Painter
1 bronze statue of Zeus
Family R xxx, Acquired 192xx

Holy cow! Renoir, Monet, and Matisse! *Big names meant big money. And a bronze statue of the king of the ancient Greek gods!* "BF vse" she knew was "black-figured vase." Naturally the rest of the family's name that began with "R" and the date were illegible.

But where were these works now?

A few pages further in the diary, she found another entry:

"October xx, 1943. Nazi shipment planned tonight. They will remove artworks from their storage place in the monastery and send them to Rome, but Sal heard a rumor that a diversion is planned and the Nazis will send at least some of our stuff to Berlin... he plans a different ending... Clxxx will drive the second truck..."

Which monastery were they taking about? Was it Monte Cassino, the one they'd talked about earlier in one of the Carabinieri meetings? Her hands shook as the implications sank in.

"Hey, folks!" Flora called to the rest of the team. "I think I found something!" Lisa and Adele leaned over her shoulders as she laid out the relevant pages and explained her conclusions. "We're looking for an Italian man named Sal, or Salvatore, and his companion whose name—given name I assume, begins with a 'Cl'—and a possibly French wife with an uncle named Henri."

"Interesting, yes, but what makes you think this is the cache in the catacombs?" Adele asked.

Flora glanced apologetically at Adele. "I've no proof, not yet. But this is the first promising lead we've had—especially the suggestion that Sal and his companion are about to interfere with a Nazi shipment of looted art." Flora showed them the relevant sections of the diary and the list of artworks. "Maybe Sal succeeded in diverting some of the listed artworks."

"I agree," said Assunta Vianello, who had arrived while Flora was immersed in her files. "This looks promising. Now we need to do some genealogical research. I know just the place: The *Archivo Centrale dello Stato* in the *Piazzale degli Archivi*. It contains Jewish records of all kinds."

The door to the conference room swung open.

"What did you find?" Irene Costa dropped her small knapsack on the table. Her brown eyes glowed with interest.

"I thought you guys were underground," Flora said.

"We were. We've come up for air, and I thought I'd stop by here and see how you're doing," said Irene with a perky expression. "Looks like you have something, the way you're all clustered around Flora here."

"Come look." Flora stood so Irene could look at the diary fragment and the list of artifacts. She also watched Irene's face, admiring her calm, unruffled manner, which hid any expression of what she might be feeling.

Irene gathered the papers together. "I'll make a copy of these and take them back to the Comando."

"The originals stay here," Adele said. "That was the agreement with the *biblioteca*."

"Of course. I'm going back to the office, but it looks like you folks have more files to go through. I'll save you some time by putting these in the hands of *Tenente* Bernini."

Adele scowled, clearly thinking Irene was stealing a march on her. But she agreed to Irene's plan. "I'll show you where the scanner and printer are," she said.

Twenty-one

Meanwhile, Bernini and his team stopped at the Carabinieri branch station on the *Via Appia Antica* to pick up more maps. Orsoni had located them after a tiresome day of dealing with officialdom. Bernini smiled as he remembered Orsoni's sour expression.

"Those *imbecilli* had the maps all the time. I can't imagine why that young woman at San Callisto didn't know that."

He'd enjoyed following Flora's suggestion to unload some of the permission-seeking and official-placating on Orsoni, who hated that sort of work but was quite good at it.

Bernini reminded himself that Orsoni would remember this assignment and resent it. Orsoni was a bean counter. If he were put in charge of an investigation and had the opportunity to return a similar assignment to Bernini, he'd do it in a heartbeat.

During the past three days, they'd covered some twenty-five kilometers underground on the southeastern side of Rome, where most of the known catacombs were located. Three teams of men and women explored both public tunnels and side tunnels. They crept through narrow passageways, bent double, scraped by rough rock on either side—the term "soft tufa" only applied to the ease of carving it. They wore hard hats and carried headlamps and industrial-grade flashlights. Bernini made teams carry orange paint as well so they could mark the entrances of tunnels already explored.

Now they were underground in the San Sebastian catacomb, also on the *Via Appia Antica*, walking in the direction of San Callisto where Flora had been followed. Bernini's heart sank as he trudged past numerous side galleries, niches, falls of stone, and other indications that their search for the lost trove of art could take months. Years, if they did not succeed in narrowing down the search territory. He sure hoped Flora and Adele had made progress in the archives after days lost in a mire of file-sorting.

He remembered a friend in the Carabinieri in Florence talking about another high-profile project. His friend had been forced to take on huge responsibility, but without resources or enough personnel to help him. Nico had called it a setup for failure, almost as if his superiors had planned it that way.

A sense of utter isolation made it worse for Bernini. He was haunted by the feeling he was blundering around in the dark, with no one fully on his side who could help him navigate through the labyrinth of professional loyalties, expectations from the top, and in-fighting among his promotion-hungry colleagues.

The agreeable personality of Davide Ricci, a young officer from the State Police, shed light in dark corners and cheered Bernini up when he felt most frustrated. Ricci took his job very seriously and performed his tasks admirably, but he never hesitated to speak up to his superiors if he had something useful to say. Bernini grew to rely on him.

Now Ricci, who marched ahead of Bernini, stopped suddenly. Bernini caught up with him in a vaulted area with rectangular *loculi* on either side. An overturned bucket sat near their feet. Small rocks mixed with chunks of plaster dribbled out of the bucket. "Someone's been digging—again." He pointed down a side tunnel, which, naturally, was not on the map Bernini carried.

The two men entered the dim passageway where the ceiling brushed their helmets, and bent down to examine the hole in the wall. It led to another tunnel running parallel to the one they were in.

Bernini grumbled. "Just like San Callisto. There's no way of telling if the diggers here are searching for the same thing we are. Or whether this happened yesterday or last month."

"I'd say odds are in favor they are. You don't see this kind of evidence of exploration on a normal basis. I checked with the head of *Sotterranei di Roma.*"

"Why is it that these folks are always just ahead of us? Anyone would think they knew where we were planning to go next."

Ricci spoke his mind without hesitation. "With the number of people involved in the search, there's always the possibility someone on our side is talking to the opposition."

"As my boss would say, you have a cynical mind for someone so young."

Ricci's lips quirked. "Not cynical, sir. Just practical."

Bernini's cell phone buzzed. He pulled it out of his pocket and saw that the message was from Flora. A second missed message came from Adele Marino. "I need to go above ground to retrieve this message. Can you follow this tunnel to its end and mark it on our map? And do you have a vial of paint?"

"Consider it done, sir." Ricci adjusted his hard hat and strode off in the opposite direction.

Bernini retraced his steps to the nearest exit, which took him about ten minutes.

He pushed speed dial to call Marino first.

"Sir," Adele answered immediately.

"What have you found?"

"Flora found a very promising lead in a folder of miscellaneous info. Looks like a French-Italian family who were art owners…" She filled him in.

"*Va bene.* Let's convene a meeting as soon as possible to bring people up to speed and regroup. How about fifteen hundred at the Comando?"

"Okay. I'll tell people here."

Next he called Flora. "*Cara,* good work. I just spoke to Adele."

Flora's voice sounded strained. "Something odd happened. Irene Costa showed up right while we were examining the papers for the first time. She didn't look like they meant anything to her, but she volunteered right away to scan and print them and take the copies to you. Adele was pissed. Irene stole her limelight."

Bernini said, "Irene's ambitious. Wants to advance quickly—that's probably all it is."

"I'm just telling you because I had a strong feeling something else is going on with her, and you said to report anything odd. Usually, Adele and Irene are buddies, but now there's some tension between them."

"There's tension all around, I think," Bernini said dryly. "This darn search affects each of us; I feel like I'm jumping at every shadow. Okay, see you at five back at the office."

"*Arrivederci.*"

~ * ~

The circle of men and women round the cigarette-scarred table lacked a few faces; not everyone had made it back on time from different parts of the city during the usual three-hour evening rush hour.

Flora, Lisa, Ellen, and Adele sat together at one end of the table.

Bernini could tell from Flora's expression that she was wondering about the whereabouts of Irene Costa. After making a play to be the first to tell the boss about new developments, Costa had vanished with her copies of the family diaries and lists. A call to her police cell went straight to voice mail.

Hmm, thought Bernini. Irene must have a good explanation. He'd reserved judgement until he heard it. Who else was missing? He checked off people in his head as he glanced around. The Austrian and French representatives sat to his left, drinking coffee and smoking. Giovanna Romano sat across from him, jotting down notes and smoking. De Luca had called to say he'd be twenty minutes late. No Orsoni.

Just then, Irene Costa waltzed in, cell phone to her ear. She walked straight to Bernini and apologized for being late; apparently she'd been stuck in a traffic jam, which was all too plausible. Irene pulled the copies of the archival papers from her satchel and placed them on the table before Bernini. "I meant to get these here sooner, you know. That was the whole reason I made the copies, so Adele and her team could keep working at the *biblioteca*."

"*Grazie*." Bernini flipped through the pages and scanned the relevant sections. He called the meeting to order. As he was summing up recent findings, the missing Orsoni joined them and took the last chair. "Sorry," he mouthed. He made a gesture with his hand that indicated he'd give his reason to Bernini later. If he remembered.

So far, Bernini observed, Costa was behaving normally. Just doing her job, and Flora's misgivings were misplaced. To be fair, they'd all been leaping at shadows, even where none existed. Not surprising after one murder and the horrible feeling that the other searchers were always one step ahead of them.

"So, folks. We must narrow our search and identify the family the diaries and lists found by the archival team point to, and look for more clues about where the missing art was hidden."

"Is the writer of the diary from a Jewish family?" asked Giovanna.

"Maybe, but I can't prove it," said Flora. "Her maiden name began with 'R.' She mentions an uncle 'Henri,' which is a French name. The family owned valuable art. Then there's the fact that the diary hints about moving artworks and tangling with the Nazis. And, I just turned up some information about two trucks of Nazi-looted art being diverted from its intended destination in Rome, making me wonder if our two men were somehow involved in that. The timing is right, the autumn of 1943."

Orsoni chipped in. "Isn't this about the same time as the heist from the Monte Cassino monastery southeast of Rome?"

"Yes. The news article I found lists of tons of stuff: medieval sculpture, illuminated manuscripts, paintings by Titian and Caravaggio, classical bronzes. Some of the artworks came from the Naples museums, the *Museo Archeologico Nazionale* and at least one other."

"But those names, Titian and Caravaggio, don't match the names of painters we saw in the list associated with the diary," objected Adele Marino.

"No, but the lists are probably incomplete in both sources." Flora turned to Bernini. "I suggest we do some more genealogical work on Jewish families with French connections and see if we can find more of that diary. Only a few pages of it were in the folder I found, and they were torn out from a larger volume along the binding."

Lisa Donahue spoke up. "We need to look at the records of the Monuments Men again. They could help us if there is a list of the works recovered after the war that came from either the Naples

Museum or the monastery. Then, if we're lucky, we can compare that list to whatever shipping lists survived for what surfaced in Rome and in Berlin."

"There must have been at least one other list," Ellen said, eyes sparkling with excitement.

Astorre Orsoni interrupted her. "You women have list mania! Why do you think everyone made lists? Or that those lists survived?" Ellen amended her comment. "There *may* be another record, probably in World War II archives somewhere in this city, of what the Nazis actually shipped to Rome. Anything not recovered by the Monuments Men could be artworks that were diverted by the men in the diary excerpt and hidden in the catacombs."

"But why would the Nazis ship anything to Rome? Then the art would be out of their control," Giovanna asked.

"Wait, wait." Bernini rubbed his face with one hand. "Let's backtrack here to the Monte Cassino operation. I recall that it was very well planned. The Nazis took wood and nails from a bottling factory near the monastery, built crates, and moved a hundred or so truckloads of art north from Monte Cassino to a villa near Spoleto, right?"

The women nodded.

"Then the Nazis looted some of the paintings and sent them to Berlin for Hitler's pleasure, but bad press about their activities made them return a large number of artworks to the Vatican in Rome." Bernini noticed that Ellen was studying something on her laptop. "So what happened next, Ellen?"

"There was a second Nazi shipment in December of 1943. Some library materials and collections from Naples were destined for the Palazzo Venezia in Rome, but that's when two of the trucks were diverted to Berlin."

Silence reigned while everyone digested this.

Flora said, "What if the two men from the diary fragment beat the Nazis at their own game by diverting artworks from one of the shipments going to Rome or Berlin? And it looks like most of this activity took place between October and December, 1943."

"That's a huge risk for those men to take," Lisa said. "If caught, they'd be shot by the Nazis."

"But maybe they were motivated by the chance of recovering specific items stolen from their families," Flora said.

"All speculation!" Orsoni objected.

Lisa ignored Orsoni. "And maybe they thought the risk was worth it, and if they couldn't find specific objects, they'd strike a blow for other Jewish families by thwarting the Nazi looters. And if your two thieves, if that's you'd call them, succeeded once in diverting a truckload, what's to stop them from trying again? There were dozens of trucks moving north, on at least two different dates."

"All interesting possibilities," Bernini said. "But I agree with Orsoni. We have a scrap of an old diary and a lot of speculation about it. While these men and their friends were scampering around the landscape diverting trucks and moving art underground in the middle of a world war, how likely is it they kept accurate written records? Or that those records survived and can be found in time to help us? Sorry I sound so cynical, but you all must realize that we're running out of time. If we don't have substantial results by the end of this week, we're all in trouble."

Orsoni smiled.

Bernini schooled his face not to glare in return. "Now, what's the report on the tunnels?"

De Luca, who had returned to them after several days on the murder squad searching for Gallo's killer, glanced at his tablet.

"We've been through most of the likely catacombs and found nothing except the evidence of other people digging. But the really interesting sections are the tunnels that intersect with other tunnels. Remember that tip we got from the archaeologists about Roman rock-quarrying under the city? Some of those tunnels intersect with catacombs, others with aqueducts or sewers. I've marked the intersections I think we should explore." He passed a sketch map to Bernini, who pored over it.

"Do any of these intersections also connect to subway stations?" he asked, looking around the room as everyone remembered that Gallo had been murdered at a subway stop, the one at Circo Massimo.

"A couple." De Luca walked around the table and pointed them out.

"Thanks, De Luca. Any progress on the murder inquiry?"

"Negative. We're still interviewing Gallo's friends and contacts. No leads so far."

"Okay, here's what we're going to do..."

Bernini parceled out new assignments, dividing the team among several archives and three more sections of the catacombs, plus some of the newly identified multiple tunnel intersections.

As people packed up their electronic devices and regrouped into smaller teams, Bernini felt the energy surging around the room. *Finally,* he thought, *this project is beginning to move. Would it be too much to hope for a breakthrough?*

~ * ~

De Luca gathered up his notes and coffee cup and followed the others out of the room. He listened to their reactions, trying to pick up scraps of information that might lead to clues about who among them had other agendas.

"… you ladies need to dig up hard facts, not just diaries, which are in themselves personal accounts not necessarily based on truth," Orsoni said to Flora and Lisa.

"A diary that we can pin down to specific dates and events is a gold mine!" protested Flora.

"And we're only halfway through that archive," added Lisa. "We may find supporting documents—"

"*May* is the operative word!" Orsoni barked. "Nothing less than 'I hid an art cache twenty meters southwest of the Cloaca Maxima entrance on *Via Appia*' will do!"

"Now you're being ridiculous; no one will find something that detailed!" said Flora.

De Luca bent his head as if staring at the floor and tuned into Irene Costa's conversation with Adele Marino.

"… don't tell me I overstepped with Bernini," Irene hissed at her companion. "It's not my fault I was delayed getting back to the Comando."

"But you took those documents, and you weren't even there when we found them!"

"Oh, stop whining! You sound like my little brother."

"The one who can't hold down a job?"

Irene strode ahead of her colleague. "Stay out of my way, Marino!"

Serious tension between those two women. It sounded like they were competing for favor with Bernini. Irene was in line for a promotion. Was that why Adele seemed so resentful?

De Luca made a mental note to learn more about the immediate families of both his colleagues.

Twenty-two
Isabelle Rossin's Diary, Part 5

October 13 [1943]. Italy has finally broken from the Axis governments and declared war on Germany. The people up north live under German control already. We fear many of the men will be forced to fight on the German side, or be killed if they refuse to participate. Sal is worried about relatives in Bologna…meanwhile the Nazi commanders are moving truckloads of all kinds of stuff (supplies? weapons? art?) around the landscape, preparing for the Allied advance.

The Germans are planning to move the Abbey library and art collections from both the Naples museums and private collections 'somewhere north' for safekeeping… I fear this includes some of my family's collection, … that they shipped to us for safekeeping after Papa's apartment was robbed. We moved some of the Rossin family art to the Monastery because Sal thought they would be safer there. He was wrong…

The Nazis appear to be collaborating with the Italian art officials, but Sal does not trust any of them. Some of our own officials are more interested in gaining favor with the Germans than in protecting Italian or Jewish heritage. Bribery is everywhere.

October 14 [1943]. Sal and Cl[emente] are up to something. I am so worried that they will get hurt or killed. Then what will the children and I do if Sal doesn't return?"

October 17 [1943]. I feel they should listen to me since some of the artworks being moved belong to my side of the family. Uncle Henri says the Rossin pieces should *not* be moved... He came down from Paris only three months ago to value the Renoir... and Monet paintings and then he arranged for a specialist in Greek antiquities to come another time and assess the vases and the bronze statue. That will take weeks, though, because travel is impossible just now.

October... 1943. Nazi shipment planned tonight. They will remove artworks from their storage places in the monastery and send them to a villa near Perugia. Sal heard a rumor that a diversion is planned and the Nazis will send at least some of our stuff to Berlin... he plans a different ending. Clxxx will drive the second truck...

... [they] will hijack the column near Spoleto. S and C plan to block the road with the help of local partisans. Somehow, they will cause an accident when the Nazi trucks enter the valley between xxxx and... divert one or two trucks... they planned to hide the loot in Rome, where C's relatives live. He knows a place underground...

Twenty-three

Flora checked the time. Eighteen thirty p.m., or six thirty according to her American upbringing. She and Bernini had agreed they both needed to stay in their offices late to catch up on regular work. They'd meet later at the apartment for a snack and a glass of wine.

Ottavia Palmiere would bite off her head if Flora didn't finish some projects quickly. She'd managed a few hours of conservation on most days, either before she went to whichever archive they were researching, or late in the day. Ottavia had given her security clearance, so Flora could work well into the night if she didn't mind being alone in the lab and would take the responsibility for resetting the alarm. Vittorio wasn't keen on this practice, but Flora reminded him of his own crazy hours—and the fact that he was in far more danger because of his affiliation with the Carabinieri.

This evening she walked, since the traffic was horrific, especially since the subway workers were on strike. People who lived in Rome permanently grew used to the continual bus, train, and subway strikes. Naturally, there were more strikes during hot weather and peak tourist season. When asked, her friends shrugged and said, "*Ci arrangiamo* (we do the best we can)."

Flora loved early evening in Rome, when people were leaving work, meeting friends in their favorite cafés for a *cinzano* or a glass of wine, and shopping on their way home. She heard metal-louvered shop doors rolling up for a few more hours of business, the clink of silverware laid out for dinner service, and the squeal of tires. The aromas of cut garlic and baking pizza filled her nostrils.

Her second favorite time, sunset during the summer, captivated her in different ways. The atmosphere was more relaxed. Less traffic, less noise. People leaning back in their chairs after a good meal, chatting with companions, while fountains picked up street lights in interesting patterns and couples or family members wandered the streets arm in arm.

Arriving at the lab, Flora unlocked the door and saw that two people, Stella and Roberto, were still at work so she didn't have to deal with the alarm.

"Hello!" she called. "Let me know when you leave; I'll lock up. I'm going to be here awhile."

"Nice to see you, Flora," Roberto smiled at her. "So you work two jobs nowadays?"

"And neglects the most important one," growled Stella in an undertone.

Flora heard the snide comment, but she ignored it. Stella's opinion didn't matter as much as Ottavia's. Besides, a smile from Roberto canceled out the grumpy attitude of Stella. Arriving at her desk, she found an urgent note from her boss.

"Finish the paint consolidation on the Lorenzetti as soon as you can (that means now)! Make sure you pay attention to 14th century pigments. The museum wants it back by the end of the week, and the curator is all over me! O."

Gasp. Well, thought Flora, *at least she still wants me here.*

She put on her smock and hustled over to her work table. After a careful examination of the paint layers, she figured she had at least three hours of work before she could go home.

Once she had laid out all her materials and begun work, her hands and eyes took over. She took short breaks to rest her eyes, and during those brief times, her mind roamed to the recent reading she'd being doing on the ancient people who once inhabited Rome.

The mysterious Etruscans, the founders of the city, built cities and tombs in the seventh and sixth centuries B.C. in central Italy. They were farmers, merchants, and traders. Painters of spectacular frescoes on tombs and scenes on pottery. Some of them had been wealthy, as their grave goods showed. Women wore jewelry made of gold and precious stones; men owned beautifully decorated armor and chariots. Wealthy Etruscans collected painted vases made in Greece and metalwork from the eastern Mediterranean civilizations to decorate their homes and their tombs.

The married couples shown on their tomb paintings lay together, half-reclining on dining couches, enjoying food and wine while dancing girls and musicians performed. Flora, turning the pages of color plates, had received a strong impression of marital equality, of women who were equally comfortable in public places and home settings.

As she mixed her pigments and matched colors to repair minute areas, she thought about how these early inhabitants of Rome might have carved and used their own underground tunnels, ones that existed before the catacombs were carved out and filled. The Etruscan sites in Tuscany were full of underground burial chambers and passageways. Didn't they have such tombs under Rome as well? What if a trader deep in debt had to hide some of his goods underground to fool a creditor? Or someone who didn't want his wealth to pass to his relatives hid it in the chambers and tunnels later reused as catacombs?

"What are you thinking about?" asked Roberto. "You look like you're a thousand miles away." He took the chair across the big table from Flora and picked up his paintbrush. "Maybe three thousand miles. Are you thinking about your family back in Chicago?"

She smiled. "You're right. I'm miles away, but in time instead of space. I've been reading about the Etruscans, who must have used the catacombs before they were catacombs. Trying to imagine other people strolling through the tunnels, hiding things in niches or chambers."

"Makes sense to me. People have always sought places to bury their dead or to hide their valuables in times of trouble. Unless they were really unlucky and didn't have time, like those poor suckers caught by volcanic ash and lava at Pompeii."

"Did the Etruscans have houses and temples and tombs here in Rome?" asked Flora, who did not want to be sidetracked.

"I think so," said Roberto. "I took a class about them once. They were the first rulers of Rome, the first builders here. Etruscans usually get short shrift; everyone wants to concentrate on Roman imperial building programs and gorgeous architecture."

They both returned to the work in front of them. Roberto left about half an hour later.

Flora finished some delicate in-painting and then let her mind wander again. She pictured Jewish families laying out their dead, decorating walls with menorahs and vines and citrons like the pictures she'd seen in a guidebook. Christian families moving bodies of their dead underground, because Christianity could not be practiced openly nor bodies buried inside the walls of ancient Rome.

Families conducting services in miniature chapels and crypts located under land owned by a few wealthy Christians…

Almost ten p.m. Flora stood up and stretched. It was so quiet. She rarely worked this late, but she enjoyed having the whole long room to herself and being able to play her own music without ear buds. Tonight she'd skipped the music, preferring the silence. She glanced at the window and noticed rain streaking down the glass. Of course, she had forgotten an umbrella. But who cared if she got wet on the way home—Vittorio wouldn't mind what he called "Medusa hair," when her moist curls sprang up like snakes. He said wet hair made her look wild, and he liked wild.

She walked up and down the room a few times to get her blood stirring again, doing a few shoulder rolls to loosen the tension in her upper back. The news media boasted frequent articles on how bad sitting for long stretches was for your health; treadmill desks were in. They might work for office jobs, but not for the finicky in-painting and cleaning with cotton swabs that conservators did. The vibrations of something moving under your work station would just make it harder.

As Flora resumed her seat on her favorite tall stool, sounds from the back door near their loading dock caught her attention. A delivery at this hour? No, couldn't be. Flora moved quietly over to the door, wishing they had a window nearby so she could peer out.

Silence.

Then she heard scratching at the keyhole, as if someone were trying out different keys.

"Who's there?" she shouted.

No one answered.

Flora whipped out her cell and made sure her voice could be heard outside as she spoke to the state police. "Someone was just trying to break into our building. The address is…"

The officer replied that they would send someone. "Wait for us, and don't let anyone else into your lab."

She punched in Bernini's number next, but the call went to voice mail. He was probably underground again. She left a message, saying she'd talk with the *Polizia di Stato* about the attempted break-in and then make her way home. As she was speaking, it suddenly occurred to her that the target might not be valuable paintings in the lab, but herself for being involved in the catacomb search. Shivering a little, she decided she'd ask for an escort going home, just in case.

Then she spent the next quarter of an hour fidgeting and starting at every little sound.

What if the intruder knew she was close to the lieutenant in charge of the search?

What if his—or her—goal was to eliminate the searchers, one by one?

By the time the police finally showed up, Flora was in a fine state of nerves.

~ * ~

De Luca was the first to hear the message that Bernini's girlfriend had been escorted home by the *Polizia di Stato*. The officer who accompanied her was a friend of De Luca's and gave him a call.

"She's a bit shook up. Better get ahold of Bernini and make sure he knows about this."

"I'll do that," De Luca said.

He tried Bernini's cell and got voice mail. He left a terse message and then called Flora at her apartment.

"How are you?"

"I'm fine, physically. But I'm scared that maybe I'm being targeted because I'm Bernini's girlfriend. Do you think I'm being silly?"

"No, I do not. Nothing is off the table in this case. I think at the very least, someone is trying to frighten you—and distract Bernini from progressing with the art search."

"What do you suggest?"

"Don't go anywhere alone, at least not at night. One of our academy students can be on call for you when you need an escort. During the day, make sure you travel with one of the other Carabinieri if Bernini is unavailable." *Common sense stuff,* he thought.

Flora said, "I hate the need for it, but I'll do as you suggest. I don't want Vittorio to worry about me. He's got enough on his plate."

"Good girl. Now get some sleep."

De Luca decided he'd be exceeding his authority if he left Bernini a second message. They'd sort things out between the two of him. He'd just make sure Bernini knew his feelings about keeping Flora safe when they next met.

Meanwhile De Luca had work to do. He wanted to interview people in the neighborhoods where Costa and Orsoni lived.

In his customary dark suit, he looked like an ordinary businessman, not a member of the Carabinieri. He'd find ways to ask questions about his colleagues' habits and movements without alerting them to his interest. Maybe pose as a friend looking for an apartment, asking questions about each neighborhood.

At least that was the plan.

Twenty-four

Thursday morning, the third day of the garbage collectors' strike, going anywhere in the city of Rome became a slow and smelly business. Plastic containers overflowed onto sidewalks and streets. Stray cats scattered chicken bones on street corners. Alternating bouts of intense heat and thunderstorms encouraged the garbage bags to swell and burst. The stench was awful.

Flora and Lisa arrived late at State Archives of Rome. They spent the morning in genealogical research. Arming themselves with lists of Jewish families living in Rome during World War II, they conducted a computer search on French personal names and surnames bracketed with Italian families.

Four hours of dusty searching later, Lisa Donahue found something. "Does the last name Buscichelli mean anything to you, Flora?"

"Seems to me I've heard—I mean read—that name before," Flora replied. She opened her lined paper notebook, the one she found easier to use than a laptop while she wandered through the aisles and file drawers of older libraries. A laptop served well for summarizing notes at the end of the day, when she could sit in one place and sip coffee or wine, but this medium-sized notebook could be propped on top of a bookshelf or balanced on an open file drawer, ready for quick notes or names she wanted to check later. It also fit well into her purse.

Flipping through, Flora zeroed in on one page. "Buscichelli, here it is. A woman named Daniella Buscichelli married a man named... Salvatore Orsoni!" Naturally, she remembered that Bernini's difficult colleague had the same last name. Just coincidence? Her quickened pulse said no.

Lisa stared at her. "Orsoni. That's a common name around here, isn't it?"

"It is."

"And it is also the name of one of your husband's police associates."

"Yep," Flora replied, returning her friend's direct gaze. "But Orsoni's not a Jewish surname, as far as I know. For the moment, let's focus on Buscichelli, which *is* one of the surnames of Jewish families living in the Rome area. And 'Salvatore' matches the male first name we were looking for. Let's research this family and see if we can build up a family tree with some modern descendants."

They set to work, using a combination of searching online, checking paper files in the archives, and carefully placing a couple of cell phone calls to verify names.

An hour later, Flora and Lisa had produced a very interesting document.

Salvatore Orsoni married a Frenchwoman, Daniella Buscichelli, in 1903. They raised two sons, Riccardo and Franco, who both married in the early 1920s. Franco's son, Salvatore II, married an Isabelle Rossin from Paris in 1940.

Isabelle Rossin came from a wealthy family in the Marais district of Paris. Her father and grandfather had amassed a substantial art collection over twenty years, most of it housed in Paris. Apparently, certain paintings had been given to Isabelle as a wedding present, as an investment for the future. Isabelle settled with her new husband in a small suburb not too far from Monte Cassino, southeast of Rome.

And in one folder, Lisa unearthed another section of the missing diary, this time with the front page intact:

"This is the diary of Isabelle Rossin..."

Flora, shivering with excitement, read the first entry:

*"**May [17,] 1940**. My name is Isabelle Rossin and I am twenty-two years old. I was born in Paris, France, in the Marais. We live in a large apartment just off the Rue des Rosiers, and I thought I would be here for many years, perhaps forever as an old maid! But today I met Sal[vatore Orsoni]..."*

She called Bernini. "Vittorio, we've got something. I think we've found the family—or at least a family—who could have hidden art in the catacombs. It's an Italian-French family, Jewish on the female side."

"Names?"

"Orsoni and Rossin. Salvatore Orsoni, who married an Isabelle Rossin early in the war, in 1940. Her family owned quite a lot of valuable art."

Flora waited as Bernini digested this.

"Orsoni, eh? Think I'll have a little chat with Astorre about his family history and see what he knows. Meanwhile, keep digging for more information on the Rossin art collection."

Remembering how personable Astorre Orsoni had been when she first met him last year, Flora wished she could be a fly on the wall for the upcoming interview. Whatever was making him so prickly now, Bernini was in for a rough ride. Would Astorre open up or not? She couldn't wait to hear about it.

"Okay, Boss. Don't say anything I wouldn't say."

"Thanks for that." Bernini broke the connection.

She smiled and slid her phone back into her purse.

~ * ~

Lisa Donahue spent another almost sleepless night, listening to street noises and the unladylike snore of her roommate, Ellen.

They'd made progress, if you could call it progress, on linking a Carabinieri family to a Jewish art owner, but that information didn't help narrow down where the art trove might be underground.

She lay on her lumpy bed and tried to imagine herself into the shoes of someone looking for a hiding place, perhaps with time enough ahead of Nazi raiders to choose an unlikely and well-protected spot. This was the opposite of their thinking up to this point—where would desperate people hide something in a hurry?

Rome sprawled over seven hills and both sides of the Tibur River. What kind of building program had taken place between the World Wars? Surely housing expansion after World War I had occurred, providing cheap places for returning soldiers to live with their families. But in Rome, that probably meant conversion of old homes into apartments, palazzos into suites for the well-to-do, and not much in the way of new footprints in an already crowded city.

A snort made Lisa glance at her roommate, who sat up and turned on the light.

"So you're awake, too?" Ellen said.

"Yes, I was lying here listening to you snore."

"I don't snore! At least, someone told me once it was a 'ladylike' snore, more of a buzz than a roar."

Lisa laughed. "Tell your friend that I respectfully disagree! You sounded like a train in a tunnel."

"My nose is stuffed up. Caught a cold, I think." Ellen plumped up her sorry pillow and leaned against it. "Speaking of tunnels, you're thinking about our lack of progress on the search for lost art, aren't you?"

"Of course I am. I'm racking my brains about locations we haven't thought about, or that we've overlooked. Do you know anything about building programs in Rome between the world wars?"

"Can't say I do, Lisa. Remember, this is my first time in Italy, and I never studied classical archaeology and European history the way you did."

Lisa explained her thinking. "If housing or renovations were in progress at the beginning of World War II, those projects presumably ground to a halt, with money and energy diverted to the war effort and obtaining enough food for Rome's hungry citizens."

"Are you talking about housing for Jewish families, or for everybody?"

"Everyone. I think we've gotten too focused on possible Jewish hiding places."

"But Rome was occupied under the Axis rule, yes? So many citizens might have moved out of the city to nearby villas and farms to stay away from the Nazis. Particularly Jewish families."

"Hmm," Lisa said, sliding her legs over so she could face Ellen. "Did art move to outlying neighborhoods, too? If so, is there any record of it? And what about moving art collections from family farms back into the city, into the possession of relatives who knew the underground?"

Ellen groaned. "Sounds like a whole new database in the making. And trying to worm information out of contractors who can't remember that far back."

"What about bombing? Didn't Rome suffer bombing by the Allied forces around 1943? Or maybe it was later," Lisa said, thinking out loud. "People must have been terrified. So did they have air raid shelters or just use nearby catacombs and sewers—"

"Not much fun for families, going underground in a sewer." Ellen made a face. "But whole families went somewhere to get away from bombs. And I bet they took their family pets, their valuables, maybe some of their art with them."

Lisa sat up straighter. "Letters! Letters and diaries! I think Flora and I will expand our search for personal documents of all kinds of Roman families, not just Jewish ones. And look for accounts of bombing raids."

"Good idea. Can we go back to sleep now?"

Twenty-five

De Luca and Bernini sat across the table from Astorre Orsoni in the Comando's conference room, a high-ceilinged apartment whose shabby elegance included gilded palmettes, vines, and fruits along the cornice, and well-trodden Persian rugs.

Gone was the affable, scholarly young man Bernini had met on the Lorenzetti case. Now a tight-mouthed, overly skinny man confronted them. Bristling with attitude, Orsoni was clearly worried about something—or someone. Being obviously on the wrong side of his boss was enough to make anyone nervous, thought Bernini. But he suspected Orsoni's problems ran deeper and he intended to get to the bottom of them.

Bernini asked the questions; De Luca was present only to make sure he got the answers he needed.

"Flora and Lisa have found a half-French, half-Italian Jewish family with the surname Orsoni. That in itself would not be of interest to us—Orsoni is a common name—but the fact that the French side of the family owned a large art collection that was dispersed during World War II certainly is. The account in the Rossin diary suggests a link to the Monte Cassino fiasco and perhaps our search for lost art in the catacombs. So, Orsoni, tell us about your family background."

"And this time, fill in the blanks you did not choose to answer on your employment application," added De Luca, throwing Orsoni's personnel file on the table.

Orsoni sighed. "My grandfather was Salvatore Orsoni. He married a French girl, Isabelle Rossin, from Paris. Their son, Giuseppe, was my father."

"And who was your mother?"

"Maria Liebermann."

"A Jewess."

"Yes."

"So you are Jewish, with both a Jewish grandmother and a Jewish mother," De Luca said. "Yet you left 'religion' blank on your form."

"And why is my religion important? It has, or had, no bearing on my qualifications for the Carabinieri!" Orsoni flared. His face twisted as if in pain.

"No," agreed Bernini. "But it would be interesting to know why you did not share that crucial fact about your background."

Astorre Orsoni looked at his clenched hands. "Easy to explain. It's because I was teased about my Jewishness as a child. Children can be very cruel; I never forgot my humiliation. I vowed that as an adult, I would never tell anyone my religious background unless I was forced to."

Bernini nodded with some sympathy. He too remembered schoolyard scenes of teasing and bullying. But in his case, he'd been teased for being small and wimpy, not Jewish. Looking at Orsoni now, it was easy to imagine him small, wimpy, *and* Jewish. Three strikes against him in the jungle of childhood. You could outgrow wimpiness; it was much harder to leave behind your birth religion.

"You are right; your religion does not affect how well you do your job here. But it may be a relevant fact in this investigation. What does your current family know about your grandmother's art collection? How was it acquired in the first place?"

"My grandmother's father, Michel Rossin, was an art dealer and connoisseur. He used family monies to build up an outstanding collection of European painting and classical antiquities."

"What happened to the collection over time?"

"Much of the art was kept in Paris, but I recall hearing about a villa in Tuscany that the Rossins used for summer vacations. I think the grandfather Rossin traded some of his collection for new pieces, so it was always changing."

A bookkeeping nightmare then, thought Bernini. "And after Isabelle and Salvatore married, what then?"

Orsoni shrugged. "She inherited a couple of paintings upon her marriage, as an investment in the future."

"Did the Nazis seize any of the collection, either in Paris or in Tuscany?"

Orsoni glared at them. "The Nazis systematically looted every Jewish collection of value, especially collections that contained what Hitler referred to as 'degenerate art.' The Rossin family was no different. Their art collection, at least the stuff stored in Paris, was seized early in the war."

Bernini jotted down some notes as Orsoni spoke. "Do you remember specific works in the larger collection, or names of painters or sculptors?"

Orsoni frowned. "There was a Renoir, and some Matisse sketches. I didn't pay attention. I was not much interested in art."

At the time, thought Bernini. *But maybe Orsoni's interest in art grew as he got older. He appeared to know about the Rossin family.*

"Was anything returned to the family after the war? Does anyone in your family know?"

"My parents knew, I think. But they are both dead. Killed in a car accident fifteen years ago."

How convenient.

"Hmm." De Luca seemed dissatisfied. "And no one else knows?"

"No." Orsoni's voice deadened, and his face revealed nothing. De Luca had more questions. "Orsoni, how about—" Bernini interrupted. "Let Orsoni get back to work. You and I can decide on the next move."

Looking as surprised as De Luca, Orsoni left the room quickly before Bernini changed his mind.

Bernini spoke his mind. "I can't believe Orsoni or his family know so little about an art collection that was—perhaps still is—a significant source of wealth to his family."

"I agree. It doesn't add up unless the art was stolen and never recovered. But he certainly knows something about the Rossin side of the family—it would be strange if he did not."

"He's hiding something."

"Yes. But how do we get it out of him? We have no proof of any wrongdoing on his part. If he is lying, he is lying by omission and telling only part of his story."

"He certainly didn't volunteer much information," said Bernini. "Or rather he volunteered some things and withheld others. I say, go around him. Get your researchers to outline his entire family tree. Find out about his siblings, his cousins, the side branches of his family. And see if they can find documentation of the Rossin collection, exactly what was in it, and what happened to it all."

"Yes, sir. I'm on it."

Twenty-six

Flora and Lisa dove back into their work, determined to find all the information Bernini had requested. Flora began by calling Adele Marino and asking for her help in looking in another set of files at the Biblioteca Hertziana while she and Lisa continued to comb files in the National Archives.

"Focus on the records of the Monuments Men, and any other sources for what was in the Rossin Collection and what happened to it after the war. Oh, I read that the Rossin grandfather, Michel, liked to trade artworks and change up his collection. Maybe somewhere you'll find his records of his sales and acquisitions."

Adele groaned. "Great, a collector who doesn't hang onto his collection. If he turns out to be a poor record keeper, we'll have a tough time."

"Just do your best."

"Right. Good luck to you and Lisa." Adele promised to send student runners around Rome for anything they couldn't locate in person or online. "We'll stay in touch."

At the National Archives, the two women split up the work, Lisa continuing to research the Rossin family and its art collections, while Flora sat with her laptop and googled the Orsoni family.

She was familiar with "White Pages," "Whois," and other people-searching websites, and the Carabinieri had given her some passwords for special accounts they used. After some thought, she decided to work backward and sideways from Astorre Orsoni since Bernini was clearly uneasy about the lack of information available in the police personnel files.

After an hour or so, she had the beginnings of a family dossier. Astorre Orsoni, age thirty-eight. Born 1972. Married to Lucia Bianchi, with two children. They already knew that Astorre's mother, Maria Liebermann, was Jewish. Flora found part of what she expected in personal names of men: the name "Salvatore" came down through the generations on the paternal side, being the name of his great-great-grandfather, his grandfather, and his brother Sal, who was two years older than Astorre. Orsoni's sister, Nicola, was the baby of the family.

Lisa wandered over to see how far Flora had gotten and look at her printouts. "Find their occupations, not just their names. It would be interesting to see if one of the brothers or uncles on the Orsoni side has other connections to the art world besides belonging to an extended family of collectors."

"Good suggestions! I'll start with 'LinkedIn' and then go backward in time."

First, though, Flora wanted to fill in some gaps about the background of Salvatore the Second—that's how she thought of him in her own mind, but Italians didn't use that kind of labeling. They didn't use "Sr." or "Jr.," either.

She trotted back to the paper files to look for Orsoni again. This time, she found a second folder that had slipped down between two others. Feeling a little frisson of excitement, she carried it back to her table, opening it next to her laptop and an illegal cup of coffee (at least it had a lid on it so it was less likely she'd damage the papers).

Salvatore, the one who married Isabelle Rossin in 1940, was the son of Franco and Matilde Orsoni. Matilde's maiden name was not recorded but could be found later if necessary. Franco's brothers were Riccardo and Salvatore. The second brother died in infancy.

New information appeared: Riccardo married Lucia in 1922, and their son Clemente Orsoni became an art dealer. At this tidbit, Flora perked up and remembered that Isabelle's diary had mentioned a man's name that began with a "C." So Sal and Clemente Orsoni were first cousins, and almost certainly the two men involved in "something dangerous!"

Feverishly, she pulled out her copy of the first part of the diary, looking for the second mention of "C." There it was: "Clxxx." Maybe not proof enough for a court of law, but good enough for Flora to feel she was on the right track. Okay, it looked very much like the two Orsoni cousins were the men planning to divert part of the Nazi shipment for their own ends.

She turned to the second part of Isabelle's diary and turned the pages with some difficulty, because liquid that had spilled on the paper had glued some of them together. Flora felt guilty for not taking proper care of the stuck pages as a good conservator should— gently re-humidifying and separating the leaves with a flat, blunt tool—but she needed the information now. Thank goodness the paper quality was decent; none of that clay-coated magazine paper that would just melt into a blob.

Flora was able to tease apart some of the pages by inserting an emery board between half-separated leaves of paper. Halfway through the second segment, she found a reference to *"... will hijack the column near Siena. S and C plan to block the road with the help of xxxx. Somehow, they will cause an accident when the Nazi trucks enter the valley between xxxx and divert one or two trucks... they planned to hide the loot in Rome, where C's relatives live. He knows a place underground...*"

Eureka! Flora called Lisa over.

"Look what I found." Flora could hear the note of triumph in her own voice.

Lisa leaned over the table, reading the section Flora had marked with a piece of scrap paper. "'A place underground!'" She smiled widely. "I'd say you can make a good case for this family being the one we are looking for!"

"Before I call Bernini, let's see if we can find any connection between the Orsoni family that lived in Rome and a favorite catacomb or other underground area they frequented." Then she thought of something. "Lisa, Adele's team might be on the wrong track in searching for lists of looted artworks from just the Rossin Collection."

"Why, what do you mean?"

"Remember that earlier discussion at the Comando? Or maybe you weren't there; I can't remember. If these two Orsoni cousins diverted only 'a truck or two,' they'd have no idea which artworks they were getting."

Lisa looked thoughtful. "Yes, I was there. I see what you mean. Unless one of these guys had access to Nazi shipping manifests—how likely is that?—they'd be operating blind. So it could be anyone's family heritage down there, not just the Rossin collection."

"Not anyone's, probably. We talked about this before. We can perhaps narrow it down to Jewish-owned works of art *not* recovered in the Rome area after the war. Items that the Monuments Men expected to find at the Vatican or in the Palazzo Venezia that never made it there."

"Did we ever find those lists we talked about in that early meeting?"

Flora pored over her notebook. "Adele and Assunta found a couple of manifests for trucks used in the transport of art from Spoleto to Rome, but they were incomplete."

"Of course. Good convoluted thinking, Flora. You could be a Nazi organizer, an employee of Hermann Göring."

"Gee, thanks. But thinking like this makes my head hurt. I wish I had the kind of mind that sees only two possibilities, and that they were always black or white, not five different kinds of gray."

"Speaking of possibilities," said Lisa, "I thought of another one last night when I couldn't sleep."

"Tell me."

"All families in Rome, not just Jewish ones, hid underground during the bombings in 1943 and 1944. If they didn't have basements, maybe they crept into tunnels, sewers, anything close to their homes. So other diaries, from non-Jewish families, might list those locations, right?"

Flora lit up. "And if they had a favorite painting or statue, they probably took it underground with them!" She paced the floor. "And if there were multiple raids, you might leave some of your valuables underground, if you found a safe hiding place for them."

"That's how I was thinking last night. If you thought more bombing was coming, you might spend time between raids looking for a really good hiding place, maybe even covering up a cache with bricks and mortar, or tufa rubble."

Flora stopped pacing. "I wonder if during any of that time period basements had direct connections to sewers, catacombs, or aqueducts?"

Lisa nodded. "All good possibilities. Construction records could help there, but I've no idea where those are stored—or how far back they go. But I guess we should go back to this diary before we explore anything else."

"Okay, back to the Rossin diary. You sit here and I'll split the remaining loose pages with you."

"These are kind of stuck together."

"Yes, I know. Ideally, a conservator would carefully separate them under controlled conditions, but we can't afford the time. Wait. Maybe I can improvise." She ran out to the restroom, grabbed some paper towels and wet them, and rushed back. "So, we moisten the pages slightly with these wet paper towels... do you have a nail file or something in your purse? The emery board I used earlier isn't thin and slick enough."

"You're in luck," Lisa said. "I snuck this through airline security." She produced a metal file with a plastic handle. The tip was pointed, but not sharp.

"Oh, that's perfect." Flora squeezed excess water out of the paper towels and laid them on the diary. Then she used Lisa's file to separate the first page from the second. "Go get some more paper towels, okay? Run them under the faucet and then squeeze them out."

"How many?"

"A bunch. About ten."

They succeeded in dampening the lumps of paper and separating most of them into individual leaves. These were spread out on the table to dry while Flora and Lisa leaned over them, reading what was visible.

"Oh, my," Lisa said suddenly.

"What?"

"Look at this: '... a hiding place near beginning of subway they are building in center of Rome.'"

"The subway!" cried Flora. She googled the Rome metro system and discovered it opened in 1955. "I wonder where the first tunnels were constructed." A few more hits and she had it. "Looks like the builders started at Termini, the train station, and built outward, with Line B being in the first phase. But here's an article stating that when World War II started, the construction stopped and the section between the Stazione Termini and the Piramide stop was used for air raid shelters."

The two women looked at each other.

"A half-finished subway system," Lisa said. "Partial tunnels, piles of debris, holes in the walls... what a perfect place to hide things."

"Yeah, with all of your neighbors watching you as you did it!"

"Not during the actual air raids. You could go down into the subway tunnel in between bombings and dig out a more permanent hiding place."

Flora pulled out her pocket Metro map. "Look, that section in the earliest construction included Circo Massimo!"

Lisa was still reading the article. "And that station... is close to one of ancient Rome's main aqueducts, the one that passes near the Palatine Hill. It's called the Appia."

Flora sat back in her chair, stunned. "Vittorio's colleague, Gallo, was killed in the subway at Circo Massimo. And two other colleagues found a disturbed tunnel down there."

"Do you suppose..." began Lisa.

Flora said, "Let's go look!"

"Haven't Bernini's colleagues checked it out already?" asked Lisa.

"Orsoni and De Luca did. But maybe, since Orsoni was there, they didn't look too carefully…"

Lisa shook her head. "Orsoni? We're leaping ahead here. You should call Bernini with this information."

Flora's hand shook as she hit the tiny buttons on her cell. Her call went to voice mail. "Crap! He's not answering."

"Leave him a text message. Tell him where we're going and why." Lisa was already bundling up her papers and purse.

Flora remembered that one person in any duo investigating underground was supposed to be a policeman, preferably an armed one.

Then she shrugged. *Act first, apologize later.*

Twenty-seven

The women took the subway, changing for the line Metro B. They exited the car at Circo Massimo and looked around the station as the train pulled out. Like most subway stations, this one smelled musty and was littered with discarded coffee cups, tissues, and cigarette stubs. A dank breeze wafted from the direction the train had taken away from them.

Lisa pointed to the right. "That way, I think."

Flora agreed, simply because they had to choose a direction, and turning right meant going around a curve into a dimmer, less visible section. Much more plausible than the straight stretch to the left behind them.

After a ten minute walk, they could see how old parts of the tunnel were. The ceiling appeared to be rock with cement patches here and there. Chunks of both materials bulged and hung down in places, waiting to fall upon un-helmeted heads. Wiring bundles protruded from niches, with some of the protective sheathing shredding off the wires. A few more paces brought them level with a ragged opening in the wall on the other side.

"Cross the tracks? What are we, crazy?" muttered Lisa.

But in fact it was easier than Flora expected. The level of the tracks rose in this part of the subway tunnel so they could easily drop down from the platform onto the gravel bed without risking a sprained ankle. They minced across, careful not to touch any rail, and hoisted themselves up onto the waist-high platform with only minor scrapes on their arms.

Flora said, "This is where we should have hard hats and better lights."

"I have the light from my cell, and it's almost fully charged since I had it plugged in at the archives."

"Good for you, Lisa. I have my cell light, too, though it hasn't been charged since last night, but I also have a little pen light in my purse. We'll save that for emergencies."

"Which, of course, we will not have."

"Ha. Famous last words." Flora led the way, saying over her shoulder, "I'm trying to remember what Orsoni and De Luca reported about this tunnel. I think they went only about two kilometers and found nothing, so they turned back."

They walked steadily, shining their cell lights on damp walls with layers of a whitish crust and patches of what could be mold. Flora thought of cave crickets and shuddered. But this is not a cave, she reminded herself. Nor a sewer, so hopefully there are no rats.

Lisa picked her way around fallen chunks of tufa and plaster. "Whatever this tunnel was, someone took the trouble to plaster the walls along here."

"Yeah, but only this part. Look ahead: it deteriorates into a channel with water on the floor and a low ceiling. We're going to get stiff necks if we go farther."

"This is just about two kilometers from where we started."

"Not very far at all. Those police officers were just plain lazy," said Flora.

"Or maybe they were eager to get back to the Comando so they could participate in the murder investigation."

"Well, either way, we should go farther."

Flora slid her arm into her purse strap so the purse lay snugly across her body. Then she stooped to avoid the low ceiling and placed her feet carefully around the puddles. "I wonder if the water means we're getting close to the aqueduct?"

Her neck and shoulders ached as they progressed.

Suddenly the ceiling rose ahead of her. Flora and Lisa popped out of the tunnel into a larger space, an underground chamber. They lifted their cells, trying to see the extent of it, but their combined light was too dim.

"There!" shouted Flora. She walked quickly to the left, where a larger opening revealed itself. Inside, a water channel cut through the rock. "This must be the intersection of the subway and the aqueduct."

Lisa had stayed behind in the tall chamber. "I can't imagine anyone would choose a watery tunnel when this bigger, dryer space was available. Look how crumbly the stone is just here. Let's walk the perimeter of the chamber and see what we can find."

Lisa led the way and Flora hung back, flashing her puny light from side to side, looking for evidence of digging or patched walls, anything to indicate a hiding place.

She stopped when she spotted a bricked-up section. "Lisa, look!"

They ran their hands over the brick, which appeared to be in surprisingly good condition. "'The Cask of Amontillado,'" Lisa said softly.

"You mean that Edgar Allan Poe story about a guy who was bricked-up alive?"

"That's it. I wonder what's behind this wall, and how long it's been here."

"Hard to tell. We have no tools, so let's look a little farther along." Flora moved ahead.

This time, it was Lisa who stopped. "Shovels!" she exclaimed.

Four shovels, a stack of buckets, and clear signs of digging. The excavators had cleared about forty feet into the soft tufa wall, revealing a shallow cave.

And the corner of a wooden packing crate.

"*Madre di Dio!*" Flora said, grabbing a shovel. "How could they get this far and just leave?"

"Maybe whoever it is decided to report the find and get some help moving it," Lisa replied, picking up one of the other shovels. "I bet we don't have much time before they come back."

Adrenaline powered Flora's arms, and she worked hard to clear more of the packing crate. "Looks about the right size for a statue, or a couple of large paintings."

"Oh, my! I found the side of another crate!" Lisa dug faster.

A fall of stones from behind them made both women pause.

"Someone's coming," Flora said. "Quick, let's scoot back into the tunnel we came from."

"Too late!" Lisa said as she turned and ran. "They're almost here!"

Flora heard a rush of footsteps and then a voice yelling, "*Ferma immediatamente!* Stop, or I shoot!"

She kept running, figuring whoever found them near the precious art trove would shoot them anyway.

Lisa tripped.

Flora whipped around and grabbed her friend's arm to help her stand.

They ran on, hand in hand.

Then Flora heard a "pop" and felt a searing pain in her shoulder.

She staggered, but Lisa pulled her into the tunnel just as the next shot missed them.

Twenty-eight

Bernini left Moscati's office feeling like he'd been tossed around in a clothes dryer and come out rumpled, with buttons and shoelaces missing. First, Moscati praised him and said he was a fine officer. Then he said time was almost up; Moscati would have to assign someone else to the top job and demote Bernini to a different assignment. Bernini had forty-eight hours to turn things around. The very thought of such a change made Bernini break into a cold sweat.

He checked his messages, hoping for some good news. "*Merda!*" he exclaimed when he listened to Flora's message. He glanced at the time displayed on his cell. The call was time-stamped two hours earlier. "Plenty of time for those two to get into trouble."

He scrolled through his texts.

The last one, from Flora just after her audio message, bore the cryptic message: "Diary points to intersection with aqueduct near Metro Circo Massimo. Lisa and I going now."

"*Oddio!*" Bernini shoved the cell into his pocket and yelled to his colleagues. "Team to Metro Circo Massimo, on the double! Bring everyone you can find, plus lights and hard hats. Don't forget your pistols."

De Luca, Orsoni, and the others piled into cars and zipped through traffic to the subway entrance at Circo Massimo.

A mountain of garbage blocked most of the entrance. Bernini shouted at his colleagues, "Push it aside. We've got to get down there."

De Luca, Bernini, and two others manhandled overflowing bags to one side. Orsoni held his nose and kicked some of the garbage out of the way. A mangy cat leaped onto the debris and found a choice tidbit of fish.

"Phew!" Bernini gave Orsoni a dirty look and wiped his hands on his trousers.

Orsoni smiled.

Bernini gave directions. "Go to the tunnel we found earlier. Follow it to the end this time! That's where we'll find them."

The police ran down the stairs, along the tracks, and nipped into the tunnel.

Bernini saw a plastic hair clip on the tufa floor. He picked it up, saw that it resembled one belonging to Flora, and was reassured. She often twisted her hair up off her neck in hot weather and fastened it with such a clip. They were on the right path. He bent double as they reached the part of the tunnel where the ceiling dropped, and was forced to slow down.

"Sir, I hear voices!"

"*Aiuto*! My friend is hurt." It was a woman's voice.

Bernini shoved the man in front out of the way and moved as fast as he could. "Carabinieri here! Lisa, is that you?"

"Yes."

"Who's hurt?"

"Flora." The two women staggered in view, Flora leaning on Lisa. "She's been shot in the shoulder. I think it's only a minor wound." A hot and filthy Lisa delivered Flora to Bernini's arms. The streaks of grime mixed with tears on Flora's face almost hid her pallor.

"Let me see." De Luca pulled even with Bernini as he reached out for Flora. "I have emergency medical technician training."

Bernini stood aside as De Luca lowered Flora to the ground so she could lean against the rock wall. Gently, he peeled away her shirt from her right shoulder so he could see the wound. "She's been lucky," he said to Bernini. "Bullet passed clean through. Once it's cleaned and bandaged up, she'll be fine. But she's losing blood fast; we need to get her to hospital."

"Wait," Flora said, her voice thready. "The art trove—we found it. Back the way we came, there's a big chamber." She described the site, and Lisa filled in details.

Bernini hugged Flora carefully, avoiding the damaged side, and kissed her forehead. "Bravo, *cara*. I wish—no, we won't talk about it now. I have to go back to the site," he said. "But you are in good hands here with De Luca and Lisa. They'll get you back to our car and to the hospital. I'll meet you there as soon as we take charge of whatever this trove contains."

They parted. De Luca and Lisa supported Flora back toward Circo Massimo while Bernini and the others headed for the open chamber Lisa and Flora had found.

The low-ceilinged tunnel twisted a few times as they trotted along, almost doubled up. Suddenly Bernini was able to stand, and he realized they'd arrived at the inner chamber. Better equipped than the women had been, the Carabinieri team flashed powerful lights around.

"Hey!" Ricci cried, spotting several dark figures clustered around a low opening about ten meters ahead. "Police! Stand still, or we'll fire on you!"

The art thieves had no intention of standing still. They fired wildly at the police and then sped away to another opening on the far side of the chamber.

Bernini's frustration erupted as he realized he had insufficient manpower to both stop the thieves and recover the art at the same time.

Quickly, he gave instructions to Romano and two of the male students. "Follow them, see where they go, but don't engage them in another shooting match. Try to find the spot where they come and go underground. I'm calling for additional backup from the *Polizia di Stato*."

Bernini motioned to Ricci and the others to follow him.

The thieves had helpfully left behind the two shovels. Bernini heaved a sigh of relief when he saw they hadn't had time to fully uncover any of the crates or drag anything away.

Ricci and Orsoni set up portable lights. "Put on your hardhats," said Bernini. "Look at the crumbling state of this ceiling! It looks like chunks of it could fall on us at any time."

"We'll be here for hours," Ricci said with a big grin. "But I think it's going to be worth it."

Twenty-nine

De Luca escorted Flora and Lisa to his Alfa Romeo and they drove to the nearest hospital. He noticed Flora's extreme pallor and how she supported her head against the head rest as if it were too heavy to hold up. Her left hand cradled the damaged right shoulder.

This was the second time Flora had been targeted. He wasn't sure what he'd do if his girlfriend were involved in a project like this. Probably ship her out of town!

"How do you feel, besides the shoulder?"

"Dizzy."

"Must be the blood loss," Lisa said. "Don't talk, Flora. Conserve your energy.

Was it an accident that Flora had been shot instead of Lisa Donahue? De Luca thought not. He suspected the thieves were still trying to slow down Bernini. What better way than to injure or kill his girlfriend?

Flora Garibaldi should be locked up—for her own good.

~ * ~

Flora woke in a strange bed. As her eyes took in white ceiling, beige walls, and crisp white sheets tucked in tautly over her legs, she registered "hospital." She was in a private room. They'd cleaned and probed her arm, bandaged it, and then told her she'd have to stay overnight. Too much blood loss, they'd said. The doctor gave her a transfusion and told her to lie quietly for at least twelve hours. A nurse brought in breakfast and raised the bed so Flora could sit up. The hospital coffee was surprisingly good. Flora had little appetite, but she downed a pastry and three spoons of yogurt and felt better for it. By crossing her uninjured arm over her body, she grasped her cell phone from the table and turned it on. It was low on juice, but she was still able to access her texts. Bernini had texted that he would be there in a couple of hours.

Pushing the breakfast tray aside, Flora lay back and tried to make sense out of the events of yesterday. The location of the trove was clearly near both the metro system and one of Rome's major aqueducts. She wondered why the original art thieves—the men who had robbed the Nazi trucks—had chosen such a location. Yes, it was near the entrance to the part of the subway used as an air raid shelter, but surely there were drier sections of underground Rome. Or maybe, the shallow cave they'd picked had not been wet in 1943. The puddles Flora had observed looked like seepage, small quantities of water trickling into the last part of the tunnel and the big chamber over time. Had part of the aqueduct collapsed since then?

Too bad she and Lisa hadn't had the time to actually see what was hidden in the alcove. Her shoulder blazed with pain, but otherwise she felt desperate to get out of the hospital and find out what was going on…

"There you are!" Lisa Donahue and Ellen Perkins entered the room. They bore flowers, hot croissants, and more coffee.

"Angels!" Flora said, sitting up again. "Is that a *macchiato*?"

"Just the way you like it," Lisa said, handing her one of the cups. She spread a napkin on Flora's lap and tipped the pastries into it.

Then she and Ellen perched on the edges of the bed, one on either side.

"How do you feel now?" Ellen asked. Flora hadn't seen much of Ellen; she'd been attached to one of the teams exploring the catacomb tunnels for days.

"My shoulder feels like it's on fire, but other than a little weakness from losing so much blood, I'm fine. Now tell me what they found in the cave! Is it really the missing art trove, the one mentioned in the rumor?"

"I'll say it is. Several valuable oil paintings, a Madonna statue, some Greek vases—"

"Greek vases! They were mentioned in the Rossin diary!"

"Yes, indeed." Lisa smiled at Flora's excitement. "When Bernini gets here, we're all going back to the Comando for a meeting. The three of us are assigned to a conservation assessment, which means we will examine the artwork, assess its condition, and begin the process of finding out what it is and who it belongs to."

Flora nodded her agreement. "Great. I wonder if my boss Ottavia wants some more business. We should call her. What about the people who shot at us? Were they caught?"

"Unfortunately not," Bernini answered as he strode into the room. His gaze ran over Flora and stopped at her wan face and her shadowed eyes. He pulled a chair up next to Ellen and took Flora's hand. "They had an escape route planned, a tunnel we didn't know about on the other side of the chamber. When Romano and the other men followed them, shots were fired to hold them back, and the criminals dashed to a place where three tunnels intersect and vanished down one of them. We didn't have enough men to search everywhere. However, the State Police spotted one of their gathering points, another metro stop with lanterns, hard hats, and digging equipment."

"Where is that?" Lisa asked.

"Piramide, southwest of Circo Massimo. You'll see at the meeting. I'll show you on our latest map," promised Bernini. His concerned gaze turned to Flora. "You look awfully pale. Did they give you a transfusion?"

"Yes. But I'm sure it takes hours for me to look normal again."

"Maybe you should stay put for a second night—"

"No! I'll sleep so much better in my own bed! And I must help with the conservation assessment!"

He patted the nearest leg. "I can't take you away until the doctor checks on you. Have you seen him this morning?"

"No. Oh, wait, here he is."

A tall young Indian physician entered the room. His eyebrows shot up when he saw Flora's three visitors. "A party, so early in the day?" His accent was British, not American. Deftly, he undid the bandage, checked the wound, and bound it up again. "You were lucky, you know. A couple of inches to the side and the shooter would have hit one of your vital organs. As it is, all you have is some muscle damage and that will heal. But you should take it easy for the next couple of days." He looked directly at Flora. "And eat lots of protein and drink plenty of fluids. You don't want to get dehydrated on top of your blood loss."

"I'll keep an eye on her," Bernini promised.

While Flora dressed in the bathroom, the other three gathered up her belongings.

She emerged. "Let's go!"

~ * ~

An hour later, everyone who could be spared from the actual moving of the recovered art gathered in the conference room at the Comando.

Bernini turned from consulting with Moscati and bade them all to sit down. "Okay, folks, now we have the art but we don't have the criminals who were pursuing it. While Ellen Perkins and Assunta Vianello lead the assessment and conservation team, the rest of us will focus our efforts on finding the people who have been digging in the Metro and the catacombs and tracking down the murderer of Benedetto Gallo. I don't think there is doubt any longer that his murder is connected to the art theft. Clearly, it's no accident that his death occurred near the location of the art trove."

De Luca looked up from his laptop. "Sir, I just got a preliminary list from Ricci, who is in charge of moving the paintings and other art pieces. He says it looks like some stuff is missing."

"How does he know?"

"There are old paper inventories in the boxes. Several paintings were unwrapped and then partially rewrapped, as if someone were checking what they were. Smaller items listed are not there, not in any of the boxes, and at least one religious statue, a Madonna and Child, is missing."

Everybody looked at each other. Their expressions varied from surprise on Irene's face to consternation on Adele's. Flora thought De Luca looked resigned.

"You mean, we're not done yet," Adele Marino said. "There's more art to be located."

"Looks that way," De Luca answered.

Bernini sighed. "Okay, some of us will return to the underground chamber where we found the first trove and fan out, looking for a second deposit of packing crates."

"Where are the items already recovered being stored?" Irene Costa asked.

"We have a palazzo not far from the Comando. It's one of our off-site storage facilities for the moment, but there is an ideal room with big tables for sorting things. Everything will fit. The conservators will have space to decide which things need treatment, and we have a security system there."

Bernini divided up duties for the next two days, sending De Luca to take over from Ricci the organizing of artworks for conservation assessment, and sending himself back underground to revisit the scene of the first discovery. Then he looked at Flora. "I was going to give you a chance to explore the tunnels, but I think your doctor would prefer you stay above ground for a few more days. So, go to the storage palazzo with Ellen Perkins and Lisa Donahue, okay? I've phoned ahead to line up some muscle to set up tables for you, lift crates, and so forth."

Flora agreed without a fuss. "I know my energy is a bit low still; I'm happy to look at paintings and such and help sort." Privately, she wished she had a week to rest up, but it would never do to reveal her weakness. That would mean exclusion from the project, and she wasn't about to risk that.

She rose to her feet. "I'm ready."

Assunta led the way, and Ellen followed. Lisa stayed behind to make sure Flora was steady on her feet, gathering up Flora's rain poncho and bag, and lending an arm.

"The Catacomb Girls are retreating to the laboratory," she said with a grin.

Flora smiled. "That's better than being buried alive in a rock fall—or drowned in an overflowing sewer."

"There's still time for that," said Lisa.

Thirty

Soon the four women found themselves surrounded by broken crates, shrouded paintings, and shapeless objects that might be statues or large classical vases.

The Carabinieri had provided a large room, once an elegant living apartment, in one of their spare palaces, the Palazzo Turchetti. It overlooked one of Rome's most beautiful public parks, the Villa Doria Pamphili, where Rome's families strolled on weekends.

Graced with tall windows and plaster scrollwork around every opening, the palazzo didn't look like an ideal art storage facility. No more so, reflected Flora, than the German churches or salt mines she'd seen pictured in old newspaper articles about art recovered after World War II. Here, at least, they had modest climate control in the form of creaking window air conditioners, hastily installed to make their task more comfortable in the sultry summer heat.

And air-conditioning would certainly benefit their patients, the paintings and other fragile works of art that had just emerged from a half-century of neglect in underground environments. A better climate would be the carefully controlled temperature and humidity in a real conservation lab, but window AC units were better than nothing.

Outside, black clouds built up like foothills as another thunderstorm threatened.

As officers carried in folding tables and set them up in a giant horseshoe, Flora, Ellen, Assunta, and Lisa walked the perimeter of the room, making decisions about which items to deal with first.

"Let's sort the paintings first," said Flora. "We can quickly determine which need immediate treatment. I called my boss on the way over and explained the Carabinieri's offer to pay handsomely for a rush job. She's happy to take as many paintings as we care to send her." And that meant extra work for Flora in her "day job," as soon as she could manage it. When would she sleep?

"Second priority: wooden statues, if we have any," Ellen added. "Wood that's been underground in alternating dry and damp environments is going to be a crumbling mess. Some of those medieval statues from church settings are worth a fortune; we need to get them out of here and into treatment as quickly as possible."

"I agree," said Flora. "Metal objects next, because of the corrosion possibilities. Stone works can be dealt with last. Stone statuary requires kinds of treatment we may not be able to handle, at least not at my lab."

"So, shall we lay out artworks by material on the tables to see exactly what we have?" Assunta said.

Lisa picked up the first painting, wrapped in damp burlap. As she pulled fabric away from the front, someone gasped.

"If that's not a Raphael, I'm no art historian!" Assunta's face shone with excitement.

The next two paintings, part of a religious triptych of Madonna with Child and flanking angels, made Flora's heart beat faster: it was a Sienese painting from the fourteenth century. Terrible condition: flaking varnish, paint lifting off the canvas, rotting wooden frame.

"Put that in the 'immediate treatment' pile," she said to one of the student helpers, referring to the table closest to the doorway. "And Giulio, take a picture of it first."

As they worked, it became clear that Ricci's initial assessment was correct: someone had removed select pieces from the crates during the 1940s, before they were hidden underground, or more recently, before the Carabinieri had found them. Almost every crate had been opened, with wrappings partially removed and hastily replaced.

Lisa, self-designated as the inventory checker, was making a new list: items missing from the crate inventory sheets, most of which were torn or otherwise defaced. She had to tape some of them back together before she could read them. "There's a pattern here," she said to the others. "Most of the works with well-known names are missing; what we have here are the 'second-best' paintings, statues, and so forth. I don't understand how the Raphael and that Sienese painting were left behind."

"That particular crate wasn't ransacked," Flora explained. "Maybe whoever was doing the sorting just didn't have time to go through all of them."

"Here's another crate that looks intact," said Ellen. She picked up the crowbar they'd been using and struggled to release the nails.

"Let me help," Lisa said. Together they wrestled two nails out and released the wooded lid to reveal the contents.

Flora picked up the first painting and carefully undid the brown paper wrapping. Her fingers slowed as her eyes took in what was in front of them. "Oh, my God…" she murmured, reaching for her cell phone.

Ellen looked at the front of the painting, only slightly damaged around the corners. "Looks like a Van Dyck," she offered.

Flora held up her cell phone, enlarging a photo she'd found online. "School of Van Dyck, a Madonna with Child and Saints. It's one of the paintings the Monuments Men never found." She smiled tremulously at her colleagues. "Wow! What a find!"

"Something to celebrate, indeed." Assunta put an arm around Flora. "Now call your boyfriend!"

~ * ~

Emilio De Luca, having supervised the transfer of art-filled crates and bundles to the palazzo, took a short cigarette break. His next task would be to set up a roster of police from both the Carabinieri and the *Polizia di Stato* to guard the storage room. He didn't want to be the one to tell Bernini or Moscati that their hard-won treasure disappeared on his watch.

Astorre Orsoni appeared suddenly at his side while De Luca was smoking and resting his eyes on the green paradise below them in the Villa Doria Pamphili.

"All the art from the underground cache is here?"

"Yes. The women are sorting the paintings and statues according to what needs treatment first."

"Huh. I'd have thought the first thing to do is to check the artists and names of works against our partial database of lost art."

"They're doing that at the same time. Identifying works, then evaluating them, photographing them, and sending those items most in need of conservation help over to Flora's lab."

"Who's providing guards for that room and for the transportation to Flora's workplace?"

De Luca felt a flash of annoyance. "Our men, of course, plus a few of the state police and students so we'll have twenty-four hour coverage." He stared at Orsoni. "Why are you asking all these questions?"

Orsoni glared right back. "I have a perfect right to ask questions. I'm still on the job, and, in case you've forgotten, I outrank you."

Uncomfortably aware that this was true, De Luca looked out the window again instead of at Orsoni's thunderous expression. Orsoni liked to remind people of his rank. Bernini, although everyone under him called him "sir," was far more comfortable to work with. He made the people around him feel like equals.

"I'm going to see for myself what the ladies have found," Orsoni said, striding down the hall.

De Luca watched him go, thinking Flora and Lisa and especially Assunta would hate being called "ladies." He was disconcerted when Irene Costa appeared in the hallway and stopped Orsoni in front of the door to the storage room. They leaned their heads together, conversing in low voices.

This was the third or fourth time he'd seen those two in private conversation, after weeks of barely speaking to each other.

Was Orsoni having an affair with Costa? Or was something else going on?

Irene turned her head and looked straight at De Luca.

A cold one, he thought. *I'd rather not be on her shit list.*

And then he wished she hadn't seen him.

Thirty-one

Evening air, clean and cool after a pounding thunderstorm, floated in the open windows of their apartment in Trastevere. Bernini sipped his wine, trying to blot out his exhaustion and his concern for Flora. She was still out, over at her lab setting up the first conservation treatments with Ottavia and her colleagues. She'd overdo it and come home exhausted; he was sure of it. Flora still hadn't fully recovered from the shot to her shoulder.

It had been a difficult afternoon. They had returned to the chamber from which the art trove had emerged. Bernini used his strongest flashlight to probe the back wall, looking for anything they had missed. He found a jagged hole in the soft tufa that had not been there the first time. Big enough for a man to crawl through.

Someone had done just that.

He beckoned to Ricci, Romano, and Orsoni, and the four of them pushed into a smaller chamber behind the first. To his horror, Bernini saw that another tunnel took off to the right. He shone his light on the little chamber's floor, picking out scraps of packing material and a telltale smear of dirt where something had been dragged along the floor.

They looked at each other. "Looks like we missed a few crates," said Orsoni. Bernini couldn't be sure, but it sounded like a note of satisfaction in Orsoni's voice. Whose side was he on, anyway? Not Bernini's, and maybe not the Carabinieri's, at least not fully.

"Did you make it into this inner chamber when you were moving the art?" Bernini asked Ricci.

"No," Ricci said in a low voice. "The wall appeared solid all the way around, so we didn't try to break through."

"One more victory for the other side," growled Bernini. "Things are not going our way!"

"Maybe Ricci wasn't up to it," suggested Orsoni, this time in an oily voice.

"Oh, can it!" Bernini said. "I'm not listening to criticisms of individuals. We're all responsible, me most of all. I should have stayed right here until the end of the recovery." He'd bounced back and forth between the art trove and following Romano. He'd left it too late to catch up with Romano and her two students, so he ended up leaving for the Comando. His guilt grew as he remembered half his mind had been on Flora, whether she'd be okay.

To say that Moscati would not be pleased with this new development was an understatement.

Maybe I won't have to tell Moscati, he thought. *Much better to find all the missing art first, then report some actual progress...*

"Orsoni, you and Romano take this tunnel as far as it goes and report back to the Comando. Ricci, come with me. I'm going outside to check for messages and then I'll meet you at the conservation station in Palazzo Turchetti. Now we'll have to look extra hard for what's missing from the first part of the trove."

On their way back to Metro stop Circo Massimo, Ricci said what Bernini was thinking. "We've got a leak on our team. There are too many coincidences with timing and someone always being one step ahead of us."

"I'm inclined to agree with you, much as I'd rather not think about it. Any ideas who?"

"Someone on the underground team, sir. The archives people haven't really had the opportunities to thwart our search underground."

"But one of the women could pass information to someone else."

"True. But I still think the underground explorers have the best chance to hinder or help us," insisted Ricci.

"That narrows the field to only about twenty-five people, if you count all the students we pulled in."

"It has to be somebody senior, someone who's attended at least some of our meetings at the Comando building."

"Maybe." Bernini scowled. He knew Ricci had a point, but he really wasn't ready to deal with a traitor of his own rank and training.

They had reached the last set of steps leading to the outdoors, and Bernini withheld his next comment to look at his cell phone.

He called Flora and was relieved and delighted to receive good news of their first real discovery, one no one had expected. He felt a brief thrill, and then realized the Van Dyck lookalike would not be enough to prevent the firestorm of reproaches he'd hear from upstairs about letting half the cache get away.

~ * ~

It was nearly ten p.m., and Bernini felt increasingly anxious as Flora stayed away from the apartment.

His cell burped.

"Bernini."

His spirits sank into the floor as he listened to the news. "There was a break-in at the Palazzo Turchetti. The storage facility's been robbed."

"*Oddio!* How did that happen? I thought De Luca set up guards there."

He listened.

"There's more, sir. De Luca was in the storage facility when the robbery occurred. He's dead, stabbed. Found just inside the door..."

Bernini let the voice on the phone babble away as he stared at the tree branches gently waving in the night breeze just outside the window. Another man dead, and most of the crates stolen. From their own facility.

Now there was no question the Carabinieri had a traitor on their staff—someone who had keys, inside information, and no respect at all for the lives of his colleagues.

Bernini picked up his cell and headed out the door into the uncaring, rain-filled night.

~ * ~

At the storage palazzo, Bernini and Ricci stared down at the body of their colleague, Emilio de Luca. His face showed surprise, perhaps because someone he knew and trusted had stuck the knife under his rib cage into his heart. Around him lay the debris of hastily moved packing crates, with scraps of paper and bits of rope left over from the conservation team's work that afternoon.

Bernini hoped fervently that Flora had taken good pictures. She was usually very good about documenting their work. Surely her colleagues at the lab already had some key pieces under treatment? So maybe this theft was not a total disaster. His gut, however, said otherwise: this was a catastrophe of the first order, one that could lose him his position as head of the investigation.

Bernini gazed out the window at the steady rain and called Flora's cell number. "*Cara*, are you home yet?"

"Just arrived, Vittorio. I'm drenched. What's wrong? Your voice sounds funny."

He told her about the robbery and the murder.

"Oh, no! How awful!" she gasped. "All that work we put in; I could just kill whoever stole the art!" Then she registered how that sounded and backtracked. "Another person dead—that's worse than any theft. How was De Luca killed?"

"He was stabbed. Very much like Gallo."

"Vittorio... you're the head of this project. That means you're in danger. You might be next."

He heard the unsteadiness in her voice. "Perhaps. But I am very well warned."

She let out a noisy breath. She understood the nature of his job, all right. "Two of your best colleagues already dead... and I really liked De Luca."

"I did, too. I liked both of them. They were good men. So how did you get on with the artworks after you called me about the Van Dyck?"

"We barely made a dent in checking all those crates and unwrapping everything. We took six paintings to the lab with us—"

"Did you take photographs of the stuff left at the palazzo?"

"Of course. Dozens. I gave the camera to one of the students, and then both Lisa and I supplemented the photography with our cell phones. And I meant to tell you earlier, but I was so excited by our Van Dyck discovery: Ricci was right—someone who knew what he was doing picked the best stuff out of that collection and took it away."

"That does not surprise me. Make sure the Carabinieri photographer has copies of your pics. At least we have some documentation of what was there and what is now missing."

"Surely the stuff has been moved together to another hiding place."

"But I bet it won't stay together. Our adversaries want to sell the art, almost certainly. As quickly as they can, for as much money as they can."

"But if we prepare a list and circulate it to the auction houses and the international conservation agencies online, the thieves will be caught when they try to sell things."

"Not if they stay out of the public eye and work with private collectors. You've heard me talk about them," Bernini said. "They're eccentric rich guys who just want to own things, so they can gloat over their possessions and withhold them from the rest of the world." Bernini didn't just sound cynical, he *was* cynical after only a few months in the art crimes unit. "Well, I have to get back to work. I have to phone Moscati and report our failure to protect the art."

"Oh, crap. That will be no fun."

"You said it. I hope I'm still in command of the investigation after this call. Drink some wine for me; get some rest."

"Good luck," said Flora. "I love you."

She disconnected. Bernini punched the numbers for his boss.

"Sir, I have some bad news..."

Thirty-two
Isabelle Rossin's Diary, Part 6

November 7 [1943]. The first salvage operation was successful and our family's paintings and many other items are now hidden under the city of Rome. Sal told me the hiding place is near the beginning of the subway they are building in the center of Rome, near a Roman monument.

...The first location is too small for all the crates; they have moved the rest about two meters to the south...

Sal and Clem have joined with members of the MFAA [Monuments, Fine Arts, and Archives] to help remove artworks endangered by the Nazi advance. Today he asked me to accompany him on a pickup. We took the truck to the church in xxx... and he asked me to distract the SS officer while he and Clem loaded the truck with art. Having no special crates, they plan to wrap things in cloth and cushion them with straw. I shudder for the valuable paintings and delicate statues, being driven on those terrible roads!

Luckily there was a bar across the street, so I lured the SS guy to come with me by saying how much I needed a drink... I had two martinis but the SS guy—his name was Hermann—downed three whiskies before Sal gave me the high sign to get away and join him in back... He teased me afterward. Said I was much too good at getting men drunk! I won't tell him about being groped under the table in the bar. Nothing happened, except I slapped his hand away. Being mauled by a Nazi in a good cause is just my little contribution to the war effort.

December 5 [1943]. Sal has recruited relatives and friends to disrupt the German theft of art by driving trucks full of valuable pieces to Rome. Rumors abound that the Nazi command promises Italian authorities they will "help" move art to safety, but then they steal choice paintings and other things for Hitler and Göring. He told me one senior officer stole two paintings by Lucas Cranach and took them away in an ambulance! His excuse? "They're Germanic art." What will be left in Italy after the war, I wonder?

December 10 [1943]. Sal is taking too many chances, driving trucks on potholed roads during bombing raids and dodging German patrols. He is in as much danger from partisan shooting as from German soldiers! I am afraid for him, for our family... he says he is doing work he must do, to save the art treasures of Italy... now that the Nazi thefts have been in the news, they promise to return artworks to Rome in a few days... Sal says they [the Germans] will make a big deal out of the return to create good propaganda.

[end of preserved part of Isabelle's diary]

Salvatore Orsoni was killed by gunfire while moving art on December 23, 1943. His widow Isabelle and her two children, Salvatore and Maria, survived. Six months later, their third child, Franco, was born. After the war, Isabelle trained as an art guide and worked at the Vatican Museums for twenty-three years.

Thirty-three

Vittorio Bernini sat on a hard chair and squirmed at his boss's expression.

"I've a mind to replace you, Bernini, as head of this investigation. Orsoni is the obvious choice."

Bernini could not restrain a wince at Orsoni's name, which made Moscati's eyebrows rise.

"Despite the fact that your team found the art trove—more by accident than by good intelligence—you've had two men killed on your watch. Both Gallo and De Luca were fine officers, men we can ill afford to lose."

"I agree, sir. I miss both of them, especially because they had just the talents we need on a project this complicated. Um, De Luca was the one to organize the roster of guards at the storage palazzo. He told me he had twenty-four-hour coverage lined up."

"So what went wrong?"

"The guard on duty told me he got a bogus text. It called for everyone on duty to report to the Circo Massimo Metro stop because of another emergency."

"Was he an experienced officer or one of the students?"

"A student, unfortunately. He was alone inside the palazzo, but his two colleagues who were stationed outside the building saw no reason to doubt the truth of the text, so all three took off."

Moscati ran his hands through his salt-and-pepper hair. "Surely De Luca told the student not to leave his post, under any circumstances?" His expression darkened. "Why was De Luca there? How on earth did he get himself killed? Don't tell me he was careless; that was not his way."

Bernini shifted in his seat. "It gets worse, sir. De Luca was probably still checking the artworks—I put him in charge of seeing that everything was organized before the women left—and he was inside the storage room when he was killed."

"Why didn't he leave when the bogus text came?"

"De Luca didn't receive it, sir. We checked his phone." Bernini waited for his boss to make the next leap.

He jumped with predictable speed. "I see! The sender had the list of fellow officers in his address book, but deliberately deleted De Luca from the message. That means—"

"Yes, I'm afraid so. We have a traitor in our midst." Bernini watched as Moscati's face settled into new hard lines. The tension between them eased as the boss focused his ire on a new target—the unknown traitor. Then Moscati's brows snapped down over his nose.

"So why exactly did you react when I mentioned replacing you with Orsoni? He's the obvious choice, and he's been with us longer than you have."

Bernini sighed. "Sir, Orsoni has been difficult to work with several times during this project. Not exactly obstructive, but combative. I thought it was just sour grapes because he got passed over, until De Luca and I interviewed him about his Jewish family connections to the Rossins." He summarized the interview.

"Hmm," Moscati said. "So you believe Orsoni is a little too interested in the art trove because of his family background?"

"Perhaps, sir. There are two other reasons why Ricci and I think someone on the inside is thwarting the investigation."

"Name them."

"One, each place we heard about as a possible location for the trove looked like it had just been searched by someone else. As if they were always one step ahead of us."

"And?"

"The stab wound that killed De Luca came from the front, exactly the way Gallo was killed."

Silence. Then Moscati said, "That implies, in both cases, that the victim knew his murderer."

"That's what I believe. Each time, the murderer was someone the victim trusted enough to allow him or her to approach closely."

Moscati leaned forward. "Who is it? Could it be Orsoni?"

"My gut says that Orsoni has some involvement, but I don't think he's the murderer. He might be shielding someone. He acts conflicted, as if he no longer knows what to do, when in the past he projected such self-confidence. And, before you ask, I have no proof for what I've just told you."

Now it was Moscati's turn to sigh. "Okay, you've convinced me. You are still in charge, but don't keep your thoughts so close to your chest. Give me a report at the end of each day with both facts and speculations. I won't ask you to meet me in person with this much going on unless it's absolutely necessary. Your first priority is to find the twice-stolen art. I'm going to ask the *Polizia di Stato* to take over finding De Luca and Gallo's murderer."

"Do you want me to report by cell phone or email, sir? With a traitor in our midst, neither is completely safe."

Moscati thought about it. "I have another email address, a private one. Send it here." He wrote on a piece of paper and handed it to Bernini.

"Thank you, sir." Bernini stood up and faced the door.

"And Vittorio?"

"Yes, sir?"

"Watch your back."

Thirty-four

Bernini didn't make it home until three in the morning. When Flora got up about seven, he lay passed out in a twisted pile of sheets. Obviously, his sleep had been restless.

She wondered if they'd manage to have breakfast together.

The past week had been so hectic they'd scarcely seen each other, except to fall in bed at night, or over the meeting table at the Comando.

Flora pulled the window down with her good hand to keep the rain from splashing on the floor. Thankfully, the shoulder was less sore today.

She fed the eager Gattino, who was mewing and winding around her feet. Then she filled the coffee pot, putting in an extra scoop of dark coffee, freshly ground. She guessed they both needed it.

Bernini dragged himself out to the kitchen. His shadowed eyes and rumpled brown hair told their own story. She waited until the coffee was ready and then poured, with milk and sugar on the table next to him, before she dared ask, "So what did Moscati have to say?"

"About what you'd expect. How did I allow a break-in at the storage palazzo? Hadn't we arranged extra guards? Of course I had, but I didn't plan on them being called away from their posts by a bogus phone call!"

"What phone call?"

"The one that said there was an emergency at the Comando building; everyone on duty should report in person, immediately. Those idiots didn't think to ring back and check if it were true; they just jumped into their cars and sped away."

Flora sat down opposite him and put a hand out. He grabbed her fingers with one hand while he took a slug of rich, dark brew.

He sighed. "Actually, he sounded pretty understanding after his initial biting comments. He understood it wasn't my fault, and I am still in command. Still, it was the sort of meeting I hope I never have to sit through again in this lifetime." Vittorio put down his coffee cup and looked at her. "There's something else, something I need your help with."

Flora took a sip of her own coffee and waited. She had a feeling she wasn't going to like this.

He said, "The second murder was in exactly the same method as the first, and it confirms my suspicion—and Ricci's—that we have a spy within the Carabinieri who is working with the art thieves. That is why they are always one step ahead of us—they've finished searching an area just before we get there, and they know things people outside of our team meetings should not know."

"What a wretched situation. Who is it?"

"I don't know yet."

"How terrible to suspect one of your colleagues."

"You can change the situation, Flora, by giving our side the information edge." He fixed his eyes on hers, willing her to agree with him. "You and your American friends—people who cannot possibly be suspects—can go through the archives and genealogical records again. This time, you'll be looking specifically for links between the Orsoni-Rossin family and our current officers. Astorre might be involved somehow, but I don't think he's the murderer. So far his conduct has been normal—that is, he does his job except for occasional bursts of negative attitude. I haven't a shred of proof against him or anyone else."

"Okay. We can certainly try."

"In the meanwhile, Moscati is putting the state police onto the job of checking alibis for the two murders and the break-in at the palazzo where the art trove was stored."

"So whoever your culprit is, he or she will be answering lots of questions. You won't be able to surprise anyone."

"I know. We will tread very, very carefully."

~ * ~

Flora, Lisa, and Ellen gathered at the State Archives again with laptops and cell phones at the ready. Assunta had been called into the museum; she promised to join them later if she could.

Bernini had furnished Flora with a list of all current officers, including a few who were not part of either the underground or the archival teams but who served as information transfer points to keep everyone up to speed.

The three women split the list up according to last names in alphabetical order. A couple of hours passed with no sounds except the tapping of computer keys and an occasional slurp as one of them gulped her coffee.

Outside, the weather remained a little cooler than usual, with pelting rain for the second straight day.

Flora batted at an annoying fly buzzing around her head and struggled to focus. "A" and "B" names had produced nothing; now she was up to "C." She reached for a folder that contained information about families living in or near Rome. Again, she made no progress.

Lisa looked up from her station. "Flora, maybe we're going about this the wrong way. Did we trace all of the relatives of Astorre Orsoni, including living cousins, nieces, and nephews?"

Flora thought about it. "No, I don't think we really finished that job. Let me pull up the Orsoni family tree." Lisa and Ellen joined her at the computer as Flora found the file.

"Seems like you went backward in time but not forward or sideways," commented Ellen.

"You're right. We have the World War II connections and before, but no cousins in Astorre's generation."

"That shouldn't take long," Flora said.

It did not. Within twenty minutes, they had filled in the family tree.

Astorre's father, Giuseppe, had two brothers: Franco and Giovanni. Franco never married, but Giovanni wed Matilde Liebermann, the sister of Giuseppe's Jewish wife Maria, during the war in 1941.

Giovanni was killed in action in the Italian army in 1945.

Three years later, his widow married Graziano Costa. Their children were Franco, Giovanni, and Irene.

The key piece of information hit all three of them at once: Irene Costa, another Carabinieri officer, was Astorre Orsoni's first cousin! Both cousins had Jewish heritage and were related by marriage to the Rossin family of art collectors.

"Holy shit," Lisa said. "This has got to be the missing link."

"Agreed," Flora said. "Before I call Vittorio, let's look at the folder with Isabelle's diary again."

Ellen pounced on two pages of the diary's second section that were still stuck together. "You couldn't have read what's on the back page," she said, as she gently loosened the pages with the ever-useful nail file.

The second page was a continuation of Isabelle's account of the transfer of the Nazi truckload from near Spoleto to Rome:

"...The first location is too small for all the crates; they have moved the rest about two meters to the south..."

"Another location! Now you have to call him!" Lisa cried.

Once again, Flora had trouble getting through to Bernini. Where was he? Was he underground again, or was his cell phone battery low? He could be in traffic as well; she left an urgent text message.

The three women gathered up their papers, computers, and cell phones and headed for the bus station in the pouring rain. It was about three thirty in the afternoon, just when some people were heading back to work after long lunches and others were on their way to meet friends for drinks or coffee and snacks at one of the ubiquitous café-bars.

To Flora's surprise, Bernini did not respond to her message with a return call, but instead sent his own urgent text message, "Meeting of entire team ASAP," while they were waiting at the bus stop.

Flora didn't like this. If the entire team included Astorre Orsoni and Irene Costa, she couldn't speak freely. Somehow she must corner Bernini and communicate privately what they'd learned about the two first cousins.

She flagged down a taxi.

Thirty-five

Bernini had his own set of complications. He'd received an anonymous message in the middle of debriefing the men who'd photographed the second chamber near Circo Massimo. It was brief and alarming: "A woman is running the operation against the Carabinieri. Do not trust your colleagues."

A woman. The two most competent women in his immediate circle were Adele Marino and Irene Costa. Giovanna Romano was less senior, but still very good at her job and clearly headed for promotion.

Costa had made Flora uneasy; very well, he would trust that instinct. Irene was one of the few team members who had moved fluidly between underground exploration and the archive group. She had all the relevant information in her head, just as Bernini did. That made her a strong suspect.

Who the hell had sent the text message? He tried everything he could think of to decipher the anonymous sender address on his cell phone and realized he'd need a laptop and IT help back at the Comando. Then, with a shiver, he realized he didn't know who he could ask without possibly alerting his adversaries. Now his head hurt. Bernini rubbed his temples with sweaty fingers.

Okay, then he'd convene a meeting but leave a few people out of the loop and see what happened. He sent a text to all but Orsoni, Adele Marino, and Irene Costa to meet at the Comando immediately. When Bernini arrived at the conference room with Ricci, he saw that Adele was already present. No doubt she'd been with someone else who'd received the text and came along as a matter of course. Well, then, he'd observe her reactions and go from there.

Then Flora came in with the two American women, Lisa Donahue and Ellen Perkins. Ellen shook herself like a dog and furled her inadequate umbrella. All three had wet pant legs and serious expressions on their faces. Flora looked straight at him and tipped her head; she had something to tell him, in private.

He waved her aside.

Flora grabbed his arm and muttered, "We need to speak outside this room." They fled into the hall and moved to a window in a cul-de-sac where no one could approach unseen.

"Tell me," he said.

She brought him up to date with their discoveries, starting with the second location for the hijacked artworks.

"I wonder if that refers to the shallow alcove we missed or whether it's a separate cache? We'll certainly check it out. But you said there was something even more urgent?"

"We dug a little deeper into the Orsoni family, the current generation, and found something crucial." Flora summarized her notes. "So Irene Costa and Astorre Orsoni are first cousins, from the same family of art collectors. They are all related to the Rossins of Paris. If you have a traitor, or traitors, in the Carabinieri, Irene or Astorre or both of them could be involved."

Bernini thought about it. "They don't appear to converse much, but that could be just their behavior in front of colleagues." He wondered if De Luca had seen a different relationship between them. "Even if they are both involved, it's hard for me to believe they'd risk their jobs, their current ranks, everything they've achieved so far, for such a risky business."

"You've said many times that the motive is usually money. Is one of them in real financial difficulties? Or maybe one of their family members is in dire straits?"

"Money and family. There you have what drives most people: family loyalty and the money to keep family members in the styles to which they are accustomed. You could be right."

"You've told me that both officers have been helpful to you, but Astorre has been the most difficult recently. Irene's newer to the Carabinieri, right? She may not have the same degree of loyalty to the police that he does."

Bernini frowned as he recalled the anonymous tip on his cell phone. "We could speculate about who and why for hours, but we need proof. Right now, we have to get on with this meeting. Be my extra eyes and ears. Watch as many people as you can. Oh, Adele Marino is here, but not Irene Costa or Astorre Orsoni."

He took her arm and whisked her back into the conference room. "Okay everyone, the reason I called this meeting is that we have some new information that will help us narrow our search. First, Flora Garibaldi and our American experts have found another page in the Rossin diary that mentions another hiding place a few meters south of the first one. That will take us into the area we wanted to explore more thoroughly anyhow, between the Circo Massimo and Piramide Metro stops."

Adele Marino was the first to comment. "I thought there must be more than one hiding place. The first location was too cramped, too small."

Bernini refrained from answering that she might have shared that insight earlier. "We don't know how big the cache is supposed to be, because we have such poor documentation. The area we'll focus on now is totally unmapped, at least as far as we know, and the walls and ceilings are notoriously unstable. "We'll need special equipment and our most experienced people to lead us."

Out of the corner of his eye, Bernini spied his boss answering a phone call and his normal poker face showing sudden animation. First Captain Moscati pocketed his cell phone and came to the head of the table. "I've just received word that a couple of geologists from the *Sotterranei di Roma* group have some information for us that may help our search effort. They've been doing some mapping of collapsed tunnels around an archaeological site near the main sewer of Rome, the Cloaca Maxima. They'll be here in about ten minutes."

Bernini decided to wait for the new information. With no immediate demands from him, people broke up into small groups and refilled their coffee cups.

About ten minutes later, a man and a woman entered the room, escorted by a uniformed officer. "Here are the geologists, sir."

After introductions, the senior geologist, *dottoressa* Lombardi, spread out a map. "This is where we have been working. It's an Etruscan site near part of the Cloaca Maxima, the Great Sewer, that archaeologists believe was built starting in the seventh century B.C. It is partly underwater now, due to leaks from old masonry belonging to Rome's oldest aqueduct, the Appia, running through the same area. I understand you are searching for something in this area that is also near the tunnels of the Metro B line?"

Bernini nodded. He wasn't sure how much Moscati wanted said in front of the geologists, so he didn't offer any details. "We are interested in the area around the Circo Massimo stop, and also the

Piramide stop to the south. There seem to be several tunnels in poor repair down there."

"Indeed, there are. That is the part of the subway that's the earliest. Construction was begun under Mussolini in the late 1930s. He smashed through archaeological ruins, and some of his workers may have cut off a corner of the foundation for the Colosseum. These are areas we are mapping and excavating whatever we can."

"Do you know of any tunnels that connect the different systems, such as the sewer and the aqueduct in this area?"

"Funny you should mention that. Yes, we have such a tunnel, one that may date back to Etruscan times. It was discovered only about three weeks ago. Also, we have found an unusual entrance into that tunnel; it goes through the basement of a private house."

Lisa and Flora looked at each other, signaling something only they knew about.

Bernini glanced at Moscati. "That is very interesting indeed. What can you tell us about conditions near your excavation?"

"The entire area is unstable, prone to collapses and flooding. If you are searching in the next few days, you should also keep an eye out for possible flooding. This torrential rain we've been having is going to cause problems all over Rome, but especially in older water systems underground."

Several team members looked apprehensive.

"Could one of you act as a guide for us, just to get us oriented?" Bernini asked.

Lombardi spoke privately with Moscati for a moment. "We have our own work to complete on a tight schedule but can certainly get you started and give you a copy of our latest map. This one has the most recently discovered ceiling collapses marked in red. Also the areas with water flowing are in blue."

"Who else works with you?"

"Our group is mostly archaeologists and geologists. Occasionally other specialists join us, and we've had visitors from the city sewer and water units."

"Any special equipment we need, besides hard hats?"

"Good lights, plenty of batteries, drinking water, cell phones—but don't expect them to work very often—reflective tape or paint for marking the turns as you go, and rope. If you go through flooded areas with water over a meter deep, you should be linked to each other by rope."

Capitano Moscati added a request. "Please, *dottoressa*, I would like a list of your team members in case we need to contact them later."

She nodded. Bernini arranged a meeting time an hour later at the Metro Piramide station and the geologists left the room.

After careful examination of the new map, Bernini said, "Okay. I'd like us to divide into three teams of five people to explore the area between the two subway stops." He pointed at a location on the map. "This looks like the most promising area because there are plenty of intersecting tunnels."

"What about the entrance through the private house?" Adele asked.

Bernini smiled. "One team will go in that way. I suspect that is the entrance our art thieves have been using that we haven't found. And we will also contact every person on the list the *dottoressa* gave Moscati to find out if they know anyone else digging under Rome."

"What do we look for, then? Anything different from the catacomb searches?" Ellen asked.

Ricci said, "What we've seen so far is a mix of dry tunnels and wet ones, and now we know there's a good chance of flooding. So, look for side chambers and sections where the color or texture of the walls changes. Look for signs of digging, recent or otherwise. Look for sections of walls that have been patched with cement or bricked up. Don't ignore wet areas; they may have been drier in 1943 when people were looking for hiding places."

Bernini looked around. "All right, here are your team assignments. Romano will take the private home tunnel, I'll start from the archaeological site toward Circo Massimo, and Ricci will lead the team from the archaeological site toward Piramide..."

Astorre Orsoni walked into the room. He looked surprised and then disturbed when he realized he'd missed the first part of a meeting.

Now I need to handle him carefully, thought Bernini. *Assign him to Romano's team so I can proceed unhampered? No, keep him close to me so I know what he's up to, that's the answer. Orsoni won't get the opportunity to communicate with anyone else or make phone calls if I can help it.*

"Ah, Orsoni. You're late. You come with my team, and I'll fill you in on the way." Bernini returned to his hastily written list and read off names for the various teams. "Don't forget to take some snacks with you. This expedition is likely to take hours."

Orsoni came up to Bernini. "Did I miss a planned meeting?"

"Not planned, exactly. Very short notice. You didn't receive my text?"

"No." Orsoni's eyes narrowed as he took in Bernini's carefully neutral expression.

"Come in my car," Bernini said, hoping to stall off other team members joining them in his small vehicle. No such luck; Adele Marino caught up with them.

"The other cars are full," she said, glancing at both men. "Okay if I ride with you?"

"Certainly." Well, he could keep an eye on both of them if they were with him underground. Or could he? Bernini felt pressure building in his head and heard an ominous gurgle from his gut. Just what he needed when they were about to go out of range of any bathrooms for hours.

They piled into Bernini's Fiat, and Orsoni took the front passenger seat. "So fill me in," he said, eyes hooded and mouth in a tight line.

Bernini talked fast and in a low voice, figuring Adele would have trouble catching all he was saying. She might tune out, anyhow, having heard it all already. He gave Orsoni an abbreviated summary of the meeting, leaving out the details about the hidden entrance in the private home and Flora's bombshell about a second cache only meters from the first.

He was unlucky. Adele had excellent hearing, and she paid attention. "Astorre, there's other news. Flora and the Americans found more of the diary and there's a private entrance to the underground..."

Damn. Bernini felt his hold on the flow of information spinning out of control. He kept his face expressionless while his brain groped for ways to keep Orsoni in line.

Orsoni's mouth tightened as he heard Adele's news. "Who's going lead the trek to the private tunnel entrance?"

"Romano," Bernini said. The three of us will start at the Etruscan site and explore north to the Circo Massimo Metro stop." He detailed the extra equipment they'd need as rain pounded on the windshield, restricting his vision.

Adele Marino spoke up. "At least we'll be dry underground."

Perhaps she'd been sleeping through some of the meeting after all and had missed the admonition about possible flooding.

Thirty-six

When they reached the meeting place, Bernini did a little last-minute shuffling of personnel. Ellen, Flora, and Lisa arrived together, already soaked by the rain but ready for the search in long pants and long-sleeved shirts. Bernini moved Ellen to Ricci's team and kept Flora and Lisa for his own team.

Three *Sotterranei*, the two they'd already met plus an archaeologist named Cellini, joined them to guide them into the excavation area. Everyone took a hard hat and a flashlight, and each team carried rope and lime-yellow marking tape.

Bernini looked at his watch. "Okay, everyone. My watch says sixteen-fifty. Check in every hour on the half hour if you can get cell reception. If you can't, call the Comando with your report as soon as you come up from the tunnels. Aim to return in four hours for a meeting on what we've found—or not found."

Romano's team set off above ground with Cellini to check out the private house and enter the tunnel system from there. The two teams slated to begin at the archaeological site bunched together and followed the two geologists, who led the way with strong flashlights.

The two teams walked the opposite direction from the Circo Massimo station in the subway tunnel. After about four kilometers, they entered a side tunnel Bernini had never seen. Immediately, Bernini felt the difference in the terrain. This part of underground Rome was wetter than many of the catacombs, with dripping water overhead and little rivulets of water underfoot. The tufa stone hung raggedly, peeling in places on walls and ceiling.

He glanced at Flora's feet and was relieved to see she'd chosen light, waterproof hikers with substantial treads. Lisa was similarly equipped.

"Has this section always been this wet?" he asked their guide, *dottoressa* Lombardi.

"No," she replied. "The water started flowing only about three weeks ago. We think there is a leak somewhere in the Cloaca Maxima sewer, but we haven't found it yet. That's why we're especially wary of flooding just now; we can't estimate how much water might flow down here."

Sweat broke out on Bernini's forehead as he realized he'd brought Flora and Lisa into this situation. They'd volunteered, of course, but he had a bad feeling that this particular trip would be more dangerous than any exploration so far. He'd never liked water that much; he didn't swim much as a child. He figured he could dog-paddle just enough to stay afloat.

They'd arrived at the Etruscan site. Bernini was amazed to see how well-lit it was that far underground. The geologists must have rigged electric lines from somewhere, probably patching into lighting for one of the subway stations. The excavation showed foundations of several small buildings and what looked like a street or passageway between the walls. The remains of an Etruscan town or housing compound? He had no idea, so he asked. "What is this site?"

"Part of Etruscan Rome." She pointed out several house structures and the foundations of another building, a little larger, that they thought might be a temple.

Bernini vividly remembered visiting the painted tombs at Tarquinia. Etruscan gods and goddesses, dancing or reclining in front of dining tables. Beautiful decorations of floral ornaments and masks on recreated house interiors. He knew Flora had been reading about the Etruscans; he must ask her to tell him some of the key tidbits she'd learned.

Lombardi pointed to the other side of the pit. "There's the tunnel you want, folks. You go in about half a kilometer and then it branches both north and south, toward the subway stations you mentioned. Best of luck, and don't venture too far off the main tunnel without marking your way back."

Bernini smiled. She sounded like a mother with a troop of children. But maybe they'd all need a little mothering during this expedition.

The two teams of five entered the tunnel Lombardi had indicated. Ricci, Ellen, and three officers went first; then came Bernini, with Lisa, Flora, and Adele clumped in the middle and Orsoni bringing up the rear. Bernini had wanted Adele to follow Orsoni, but he hadn't had time to rearrange the order before they started. He'd do that when they arrived at the north-south branching tunnel.

They passed several smaller openings in the heavily worn and pockmarked tufa walls before they reached a flat wall where the tunnel branched to the right and the left. "There's your path, Ricci. I'm going left," Bernini said.

"Talk to you soon, I hope." Ricci replied, and then he was gone.

Bernini made his arrangements. "Adele, how about you lead? Then Lisa. Flora, stay just in front of me. Orsoni and I will follow at the rear."

Orsoni's eyebrows shot up in surprise, but he complied without complaint. "Sandwiching the civilians between the police officers, are you?" he whispered.

"Something like that," Bernini said as he shifted the coil of rope he carried to a more comfortable position. He knew this short section where it was wide enough to walk two abreast would narrow soon. It did. After a short stretch of relative comfort, when the searchers could stay upright, the ceiling dipped and the walls leaned in. Bernini found himself hunched over, with Flora's hand lightly hooked into his belt. Orsoni moved like a crouched dwarf just behind them.

Bernini assumed this tunnel would eventually lead to the vast chamber where the first cache had been located, but he was mistaken. The floor tipped downward and they progressed at an uncomfortable angle until they were deeper underground than he had ever been.

He didn't like it, especially when the sound of water grew louder to their right. Visions of his head bobbing just above filthy water danced in his brain. Ugh. None of them had signed on for an underwater expedition. Sure enough, in a few more meters, they reached a section of the tunnel that was half under water.

The team gathered together in a clump to talk about how to go forward.

That was when Bernini discovered Orsoni had disappeared. "Did you hear him go off to one side or the other?" he asked Flora, who had been between the two men.

"I didn't hear a thing. But he could have just stepped aside quietly and waited until we'd moved around a bend before he moved again. We were all making enough noise to hide that."

Bernini thought hard. He suspected Orsoni would not have turned aside unless he had prior knowledge of these tunnels. There had been a branch about a half kilometer back.

"We go back to where that last tunnel branched and follow him, if he went that way." Bernini told himself that the water ahead of them had not influenced his decision.

Adele said, "I am not surprised he has a different agenda, sir. He's been acting strange for days now."

Bernini grunted as he took the lead. Again, he wished Adele had told him she thought Orsoni was acting strange, but maybe she thought it wasn't serious. Cops had moods like ordinary people—certainly he did. He was pretty sure he had been a bit bearish and less than sympathetic since this project began. Bernini decided that assuming more responsibility didn't make him a better person, just a more harassed one.

And so much for keeping track of Orsoni. His only hope now was to discover where the branching tunnel led without Orsoni's assistance. Could it be a shortcut to the large chamber where they'd found the first cache of artwork?

Abruptly, the passage they were in made a right turn, dropping down to a new level. Water flowed past the opening. Bernini saw water along the edge of the drop, making it likely Orsoni had splashed as he jumped down. So, assuming there was something worth seeing further in, they would follow. Bernini put in a cautious leg and discovered it was thigh deep on him, so it would be almost waist deep on Flora. A profound uneasiness possessed him.

He eyed the women, who all looked resolute if not enthusiastic. Flora's face was paler than usual, and again Bernini felt a pang of guilt for dragging her along. His protective glance asked her, "Sure you're up to this?" and her answering glower replied, "Of course!" He couldn't force her to go back, and his instinct said he'd better not try. She wanted to be here with him and her American friends, and her defiant dark eyes added, "Don't you dare send me away!" Her shoulder wound was high up; if they got into water deeper than this, they'd all turn around and he'd send in new people.

"Ready for this?" he asked. "We'll be half soaked, but no worse. If we rope ourselves together, we can continue unless it gets too deep. Good thing I brought the headlamps; you can strap them onto your helmets and put everything else on your backs." He'd made sure each team had plastic bags for storage of valuables, especially extra flashlight batteries and cell phones, and knapsacks to carry everything while freeing up arms and hands.

Everyone readjusted their gear, put on the miner's lamps, and moved cell phones and wallets into their plastic bags and knapsacks, cinched high on their backs.

"Now for the rope. Loop it around your waist, tie a fixed knot so the rope won't strangle your midsection, and pass the rope to the next person. Keep at least two meters of length between you so you can maneuver easily. Last person—that's you, Marino—tie up the excess rope and stuff it into your knapsack. Ready? Let's go."

~ * ~

Flora took her place on the rope behind Bernini. She hated to admit it, but the attack and the night in the hospital had sucked the energy out of her. She felt almost weightless, except for the throbbing in her damaged shoulder. Maybe that was the painkiller the doctor had prescribed. Her thoughts drifted and her brain was pleasantly fuzzy. As long as no one asked her to make a decision or perform heroic acts of strength, she could manage this trek through the watery tunnel. She hoped so.

Lisa patted her on the unwounded shoulder as they began to move, giving Flora a warm glow of reassurance. With Bernini in front and good friend Lisa behind her, she could relax a little. And if something happened, they were all in it together.

Flora's legs grew heavier as they slogged forward through swirling water. Her drip-dry travel pants flapped against the skin of her thighs and the knapsack shifted uncomfortably on her back. Dank odors assailed her nostrils and her headlamp picked up areas of yellow-white slime on the walls. Uh oh; the level of the slime matched a faint water line above her head; this tunnel had been completely underwater not too long ago.

Behind her, Flora could hear Lisa's breathing roughen as the current around their legs picked up. Had Lisa noticed the water line? Was the water rising now? She was too busy keeping her balance and focusing on what was right in front of her to be sure. Her own breathing accelerated.

Bernini shouted ahead of them, but his voice faded in and out like bad cell phone reception. Flora yelled, "What? We can't understand you!"

He turned his head slightly. "I said, we're going up again!"

As he spoke, Flora felt the floor level of the tunnel rise and soon her knees appeared above the water. Five minutes later, they reached another hole in the wall. They had to climb over a lip of tufa to reach the new tunnel.

Bernini stood ready to give her a hand, which Flora took gratefully. He boosted her up and she crawled out onto a nearly dry floor. Behind her, Lisa received a boost and soon she was brushing herself off next to Flora. They both squeezed some water out of their pants.

Lisa laughed. "I don't know why I'm bothering. We all look like drowned rats, and I wouldn't be surprised if we have to go back the same way after we're done exploring."

"You may be right. I'm just glad to be out of that water."

Adele Marino joined them, then Bernini. Neither of them bothered to squeegee water out of their clothes.

Bernini glanced at his cell. "Five-thirty. We've been underground about an hour. Feels like longer." He glanced at Flora's face. "Hey, you don't look so good. Drink some water, here." He unscrewed the cap of his water bottle and thrust it at her.

"I'm okay. Ignore the hospital pallor; it's my normal look."

"No, it's not, but I won't argue here. When this is over, you're taking a full day off."

"Yes, boss," Flora answered with a little smile. Instead of annoying her by being bossy, Bernini's concern made her feel cared for, protected. She was starting to like that feeling, that plus not being in charge of every aspect of her life all the time.

The four of them replaced water bottles in their knapsacks, untied and stowed the rope, and started out again. This time, Adele Marino took the lead and carried the strongest flashlight. Bernini followed behind Flora and Lisa.

Flora trudged along, fighting her fatigue, wishing that perhaps she'd stayed behind after all. The ceiling dipped and she crouched lower, thigh muscles clenching. How long would the search go on before Bernini called a halt for the day? Cops worked crazy hours, she knew that already. What if she—

"We're at the big cavern!" called Adele. She stepped through another ragged opening and Flora followed.

What a relief to be in a larger space again! Flora watched as Adele played the beam of her flashlight around the walls.

"There!" said Flora. "That's the direction of the art trove. We should start there, right, Vittorio?"

"Yes. The second cache—if there really is one—should be near where we found the first art cache."

He took the lead again, crossing the bumpy surface of the cavern and sweeping from side to side with his light.

They had arrived at the smaller, empty alcove where the first crates had been discovered.

Bernini turned to Flora. "Didn't the diary mention a direction?"

"To the south, by a few meters."

He pulled out his cell. "I have a compass app. It would be a miracle if it worked down here." He clicked the icon and watched incredulously as the virtual needle moved on the compass dial. "If this is working correctly, we're facing northwest." He swung around to the left. "And that way is south."

They walked along the wall about three meters to a projection in the rock. "There's another tunnel!" Flora cried as she spotted a hole barely large enough for a woman her size.

"The opening is half-hidden by rubble. This tunnel could have easily been missed before, sir," said Adele to Bernini.

"Yep, I know."

One by one, they squeezed through and crawled forward. Bernini had to turn his torso sideways; it was a tight fit for his big shoulders.

The tunnel widened a little bit, and soon all four of them could stand upright again.

And then they heard voices, somewhere ahead of them.

Thirty-seven

The first voice was female. "It's supposed to be here! That diary said so... who could have taken it?"

Irene Costa.

Now Bernini had no doubts about the identity of his traitor, the woman with inside knowledge of the Carabinieri and all its plans. But was she also a murderess? They still had no proof of anything against her.

Around the next bend, where the tunnel widened enough for several people to stand together, he saw them. Not just Irene, but three young men and a policeman, Astorre Orsoni. Shovels lay at their feet, and behind them was a hole in the soft rock wall. Remnants of packing material showed that something had been stored there once, but all of it was gone.

All eyes turned toward Bernini.

"So you finally caught up," Orsoni said. He didn't look at all worried.

Irene Costa squared her shoulders and faced Bernini with a defiant expression on her narrow face. "Say what you will; I had my reasons for pursuing the art trove on my own."

"You are related to the Jewish family that owned some of the art, as is Orsoni here."

"I won't deny it. But my family is in financial trouble. We need cash, quickly, and we can't afford to wait for the wheels of the law to turn in our favor. Some of these cases, like the Klimt 'Woman in Gold' one, took years to resolve."

"Didn't it occur to you that if you talked with the colonel, the police might help you with a loan?"

Irene stared at Bernini. "I've never heard of such a thing."

Bernini sighed. "You wouldn't know how generous he can be unless you tried. Now it's too late. But you might get a reduced sentence if you share what you know and work with us instead of against us."

Irene laughed. "You have no proof of anything. It's not a crime for me to hunt for the art trove on my own."

"It is if your search is conducted on police time. And your recent conduct is certainly against the oath you swore to the Carabinieri not to reveal information outside the Comando."

"Oh, don't moan to me about rules and personal conduct!" Irene sneered.

Bernini nodded at the three young men, one of whom resembled Irene closely enough to be her brother. "Who are these guys?"

"You don't need to know."

Astorre spoke up. "Irene, maybe this is the time to come clean—"

"Shut up, Torre."

"But there's nothing here; you have nothing to gain. Why not cooperate?"

She glared at Orsoni. "I thought you were with me, Cousin. Now I see you've got no guts. Don't you want your cut?"

"Not at the price of another death. And I could help your family, as I offered to before—"

"The Costas don't take handouts!" The speaker was the young man who looked so much like Irene.

"My brother speaks the truth," added Irene. She stood shoulder to shoulder with him, presenting a united front of short-sighted defiance.

Astorre Orsoni backed up so he flanked Bernini. "I won't have any part of this operation from now on. You can go to hell without my assistance."

"Trying to protect your ass, are you?" Irene drew her service pistol and pointed it at Orsoni. "Well, you're too late."

"Costa! Put that down. If you shoot another officer, there's nothing I can do for you!" Bernini yelled. He pushed Flora behind him.

He had forgotten Adele Marino until movement in the brother's eyes alerted him that she'd changed position.

"Put the gun down, Irene. I've got you covered, and I'm not afraid to shoot a rogue officer." Adele's voice sounded to Bernini's left.

Everyone froze as the two women confronted each other.

Then Flora said, "What's that noise?"

The rushing of water filled all their ears.

Bernini remembered what the geologist had said. "Must be a break in the aqueduct somewhere close! We've got to get out of here!"

The sudden pallor on Irene's face matched Flora's as she weighed her options. "Follow me," she said, pocketing her gun. "There's another way out." She and her relatives turned back the way they'd come.

There was no time for ropes. Water poured through the opening Bernini and the others had used a short time ago; it surged around their feet as they ran.

Flora discovered she had enough energy left after all. Fear of drowning and the resulting rush of adrenaline helped power her legs. She stumbled on the uneven surface but kept pace with Bernini as he stooped and slithered just ahead of her.

Another surge of water from behind Flora swept her off her feet. Her head dipped under the filthy stream and she struggled to the surface. She spat out the water and moved her arms just enough to stay afloat. The sore shoulder protested.

Blackness, rushing water. No light ahead.

She treaded water against the current and stuck one hand up. It touched the ceiling.

"Vittorio! Lisa!"

"Here!" he answered just in front of her. "Swim for it!"

"I'm behind you!" called Lisa. Her miner's lamp suddenly flashed back on, providing a bobbing illumination for the swimmers ahead.

Flora glanced up and saw the ceiling of the tunnel barely a meter above her. Her breath came in gasps as she let the current carry her, fluttering her feet in an effort to stay on the surface. She was a good swimmer, but that skill wouldn't keep her alive if the tunnel filled to the top with water.

She felt something bump her underwater. She grabbed a handful of clothing and pulled with her good arm. Adele's head rose next to Flora's face. She coughed up water and moved her arms.

"I'm okay," she sputtered. "Got knocked out when the surge came."

Flora let go of Adele and concentrated on keeping her own head above water and her breathing even. She knew she was losing that battle because fear closed her throat every time her head bumped the ceiling.

The water rose further.

"Vittorio! Are you there?"

He answered in a waterlogged voice. "Just ahead! Keep swimming!"

Ahead of them, Irene called, "… opening ahead… underwater… Dive for it, then swim up!"

Huh? Swim down and then up?

A few more strokes and Flora banged into Vittorio. He grabbed her and spoke in her ear. "We're at a wall. I can feel the opening below, about the length of your arm downward. All you have to do is dive underwater a bit, and then the new tunnel slants upward. Take a big breath now."

Flora shuddered in his arms. The dancing light of Lisa's miner's lamp shone on Vittorio's face. He looked perfectly calm.

She kissed him, took a big gulp of air, and ducked under with both hands out to feel whatever was in front of her. The tunnel, barely wide enough for a single human to crawl or swim, sloped gently up from the opening. Flora pushed against the walls with her booted feet, trying to gain a little speed so she could get her head above water again.

Just when her lungs felt like an over-full balloon, the water poured off her face and she could breathe. Two meters farther and she crawled out onto a slimy rock surface.

Flora rolled like a seal to get out of the way of the others and lay gasping in the dark. She had survived; she was okay.

Then she felt two strong hands grab her wrists and drag her backwards.

Flora screamed in surprise and pain.

"Shut up," Irene Costa told her. "I could shoot you, but I need you as a bargaining chip with Bernini."

Flora screamed again. "I can't help it! My shoulder... one of your men shot me there! Damn, it hurts!"

Irene muttered under her breath and shifted her grip so her strong arms wrapped around Flora's chest. Still dragging Flora, she stooped to enter another tunnel, one that led away from the wet landing place where Flora had emerged from the water.

Whimpering, Flora scrabbled with her feet to keep her legs from bumping over the floor but the pain in her shoulder was excruciating.

She passed out.

Thirty-eight

Vittorio Bernini took a huge gulp of air as his head rose from the water. He dragged himself forward, hearing gasping and retching around him, and crashed into Adele and Lisa in pitch blackness.

"Who's that?"

"Me, Adele."

"Flora?"

No answer.

"Lisa?"

A watery cough. "I'm here."

"Flora, where are you?"

It took them a few minutes of fumbling around and listening to each other's voices to be certain there were only three of them.

Bernini was beside himself. "*Madre di Dio!* Who's got a light that works?"

"Mine did, but it's gone out," Lisa said.

"Okay, let's fan out and grope around until we find her. She must have passed out from pain or exhaustion."

Five minutes later, it was clear to Bernini that Flora—or Flora's unconscious body—had moved out of reach. His anxiety rose to blood-pounding levels. *Find her!*

"I felt another tunnel opening," Adele said. "I think it's the only one out of this little cave."

"Let me go first. Lisa, grab onto my ankle until we're all in the tunnel. Adele, you bring up the rear."

Bernini crawled, one hand reaching out to check for obstacles in the dark.

He had to find her! Flora was his life!

Head and body fought each other. His brain shied away from the possibility that she might be dead, drowned in the few moments between his gentle push and her body washing over the low lip of the little cave. His body feared the worst: his limbs shook and cold sweat mixed with the moisture already on his face. He kept blinking his eyes, trying to make them pierce the darkness around him.

The surface of the tunnel might be of soft tufa, but pebbles of harder rock grated on his knees. Depressions in the floor, if it could be called a floor, trapped his toes and jarred his legs. Muscles he didn't know he had ached from the earlier journey. Something new and wet dripped down his forehead—was it blood? He wiped his forehead with the back of one hand, but the maddening drip continued.

He must have banged it coming out of the water.

Time passed. He could hear the rasping breaths of the exhausted women behind him, accompanied by sharp yelps or groans as one of them barked a shin or scraped some skin while struggling forward. Just when Bernini figured they needed a break, even here in the dark, a dim light shone from behind him.

Lisa's headlamp still had a little life in its battery, but it flickered ominously.

At the same time, the tunnel widened slightly. Three soggy people sat in a huddle and surveyed each other's faces.

"Everyone okay?" asked Bernini.

The women nodded. Lisa's face shone with water and sweat, her features festooned with wet blond hair. Adele's shorter hair bushed up around her ears, making her look wilder than usual.

"You've got a cut on your head," Adele said to Bernini.

"I know. Nothing I can do about it. Anyone got any fresh water left? My water bottle must have pulled loose earlier; it's gone."

"Here," Adele said, unclipping her bottle from her belt.

He took a swig and handed the bottle to Lisa. "Take some."

"It's okay, I've still got my own water."

"Okay, onward. This tunnel has to come out somewhere. Irene and her people went this way. Flora has to be ahead of us; there's no other way for her to go."

"We didn't miss any side passages, did we?" croaked Lisa. "I certainly didn't feel any."

"Believe me, I checked," Bernini said.

"So did I," Adele agreed. "I patted the walls on either side of me as I moved."

"Then we will find her."

As Bernini said this, he realized there was another possibility for Flora's disappearance. Instead of being unconscious, she might have been captured. Irene, deciding she couldn't shoot anyone with Adele's gun trained upon her, had chosen to use Flora as a bargaining chip...

Lisa's light lasted only a short while longer.

Luckily, it went out for the last time just when the three of them reached a point where the ceiling rose and they could stand. After their eyes adjusted to darkness again, they moved forward carefully, feeling the tunnel walls on either side for openings and testing each step for sudden drops or obstacles.

Then a faint light appeared ahead.

Bernini broke into a run. Around the next corner, a rickety metal ladder bolted to the rock wall reached up into the gloom. He began climbing it just as Lisa and Adele reached the bottom.

"One at a time," Bernini hissed as Adele laid hands on the bottom of the ladder. "The metal bolts look corroded and the ladder wiggles like it's going to come down at any time. Climb as quietly as you can. We don't know where this comes out."

The bolts holding the ladder gave way just as Lisa reached the top. Bernini and Adele grabbed Lisa's hands and hoisted her up. She skinned one knee but was otherwise unharmed.

Soon the three of them found themselves in a derelict kitchen that looked like no one had cooked there for at least a decade. But discarded coffee containers and the remains of *panini* littered the surface of a small table.

"This is the safe house Irene's group has been using!" whispered Bernini. "Guns out. Let's see who's here." He hoped fervently that the plastic bag had kept his pistol dry.

Adele moved up to flank Bernini, and Lisa stayed a few paces back. "Don't get yourself shot," whispered Adele to Lisa.

"Don't worry, I'll stay back," said Lisa. "I'd rather not be a target."

They tiptoed down a short hallway and faced a closed door. It hung crookedly, clearly decades old. Bernini motioned for Lisa to stand to the right, so the door would cover her when it opened.

Then he listened.

"… you think you're so smart, joining the Carabinieri on this search."

"It was Vittorio's idea. I've been helpful." Flora's voice sounded weak and strained.

"Of course it was! Well, he can pay the price for dragging his American girlfriend into a police matter."

A new voice: Astorre Orsoni's. "Irene, this is madness. Let her go. You still have a chance of reducing your sentence if you cooperate with the police—"

"Oh do shut up, Torre! I thought you said back in the tunnel that you wouldn't be involved in my operation again."

"I've no intention of being part of this kidnapping. I'm trying to see that you don't spend the rest of your life in jail."

"I won't as long as I don't murder someone myself," scoffed Irene. "And the police have no proof except the testimony of two officers. I doubt they'll believe you anymore."

"Let me go," Flora's voice sounded very weak. "Bernini has figured out by now that I'm in your custody. You'll be caught. And if you killed Gallo and De Luca—or had them killed—the Carabinieri won't rest until you're captured."

Irene laughed. "Trying to get me to confess? I'll admit nothing— not to you."

"Let Flora go," Orsoni insisted. "Can't you see she needs medical attention? If she dies of infection after being submerged in that filthy water, you'll be responsible. Untie her now, or I will."

That statement make Bernini quake with fear behind the door. He would wait until a calmer moment to break in, and then...

"Oh yeah? Are you really going to untie her when I have my gun trained on your head?"

The slam of another door indicated that a fourth person had joined Orsoni and the two women.

"Irene, I have bad news."

"What idiocy have you committed now, Giovanni?"

Bernini thought Giovanni must be one of Irene's brothers.

"Franco drowned. He fell behind us in the second underwater tunnel... I couldn't get to him in time." His voice was thick with tears.

Irene shrieked. "*Oddio*! No, I don't believe it!"

"It is true, little sister."

The clang of metal on the floor suggested someone had dropped a gun.

Loud sobs ensued.

Bernini nodded at Adele, and they broke down the door together.

The first person he saw was Irene, who had collapsed into a chair, crying bitterly. Flora lay in the corner, near a second door that was wide open.

Bernini used Adele's belt to tie up Irene—neither of them had remembered to pick up handcuffs from the supplies furnished by the state police. Adele kept her pistol trained on the older brother.

"Where's Orsoni?" she asked, looking around the small kitchen.

"Gone. Again," said Bernini in disgust. "So is the older brother."

Lisa went straight to Flora, who lay in a wretched heap on the floor. Her pallor was extreme, and tracks of tears showed on her dirty face. "My shoulder," she gasped. "It's really bad."

Bernini completed his phone call for backup and an ambulance. He crossed to Flora and squatted down, using a pocket knife to slice the rope that bound her arms. He rubbed her good arm to restore circulation, but she winced when he tried to massage the other arm. "The medics will be here as soon as they can. Just hang on a little longer."

"Shoulder hurts," she mumbled against his chest.

"Of course it does. You were shot, remember?"

A weak giggle from Flora.

"I still say you'd make a great officer. Sure you don't want to change your profession? After all, you've already had excellent practice in dealing with thugs, crawling through tunnels, and running for your life."

Flora gave him a teary smile. "Shut up and hold me."

Thirty-nine

The lost art seekers met the next morning at nine, as early as Bernini thought reasonable after their long trek through the tunnels and fight with the flood. The Carabinieri secretary provided coffee and pastries for everyone at Moscati's request.

Bernini was sore in every muscle; he assumed Flora felt worse. Before he left the apartment, he told Flora to stay in bed this morning, resting the damaged arm on an extra pillow to elevate it. To his surprise, the gunshot wound had not reopened in the tunnel. That doctor had done a good job of stitching and bandaging, and Flora said she'd already had an antibiotic shot. She'd also wrapped her bad shoulder in a second bandage and plastic wrap before they'd gone underground.

"So you knew we would end up under water?" he teased.

"I didn't know for sure, but I knew it was possible. I also knew I should have stayed home, but I just couldn't bear missing out. Got a little more excitement than I bargained for."

"That's my Flora."

He made sure she'd taken her pain medication and filled her water bottle. Far from protesting being ordered around and cared for, she gave a sleepy grunt and smiled. The kitten curled around her elbow and purred.

At the Comando building, the mood was glum. The art-hunting teams had turned up nothing, either from underground caches or from the paintings and sculpture stolen from the Carabinieri's storage palazzo.

Bernini explained the Orsoni-Costa family connection, and told the others Irene had as good as admitted her role in blocking the Carabinieri. He added that they had no proof of any crime or criminal intent except what they'd overheard Irene saying. And, of course, they had Flora's testimony that she'd been kidnapped and dragged to the private home at the tunnel's end.

Adele Marino interrupted. "We do have proof, sir."

"What's that?"

"I pushed 'record' on my cell phone, and to my great surprise, it worked. I have an audio file of her first conversation with you and Orsoni, the confrontation before the flood."

"Good work! I don't suppose you got video of her drawing a gun on her colleagues, did you?"

"Sorry, no."

Bernini's voice assumed a more upbeat tone. "We still have no idea who killed Gallo and De Luca. It could have been Irene, one of her brothers, or someone unknown." He smiled for the first time in days. "It's progress, though. I'll have to work on Orsoni and see if he's willing to be a witness against her."

"Where is Orsoni now?" Ricci asked

"We don't know. He escaped the flooded tunnel on his own, then disappeared while Irene kidnapped Flora, and reappeared in the kitchen of the house where we had our little showdown. Then he took off again. I'm hoping he will turn himself in since he has broken with Irene Costa."

"If he were really remorseful, he'd have stayed and helped rescue Flora," Adele said bitterly. "I think he's still conflicted about whose side he's on. I hope he does turn himself in."

"Yeah, that would be one less thing for us to worry about," said Ricci.

The other officers stayed silent and grim-faced, probably thinking the Carabinieri would cease to function if it lost any more men.

Bernini absorbed his colleagues' somber expressions. "Cheer up, folks. We've had terrible setbacks, but we are beginning to crack this case. Since the Orsoni-Rossin-Costa family connections are at the center of this mess, let's pool our resources." He asked everyone to review what they knew about Irene Costa and Astorre Orsoni and their living family members. "Who are their closest relatives, what is their financial situation, what kind of property do they own?"

"Aha," Ricci said. "Property that might be used to hide stolen art, either above ground or under it."

"Exactly."

"You know," added Ricci, "De Luca was looking into the Orsoni and Costa families before he was killed. He told me as much."

Bernini scowled. "A clue to why he was killed, but not who did it. What else do we know that you haven't told me?"

Everyone agreed that neither Orsoni nor Costa talked often about their families, although Ricci remembered Irene complaining that her younger brother couldn't find a job. Ricci also said that Astorre preferred to keep work and home separate. He was married with a young son; that was about it.

Bernini shook his head. "Those of you with laptops handy, do some Internet searching. See what you can find out about their families, especially those living in the Rome area. Names, addresses, occupations, connections with the modern art world—everything."

His cell phone buzzed. He took the call.

"We've got Irene Costa ready for her interview, sir."

"Okay. Put her in interview room five. I'll be right down."

Bernini beckoned to Adele, who had moved around the table to make suggestions to a colleague searching on personal names and occupations.

"Come with me. We've recovered Franco Costa's body from the tunnel. I'm going to interview Irene now. I think you know her as well as anyone. You can help."

Adele squared her shoulders. "I'd be delighted. I have a few questions of my own to put to her."

He pinned her with a severe gaze. "I'm sure you do, and I'm sure that some of your questions deal with the tensions between the two of you. But let me take the lead; you can chime in when I run out of ideas or get stonewalled."

Adele nodded and her face closed up.

Bernini turned to the others. "We've got Costa in custody. Marino and I will interview her and report back in an hour or so. Keep grubbing for information, okay?"

Lisa and Ricci nodded and bent over their computers and notes.

~ * ~

Adele Marino followed Bernini into the interview room.

An almost unrecognizable Irene Costa perched on the edge of a chair. Her thin arms hugged her chest and tears streamed down her filthy face. Her normally perfect hair hung in wet snakes at chin level and her clothes were torn and soaking. Her sobs filled the room.

Bernini and Adele took chairs opposite her.

"I'm sorry about your brother, Irene." Bernini spoke in an even, friendly voice.

She didn't look at him or say a word.

"I gather he was helping you supplement your police income—"

"As if you knew anything about him or our family!" Irene sputtered. "My parents are almost destitute after caring for my grandmamma. My salary was pitiful. Franco…"

Fresh sobs stifled her voice.

"Franco?" prodded Bernini.

Irene raised her head and glared at him. "Franco was the brother I raised; I taught him everything he knew. I found a job for him only yesterday."

Bernini sighed. "A waste, a tragedy. Again, I am sorry." He paused. "Irene, we just recovered your brother's body. If you help us immediately, you might be allowed to attend his funeral—"

"I don't care if I go or not! He's dead; he can't be brought back to us."

He tried again. "You are in a bad position. Adele here recorded our conversation in the tunnel with her cell phone…"

Irene's hostile gaze focused on Adele. "Thanks for that!"

"You had it coming," Adele said, crossing her arms over her chest.

"So now your best course of action is to help us in exchange for the possibility of a reduced sentence," Bernini said. "Although that will be difficult if you are proven a double murderer."

"I didn't kill anyone." She put a slight emphasis on the "I."

So you got someone else to murder Gallo and De Luca, thought Bernini. Out loud, he said, "Where are the paintings and statues that were stolen from the Palazzo Turchetti?"

Irene remained silent.

"You know our men will search all possible hiding places, including every piece of property your family owns."

"Search away!"

Bernini let her mull on her situation for a moment and then tried a new tack. "You were always ahead of us in the search for missing art. What were your sources of information? How did your cousin Astorre become involved? What happened to the rest of the trove we found, the one you so confidently expected to find near the Metro stop Circo Massimo? Why—"

"Oh, *stai zitto!* Shut up! I'm not answering any of your questions without a lawyer. Not that I can afford one. But until then, I'm not saying anything else." She wrapped her arms tighter around her torso and turned her head to the side, shutting them out.

"Irene—" Adele said.

"Oh, you! You think you're so smart! No doubt you'll advance in the Carabinieri because you had the presence of mind to get an audio recording of me in the tunnel! Don't expect anything from me, I won't talk. Go away and let me grieve." Costa resumed her defiant and silent pose, her body facing the wall.

Bernini motioned to Marino to stand. "Let's go. We'll try again later," he mouthed.

To the junior officer stationed outside the door, he said, "Take her to a cell. Give her water, but nothing else." Sitting for hours in filthy wet clothes and getting hungry might change her tune.

~ * ~

Vittorio Bernini and Adele Marino walked up the stairs toward the conference room.

"That was a bust," offered Adele.

"Not entirely. We got a little more information about her younger brother Franco and the relationship between them."

"I wish I'd asked more questions about her family," sighed Adele. "I had no idea they were so badly off."

They entered the conference room to find a buzz of conversation.

"What have you found?" demanded Bernini.

Davide Ricci spoke up. "The Costa family owns a warehouse along the Tiber. We think it might be just the place to store the art stolen from our palazzo."

"Excellent. Who's going with you to check it out?"

"I'll take some of the *Polizia di Stato* with me."

"Okay. Report back as soon as you can."

Forty

Bernini focused on the search for Orsoni while Ricci was gone. Despite what he'd said to his colleagues, Moscati expected him to check all the places Orsoni could be hiding out.

He questioned Orsoni's wife, Lucia, tracking her down at her workplace.

Lucia Orsoni sat uneasily on an office chair in an empty office at the insurance company. She was petite, a small dark woman trying hard to project invulnerability.

"Did your husband come home after he escaped from the tunnel?" Bernini asked.

"What tunnel? I know nothing of any tunnel."

"When did you last see him?"

"Yesterday morning, at breakfast. He left for work at the usual time. He took Sal to school on his way there." She sniffed, wiping a tear away with her hand. "What has he done?"

"He's been helping his cousin Irene Costa obstruct our investigation in the catacombs."

"Irene! That witch! I always told him he shouldn't trust her! Why, I—"

"Signora, please focus on your husband's possible whereabouts. Where does he like to go when he's not at home or at work?"

Her gaze turned hostile. "He does not have a mistress, I promise you!"

"No, of course not. Does he visit family in town?" Bernini found questioning someone so combative very tiresome.

"Only Irene and her brother. They live near the Janiculum Hill." They went back and forth, until Lucia lost it.

She wept and twisted her hands together. "My little son! What will become of us? How could he be involved in something like this?"

A dead end. Bernini told Lucia she was free to return to work. As she left the room, her tears dried up with suspicious speed.

He'd come back a second time if necessary.

~ * ~

Bernini's cell phone buzzed. "Yes?"

Ricci said, "We found nothing, sir. The warehouse is packed with canned goods, but no art. What would you like me to do now?"

Bernini sighed. "Return here to the Comando. We'll see how the others are getting on with their research."

He entered the meeting room and several people looked up.

Lisa Donahue waved her hand. "Sir, I think I've got something."

"Let's hear it."

"When Flora and I first researched the Rossin family, we found a mention of a man whose name was incomplete but started with 'Cl.' We now know his full name was Clemente Orsoni, and he built up a reputation as a dealer in fine art during the 1930s and 40s. He bought and sold many artworks, especially paintings. His son, Danielo, joined him in the business but changed his last name to Buscichelli after a family fight. Does that ring any bells?"

"No, but let's take it further. Anyone?"

Silence reigned except for the tapping of computer keys.

"Here we go!" cried Adele Marino. "Danielo Buscichelli is retired now, but he still lives in Rome. He took over from his father after his father's death and is said to have a large personal collection."

Bernini and Adele looked at each other. "Could it be that this relative of Salvatore and Isabelle rescued some of the art from its underground hiding place? And either kept it or sold it?"

"Worth checking out," Adele said with shining eyes.

"He still lives in Rome? Where?"

Ricco had googled the name and found an address. "In Trastevere, sir, on the *Vicolo S. Francesco a Ripa*. Not too far from your own apartment."

"Okay. We'll pay him a visit."

"What happens if he won't let us in?"

"Then we go to the Public Prosecutor, obtain a warrant, and mount a raid."

Forty-one

Flora's cell buzzed. Eyes still shut, she groped among the sheets and blanket until she felt something hard that vibrated in her hand. She pushed the "receive" button just in time.

"Pronto."

"I'll pick you up in twenty minutes," said Bernini.

"Huh? Did we have an appointment?" Flora said, rubbing the sleep out of her eyes.

"No, but you won't want to miss this." He rang off.

Flora, feeling much better after a morning in bed, put on yesterday's capris and found a clean sleeveless top and her sandals. As she brushed her hair in front of the bathroom mirror, she decided she felt almost human again. After a quick application of mascara and lip gloss, she grabbed keys, wallet, and water bottle and hastened downstairs.

Bernini pulled up five minutes later with Adele Marino and Davide Ricci in the car.

"We saved the front seat for you," Vittorio said with a smile.

"Where are we going?" Flora asked as she strapped herself in.

Adele told her.

Flora's heart jumped. What if they found some of the Rossin pieces? How much could be stored in one of the older, more spacious Rome apartments? Since some of them were entire floors of abandoned palaces, quite a lot... *darn*, she hadn't brought her laptop or notebook.

Bernini parked the car only a few streets away from their apartment in Trastevere.

The four of them climbed out and approached a plain entrance with a buzzer. When Bernini pressed the button and the landlord asked who he was, Bernini answered, "We're here to visit Signor Buscichelli." The glass doors opened on a beautiful foyer, with three apartment doors around the perimeter.

Bernini, after consulting the short list of names near the mailboxes, pounded on the door of number three.

"Who is it?" a quavering voice asked.

"My name is Vittorio Bernini. I need to speak with you."

Smart not to say they were police right away, thought Flora. Perhaps the occupant would respond more favorably to what sounded like an ordinary citizen instead of the Carabinieri.

They heard sounds of rattling as bolts were drawn. The door opened as far as a chain would allow. "What do you want with me?

Flora saw the wrinkled face of an old man, somewhat shorter that she was. Behind him, a painting on the wall caught her attention. Caravaggio! And next to it was surely a Titian? Her blood pounded in her head and her mind whirled. In her excitement, Flora couldn't remember the titles of most of the paintings she'd come across during her research. She was helpless without her computer files.

"Signor Danielo Buscichelli?

"Yes. What do you want? And who are you?"

By now Bernini had a foot in the doorway and his hand braced upon the door to keep it open. "We have some questions about your art collection, sir. We're from the Carabinieri, the *Comando per la Tutela del Patrimonio Culturale*."

"Do you have a warrant?"

"Not yet, but already we've seen enough on your walls to obtain one by the end of today. So you might as well open up."

The old man considered. "No, I will not let you in. Go get your warrant."

Expecting this, Bernini placed a phone call for men to cover the front and back of the building so that nothing could be moved out of the apartment without his knowledge. He asked for a third man to patrol the inside of the building to prevent Danielo from moving objects within the building. He doubted the frail-looking old man could muster the kind of help needed for moving before they returned with a warrant, but he wasn't about to take chances this close to their goal. Danielo might have some small and portable goodies he cared about that could be hidden within the building.

Then, Bernini called the Public Prosecutor and made his case for a search warrant.

Adele listened eagerly to his explanation.

"It will be ready at seventeen hundred," said Bernini as he pocketed the cell.

"Good work, sir. I can hardly wait."

Forty-two

Bernini dropped off Flora so she could rest again until a little before seventeen hundred. The three officers returned to the Comando building.

They checked on the progress of the team researching the Orsoni and Costa families, but the researchers had learned nothing new. He dispatched a team to interview Costa and Orsoni relatives about Astorre's whereabouts.

But just a few minutes after Bernini had dispatched his team, Orsoni entered the Comando. He gave himself up, just as Bernini had hoped.

Bernini decided to interview Orsoni immediately, hoping to get new information out of him. He took Adele Marino with him to this interview as well.

Orsoni looked exhausted, but far less surly than usual. Perhaps the fight had gone out of him with the knowledge that his career as an officer in the Art Squad was over. Or perhaps he felt relief now that he'd turned himself in.

Bernini and Marino sat opposite Orsoni, and Adele turned on the tape recorder.

"I interviewed your wife a little while ago. She had no idea where to find you."

Orsoni closed his eyes. "She called me. That's what made me decide to come in; I don't want my family to suffer any more harassment."

This irritated Bernini. "I was quite gentle with her, considering."

"She likes to complain," replied Orsoni, summing up his marriage in a few words.

"Irene is in custody, too. Why don't you tell us about your role in helping her? Obviously she inspired strong family loyalty."

Orsoni's expression hardened. "You heard her in the tunnel. Her side of the family has always had money problems. Her father drank, her younger brother couldn't keep any job more than two weeks, and the mother is disabled. But their lifestyle has always been beyond their means—they like good furniture, good food and wine. They always want more."

This explanation went some way to explain why Irene would risk a good job for stolen art.

"Knowing that history, why did you get involved with her and her obviously dubious schemes? Finding the art trove was never a sure thing. Nor is selling it to realize the cash value once you lay your hands on it."

"Irene planned to use her knowledge of the black market to find distributors and buyers for the stolen art. She is an excellent database searcher. She loves accessing obscure information; I used to see her spending her lunch breaks at the computer rather than going outside the building."

"Where is the art that was stolen from our palazzo?"

Orsoni looked as if he no longer cared. "I've no idea. The Costa family has plenty of connections. I wasn't there for the raid; Irene organized that. Her underlings hid the art."

Bernini regarded him as if he came from another species.

"Why on earth did you risk everything you've worked for, especially with a young son to support, by working with Irene?"

Orsoni shrugged. "She's family too; we grew up together. And at first it was almost a game, to see if I could be useful to both sides. Participate in the search with the Carabinieri, feed information to her cousins and our *Sotterranei* buddies, stay one step ahead of you guys when tips about where to search came through. I enjoyed that part."

A lightbulb flashed for Bernini. It was Orsoni's early mention of the *Sotterranei* that had niggled at Bernini's brain. The clue that was right under his nose: Orsoni's familiarity with the underground organization and all it implied.

Marino pounced. "Oh, so *both of you* were deep in with the *Sotterranei*? That must be where you gleaned your insider knowledge of those tunnels and how to navigate them."

"Irene took climbing lessons. Learned how to rappel down walls underground. She's good at snorkeling and scuba, too. She can hold her breath longer than anyone I know."

Bernini changed gears. "What do you know about the murders of Gallo and De Luca?"

"I didn't kill either of them, if that's what you mean."

"Did you hear anyone planning those killings? Or the reasons for committing them?"

Silence.

"Oh, come on, Orsoni! Surely it's time to talk! Just get it over with."

Orsoni looked up, pain in his eyes. "I heard Irene say both men should be eliminated. They were getting too close to her operation. Gallo followed her team into the subway; that's why he was killed. I don't know what De Luca found out, but he seemed especially interested in what Irene did with her time off." He remembered something. "Irene spotted De Luca down the hall from us while we were talking at the Palazzo Turchetti. She may have thought he overheard something vital."

"Do you know who did the actual killing?"

"No. It could have been one of her relatives, or even one of her buddies in the *Sotterranei*. Personally, I suspect older brother Giovanni. But I don't have any proof."

"Anything else you wish to tell us?" asked Adele after a few moments.

Orsoni thought about it. "I was the one who sent you anonymous tips by text and email," he said to Bernini. "You might consider that worth putting in a good word for me during my trial."

"The one about the leader of the clandestine operation being a woman?"

"Yes."

"Can you prove you sent those messages?" asked Bernini drily.

Orsoni's lips pursed. "Our IT guys can compare my computer records with the email address I used to send the messages. I used my personal cell, not my work one. It's easy enough to disguise the source of a message if you know how. It's a little harder to go in the reverse direction, but it's possible."

"Huh," Bernini said, shaking his head. "We'll talk with you again, Orsoni. Count on it." He knew the Carabinieri brass would not give up easily on solving the murders of their own officers. But for now, they'd have to settle for less than the complete truth.

~ * ~

Bernini, Marino, Ricci, and Flora returned to Danielo Buscichelli's apartment in the early evening. Bernini asked the officers guarding the building to stand by; he might need them later.

Again, he pounded on the door.

The old man repeated his question. "Who are you and what do you want?"

"Police. We were here this morning. This time we have a warrant. Open up or face the consequences."

Danielo released the chain so he could inspect the warrant as Bernini held it up.

Resignedly, he removed the chain and opened the door all the way. He shuffled ahead of his four visitors into a large room filled with light from the tall windows.

A perfect display space for its contents. Valuable paintings graced every wall. Greek and Roman statues lurked between the sofas. The glass coffee table displayed ivory miniatures and a jewel-encrusted reliquary.

"Sit down, please," ordered their host. Now that the inevitable had happened, his manner became almost affable.

Obediently, they sat. Adele, Flora, and Ricci stayed silent, content to look around the room. Flora could almost see the wheels turning in Adele's brain as she began a mental inventory.

Van Dyck, Caravaggio, Titian, Rafael, Lorenzetti, Renoir... she identified a missing Lucas Cranach painting, stolen early in the war and never recovered. Could the Renoir on the wall closest to her be the Rossin family painting? She ached for her list, unfortunately still on her laptop at home because she'd never made it back to the apartment after joining Lisa at the Comando. *How stupid not to arrive better prepared!*

Bernini took a deep breath. "Were you born Danielo Orsoni?"

"Yes, that is my name. I took my grandmother's name after a fight with my father, Riccardo Orsoni." Danielo held himself proudly, as straight-backed as his advanced age and arthritis would allow. He seemed perfectly calm, not in the least worried by the presence of police in his domain.

"Tell us about the history of your art collection. How you acquired these paintings and statues. Everything in this room."

"This will take some time," said the old man doubtfully.

"We have the time, sir. What we need is all the information you can give us. We are particularly interested in art you acquired during World War II, and just after the war. Who sold things to you, what you found or purchased for yourself, what you sold over the years."

Marino and Ricci pulled out notebooks, and Marino kept her smartphone handy in case she needed to verify something online. Flora had nothing to write on except a receipt in the bottom of her purse, so she did her best to remember everything she saw and heard. They could compare notes later and fill in any gaps.

Buscichelli rang a small bell. A middle-aged woman appeared in the doorway. "Catarina, some coffee for my guests."

She nodded and disappeared.

The old man began his recital. At intervals, he hoisted himself up and pointed to various artworks around the room. He retrieved a large, leather-bound notebook from his desk that listed sales and acquisitions over the years.

It was a gold mine of information, as good as anything in the State Archives. A substantial record of provenances, prices, owners, exchanges, from the 1920s until the present. Flora, skimming the entries, noted some gaps of many months in the records and wondered about them: did Danielo not buy or sell during those periods? Or was he ill? Or maybe he just didn't record all of his transactions?

Three hours later, the stunned team left the apartment. They gathered around Bernini's Fiat to catch their breaths.

Adele spoke first. "I will never forget this day as long as I live. What a find! What a collection!"

"You are so right," agreed Flora. "As an art historian, I am overwhelmed. It's like an entire course in the history of Western painting in three hours, with the best documentation I've ever seen. Danielo is a fabulous curator, even if it turns out some of his records are incomplete."

"Since he has been so cooperative, I think we can honor his request that the collection stay intact while experts evaluate it. I will send photographers and inventory clerks over first. Then you art historians can have at it, and match up as many items as you can against the lists of lost artworks."

They stood in the spring dusk in a small piazza across from a bar that was just coming to life for the evening.

"Let's have a drink," suggested Adele.

Bernini smiled, the biggest grin he'd managed for weeks. "This is the day for it! My treat."

Forty-three

Three days later, Flora drove Lisa Donahue and Ellen Perkins to the airport to catch their flight back to the United States.

All three were quiet during the first part of the journey. There was so much to think about.

Flora turned to Lisa, who rode in the front passenger seat. "So, what are your impressions of Rome after this little adventure?'

"I have such different memories from my last trip," Lisa answered. "The first time, I took away mental snapshots of monuments, crazy traffic, feral cats wandering around, favorite restaurants and cafés. Now my mind is overwhelmed with images of paintings, statues, flooded tunnels, and the faces of the Carabinieri."

"Yeah," Ellen said. "The faces of heroes, traitors, and ordinary cops. I still can't believe Irene Costa risked her peachy job with the Carabinieri for a chance in a thousand to find that art trove."

"I can't either," Flora agreed. "It was such a long shot that we'd find anything in that incredible labyrinth underground."

"So what do you have planned for the hunky policeman?" teased Lisa.

Flora smiled with a touch of malice. "Vittorio doesn't know this yet, but I'm going to introduce him to all my Chicago relatives next month. If he survives that experience, we'll probably get married later this fall. But first, I get to meet his mamma, probably next weekend."

"Uh oh," Ellen laughed. "Going to be inspected?"

"Yep. She'll do everything except take my measurements to see if I'm good enough for her Vittorio."

"You'll pass muster, Flora. I'm betting on it." Lisa said.

"What are your post-'Roman holiday' plans, Ellen?"

"I'm going to join a spelunking society. Now that I've got my feet wet, literally, I want to visit all the caves in the U.S."

~ * ~

Two weeks later, Vittorio and Flora knew that they'd been hoodwinked by Danielo Buscichelli.

They'd had several interviews with the art dealer. The wily Danielo had recorded all the transactions he was involved in for non-family members. But when it came to relatives, there were no records—or no records the Carabinieri could find.

Why? When asked, Danielo said simply it was nobody's business except his own. The pieces of art that had belonged to the Orsonis, the Rossins, or any of their larger extended Jewish families, were "off the record." While Flora suspected he remembered most of the information, he would never write it down for them.

Bernini told Danielo he could be charged with hindering the police, and that might mean a lengthy jail sentence. Danielo replied that he didn't care; he was old. If he died in prison, at least he wouldn't have to pay for food and rent.

The Carabinieri found his attitude toward money was surprisingly frugal. Didn't the old man realize that he'd lived surrounded by a fortune in art?

Signor B, as he became known around the Comando, also neglected to mention the existence of two warehouses of art. Naturally, they didn't look like warehouses; they were former mansions or palazzi near the Villa Doria Pamphili. One of them contained the art lifted from the police storage facility... but not all of it. During the month or so of interviews and cataloguing, Danielo had directed someone to begin selling off his accumulated holdings.

When Bernini discovered this duplicity, he made sure Signor B spent some time in a prison cell with no computer or cell phone. Bernini allowed the old man basic comforts, such as a decent mattress and a reading lamp, but there were no frills. The Carabinieri, in pairs and singly, continued to interview him, hoping conversation would loosen the old man up.

They failed. Danielo Buscichelli was the most stubborn, reticent man alive.

Adele tried to appeal to his better nature, saying how much he could help reconstruct what had happened to the incredible art that had passed through his hands. He, Danielo, could help repatriate artworks, stolen by the Nazis, to their original Jewish families. Wouldn't that make him feel useful?

Danielo shrugged.

Adele and Flora looked at each other. When he died, the only chance of finding out the final disposition of certain paintings or statues was to find the current owners by chance.

Bernini said it would take many months, if not years, to locate all the stolen artwork, find original owners or their heirs, and return the items. In this endeavor, they were not alone: experts all over Europe were engaged in the same search. A recent estimate obtained by Moscati told them that over two thousand artworks originally stolen were still missing. The search continued, not just in Italy, but all over Europe and in other countries that traded in fine art.

Clearly the catacomb project and its aftermath would not answer all their questions about the Rossin-Orsoni-Costa network of art collectors and thieves.

Bernini thought this particular project had wrapped up as well as could be expected, considering they'd lost two officers to murder and two more to treachery. He calculated that First Captain Moscati would assign him to something new, any day. Perhaps Bernini would earn a promotion, now that most of the art had been recovered. However, the Carabinieri were unpredictable in how they awarded promotions; Bernini would not exceed his income in anticipation. And he knew, to his shame, he had not found the killer of De Luca and Gallo; the *Polizia di Stato* had done it. They obtained a confession from Giovanni, the older brother of Irene Costa.

One afternoon, as he was crossing the Piazza Navona just before the rush hour began, his cell rang.

"It's Elettra Lombardi. Remember me? I'm the geologist who briefed your group about our excavation in the subways."

"Yes, of course."

"I've a bit of news. Our archaeologists broke into a chamber not on our map. Turns out to be right behind the one where your team found the lost art, the stuff that was in the news recently. But our chamber was different: instead of being full of Nazi-looted art, it's full of Greek antiquities, and the stuff was buried by an Etruscan."

"How do you know when it was buried, and by whom?"

"The lead archaeologist says he can date the objects found in the same stratum with the Greek artifacts, because a nice layer of rubble and brick seals it in. Carbon dating of some scraps of fabric in the same deposit will confirm the dates. And they found a seal belonging to someone whose name appears in an Etruscan inscription nearby. The consensus so far is that it looks like a hidey-hole this Etruscan used when he was afraid he would lose his valuables, or maybe his sales stock if he traded in what was then contemporary art."

Bernini thought about this. Underground, in pre-Roman times, someone had hidden precious objects in a small cave. He remembered Flora's dream. "History repeats itself," he said slowly.

"Indeed, it does."

He couldn't wait to tell Flora.

~ * ~

Flora prepared a special meal to celebrate the end of the catacomb case. She sautéed chicken slices that had been marinated in a mixture of herbs, olive oil, and Parmesan cheese in butter and prepared a risotto. A bottle of Pinot Grigio—a cut above what they usually bought—chilled in the small refrigerator.

Vittorio's key rattled in the lock. He came into the kitchen, tired and rumpled, but with an expression of relief on his narrow face that made Flora rejoice. She had her guy back, not the tense, overworked almost-stranger who had shared the past few weeks with her.

"Hi!" she said with a big grin.

"Hi, yourself," he returned with an equally big grin. "Something special for dinner?"

"One of your favorites, *etti di pollo impanati*. And a mushroom and cream risotto, with a green salad."

"I have something to tell you," he said, dropping his bag and taking off his suit jacket. He hung it on the kitchen doorknob as usual and poured some of the white wine.

Flora rinsed the lettuce leaves as she listened to his story of the phone call from *dottoressa* Lombardi. She turned around from the sink, stunned.

"Rather like my dream!"

"Yes. Maybe you should write a novel—give free rein to that imagination of yours." He laughed as she threw some lettuce at him.

"I have something to tell you as well."

"Oh?"

She pulled out her chair and sat facing him. "I'm ready to meet your mamma."

His face lit up. "That's wonderful! We'll go this weekend."

Flora lips curved. "And, my family has invited us to Chicago in August, when you have some time off. They're planning a reunion. You'll get to meet my parents, my sister, my aunts and uncles. An overload of Garibaldis, all at once."

Vittorio's expression went through several comical variations and settled on cheerfully resigned. He got up to fetch the wine and refilled both glasses. He sat down again and looked at her.

"It's a deal."

Afterword

The research for this novel was especially fascinating. I began with research on the Monuments Men and the systematic looting of Jewish-owned art during World War II by Nazi forces. Then I used pictures and notes from a trip to Rome, along with numerous maps, guide books, and websites about the catacombs. I recommend these sources:

Robert M. Edsel, with Bret Witter, *The Monuments Men: Allied Heroes, Nazi Thieves, and the Greatest Treasure Hunt in History*, Center Street/ Hachette Book Group, 2009.

Robert M. Edsel, *Saving Italy: A Race to Rescue a Nation's Treasures from the Nazis*, W. W. Norton & Co., Inc., 2013.

Other notes: The *Sotterranei di Roma* is a real group of collaborating geologists, archaeologists, spelunkers, and others who explore and map the underground city:

http://www.romasotterranea.it/

Some of the stories in my novel are based upon true events, for example the discovery of an apartment full of looted art owned by a retired art dealer. In *Catacomb*, this event took place in Rome, and the dealer is fictional, like the rest of the Orsoni family. In reality, this event took place in 2012 in Munich, Germany, and the dealer's name was Cornelius Gurlitt. This incredible discovery was widely covered in the news at the time, and accounts can be found on the Internet.

Meet Sarah Wisseman

Sarah Wisseman is a retired archaeologist. Her experience working on excavations and in museums inspired two contemporary series, the Lisa Donahue Archaeological Mysteries and the Flora Garibaldi Art History Mysteries. Her settings are places where she has lived or traveled (Israel, Italy, Egypt, Massachusetts, and Illinois) and her favorite museum used to be housed in a creepy old attic at the University of Illinois.

VISIT OUR WEBSITE
FOR THE FULL INVENTORY
OF QUALITY BOOKS:

www.books-by-wingsepress.com

Quality trade paperbacks and downloads
in multiple formats,
in genres ranging from light romantic comedy
to general fiction and horror.
Wings has something for every reader's taste.
Visit the website, then bookmark it.
We add new titles each month!

CPSIA information can be obtained
at www.ICGtesting.com
Printed in the USA
LVOW04s0313190816
500953LV00031B/805/P